Chocolate Sauce
&
Malice

Chocolate Sauce
&
Malice

Arline Potter

Writers Club Press
San Jose   New York   Lincoln   Shanghai

Chocolate Sauce & Malice

All Rights Reserved © 2000 by Arline Potter

No part of this book may be reproduced or transmitted in any form or by any means, graphic, electronic, or mechanical, including photocopying, recording, taping, or by any information storage or retrieval system, without the permission in writing from the publisher.

Published by Writers Club Press
an imprint of iUniverse.com, Inc.

For information address:
iUniverse.com, Inc.
620 North 48th Street
Suite 201
Lincoln, NE 68504-3467
www.iuniverse.com

ISBN: 1-58348-849-9

Printed in the United States of America

Dedications

To Carl, my true love, whose support makes it possible for me to play my games of *make believe*. I remain in abysmal ignorance of all things technical and would hardly survive in this new world without your help.

To my son, Bob, whose help in understanding the workings of a modern TV studio was the cornerstone on which this story rests. Thank you.

CHAPTER ONE

JAMES GARDNER VANDERSAGEN, CEO of the JGV network, had just left his very angry wife, Adele, in the Green Room, where she had threatened, "If you try to push for a divorce so you can marry that blonde bitch out there, just remember, I own at least half of your precious empire, and I won't think twice about taking the other half."

Jim was furious as he slammed the door and went out to the set where a kitchen was arranged for Kate Cassidy's show to be taped before a live audience. Today's guest was a weight-loss cooking expert. Her book's title was How to Have your Cake and Grow Thin too.

On the counter was a fully-baked but undecorated cake. Beside it were small containers of various ingredients. As he often did on the set of a cooking show, Jim put his finger into an open jar of chocolate sauce for a quick taste before shooting started. He had a notorious sweet tooth and chocolate was his particular favorite flavor.

The studio was a cacophony of noise as workers bustled about the set. Lights were being adjusted and camera operators were setting up various shots. As Vandersagen brought his finger to his mouth, about to taste the sauce, he heard no particular sound above the others. For a millisecond, in his peripheral vision, he saw the huge overhead mirror which had broken loose from two of its four lashings, pivoting downward, headed for the spot on which he stood.

Not only was he furious with Adele, he would let the producer, Rudy Macklin, have a choice word or two, as well. What kind of studio management was this anyway? Rudy had better explain why the overhead mirror was rigged so poorly. He ought to know how dangerous...

Vandersagen's brain may have registered pain and shock but little else. As the second set of lashings broke loose, the entire weight of the mirror crashed into his head, smashing the bones of his skull and snapping his neck.

Jim's eyes were open and staring as his body lurched forward under the impact of more than 200 pounds of shattering plate glass. Frozen like a deer in headlights, Kate Cassidy took the full weight of Jim's body against her own, only a foot from where he had been standing. She barely felt the pain of hundreds of glass shards as they pierced the skin of her left arm.

In the studio, witnessing the event, were more than a dozen people, most of them working on the show. Maureen Cassidy, Kate's mother, was on the set, out of camera range. High in the rear, in the audience area, and barely visible, was Maureen's ex-husband, and Kate's father, Tom Cassidy. Maureen didn't know he was there, for he had not sought her out to say hello.

The studio audience was in the hallway, patiently waiting to be allowed into the seats rising in steep tiers from the stage. If they were lucky they might be called upon to participate in the show, where each week, Kate Cassidy, the host of Come Home With Kate, interviewed guests and took questions on camera.

The show's focus, home, gave Kate a wide range of guests from whom to choose. One week it might be a famous decorator who, before a live audience, would take a collection of objects and arrange them to create either an entire room or part of one. Often there was a requirement for a kitchen set, for food and cooking were frequent themes.

During the eight months of its current run, ...Home... had hosted builders, plumbing experts, gardeners and, just the previous week, a pet-behavior specialist, complete with dogs, cats and a pot-bellied pig.

As Jim Vandersagen described it to the press, "Come Home With Kate is not about transvestites and sado-masochists. It's about the things that people really care about, what happens in the places they live. This is one show your children can watch." He was making oblique reference to the competition which had been recently excoriated in the conservative press as totally unsuitable for prime time, what with frank discussions of subjects generally considered obscene. Only last week they had a panel of parents and their children whom they had molested.

Kate's show got good press coverage, thanks to the Vandersagen newspapers in major U.S. markets. It also got favorable reviews from independent writers who liked the format, an hour of more activity than talk. And, to judge from the fan mail, everyone liked the host, Kate Cassidy.

Immediately after the mirror fell, the studio was the scene of chaotic frenzy. With gloved hands, people were picking up shards of glass. Someone turned Jim Vandersagen over on his back. From the way his head lolled, it was evident, his neck had been broken. He was not conscious.

Kate Cassidy, barely conscious, lay, bleeding where she had fallen under the impact of Jim's body. A man leaned near her head. "She's breathing!" he screamed. "Get the first aid kit!"

Maureen Cassidy, using all her strength, shoved her way to her daughter's side. "Where's that first aid kit, dammit, she's going to bleed to death!" She had removed her half-slip and was using it to mop at Kate's arm. "Kate, Katy, it's Mommy. Can you hear me?" She was rewarded with a deep groan.

The 911 response was quick and the team of paramedics went to work without any lost motion. One of them shouted to nobody in particular, "Would somebody please get this lady the hell out of our way so we can work?" A different voice said, "The guy's DOA."

Maureen, hearing herself referred to as "this lady," just another obstacle, looked up and said, her voice trembling, "I'll stay right here with her until you get her into the ambulance and then I'm going along with her. Don't anybody try to stop me. I'm her mother."

The paramedic, continuing his work, said evenly, "Lady, "I don't care if you're the Mother of Jesus or Mother Theresa, even. Stay the hell out of our way!"

Maureen nodded and backed away, helped to her feet by her ex-husband, Tom. She registered no surprise at his sudden appearance. Like automatons, together they moved well aside while the medics worked deftly to stem bleeding and set oxygen tubes into place.

The older couple, together now, though they had been divorced for years, watched silently as their daughter was lifted onto a wheeled table to be taken through the exit to a waiting ambulance. They said nothing to one another. When Kate moaned, "Mommy" a medic led Maureen to her side and said she could ride along. Tom was strong-armed away. Maureen thought, he'll have to get there on his own.

At Roosevelt hospital, Tom and Maureen sat in grim silence while Kate was wheeled into an operating room. The staff doctor had assured them she was not in critical condition and that the surgery was primarily to repair the cuts to her arm.

The wait seemed eternal. Maureen, still shaken, said, "Oh Tom, we nearly lost our Kate. Thank God, that monstrous mirror didn't kill her. I feel bad about Jim Vandersagen, of course, but our daughter...."

"I know. We're just incredibly lucky."

"But someone was trying to kill her, I know it. Jim just got in the way. That means somebody's out there. Oh my God, Tom, they'll try again. What are we going to do?" She began to cry.

"Shsh, it's alright. You heard what the doctor said. It's just superficial. He'll have her fixed up in no time."

"That's not the point, dammit! Somebody tried to kill her. Don't you understand? There's somebody out there trying to murder our daughter!" Her voice had reached its upper register.

"For God's sake, Maureen, do you want the whole building to hear you? Lower your voice."

Damn him, she thought, his daughter is nearly killed and all he cares about is appearances. Screw the building. "Goddammit, Tom, stop telling me what I can and cannot do! I'll yell, if I want to. There's a killer out there." She pointed vaguely toward the elevators. "Maybe somebody tried to kill my daughter and he's running around loose, ready to try again. And all you give a damn about is me raising my voice." She didn't add that she could smell the booze on his breath. Must have stopped for a pick-me-up before getting in a cab to come here. So typical of Tom, she thought.

"Look, we don't know if someone's trying to kill Kate. You did notice, didn't you, that Jim Vandersagen was dead when the medics got there? Your daughter, our daughter's in there." He pointed to the operating area doors. "As far as we know, she's going to be perfectly alright."

He was speaking softly, his speech perfectly clear. Tom didn't slur until he had drunk a great deal, and then he would suddenly become incoherent and staggering. Maureen read somewhere that it was the pattern of advanced alcoholism.

"The fact is," Maureen was still fuming, but she spoke as softly as Tom. "we don't know whether that mirror was set to kill Kate; it probably was. After all, Jim Vandersagen isn't always on the set. He just shows up now and then."

"That may be true, but from what I heard, he's been to every show in the last few months. Getting pretty tight with Kate, wasn't he? Anyway, that's the rumor I was hearing out on the Coast."

"Yeah, I heard rumors about it too," Maureen admitted. "But, still, that mirror could have been intended for Kate and she could have been killed." She began to cry again. "My God, it was so close!"

Tom was contrite. "I know. But, it's okay now. She's safe, really she is." Then he went on as if there had been no angry exchange. "Who would do something so vicious? And more important, why? Kate doesn't have any enemies that I know of. You know anybody who'd want to harm her?"

Maureen mopped her eyes. "No. My God, Kate's the sweetest, the kindest, the all-around best person. Everyone loves her. But whoever set that mirror to fall has got to have some reason…"

The surgeon emerged from the double doors to the operating-room area. They rose to their feet. "How is she? Is she alright?" Kate and Tom spoke together.

"She's fine. She's in recovery now. You can see her in an hour or two when she gets settled in her room. She was very lucky. The cuts were deep, of course, but nothing vital was severed, so I'm sure she'll have full use of her arm again and the scarring will be minimal. I'll look in on her before I leave."

The doctor backed away, then turned before either Tom or Maureen could ask further questions.

Maureen had not so much as greeted Tom during the excitement immediately after the accident. She had barely acknowledged his presence when he helped her to her feet. Now, calm, she said, "I didn't know you were in town. When did you get here?"

"Last night. I had a couple of meetings."

"Did you see Kate when you got in? I talked to her last night; she didn't say anything about your coming. Did you call her?"

"No, it was too late. But I stopped by the studio this morning. I was going to watch the taping, then I had planned to take her to dinner tonight. That leaves me at loose ends. I don't suppose I could persuade you to have dinner with me, could I?"

"Um, no, thanks, Tom. I've got too much to do. You know how it is." Maureen declined to spend any more time with Tom than necessary. It was one way to avoid what she knew would be hours of watching him drink himself into a stupor while his dinner grew cold. "And right now, I've got some phone calls to make. I'll see you later, won't I? In Kate's room?"

Tom nodded.

"Mr. Cassidy?" It was a tall, black man, holding up his NYPD detective's badge. "Could I have a word with you?"

Tom looked at Maureen. "You going to be okay?"

"Yes, yes, go ahead. I have lots of things to do right now." No point, she thought, in hanging around waiting for Tom. She knew they would just get into another meaningless wrangle where each of them might say ugly things to one another.

"We can talk in here." The detective ushered Tom into an alcove. Maureen walked quickly toward the elevators.

God! she thought, at least I don't have to spend the rest of the afternoon with Tom, listening to him tell me I'm being paranoid. Of course she was afraid. And she was certain there was good reason to be afraid. One person was dead. Thank God, it wasn't Kate. But, had the killer made a mistake? Was the victim really meant to be Kate? Merciful Jesus, does anybody know anything?

She was still furious with Tom. His daughter was nearly killed, and for all she knew, Kate might still be the target of a maniac trying to finish the job, and Tom just breezed along. He probably would finish the evening by getting blind drunk. Well, at least, he was no longer her problem, though she knew that Kate's affection for him had never wavered and, drunk or sober, he was her Daddy. Maureen, she told herself, try to think a little more kindly about him. Sure, her other self answered, I'll try, but thinking kindly about Tom doesn't come easy.

It was one o'clock in the afternoon and very quiet in Kate's cramped room. She opened her eyes and saw, hovering over her, the anxious face of her mother. "Oh good, Kathleen, you're awake. How do you feel?" Her mother never called her Kathleen unless there was real trouble.

Kate was thoroughly bewildered. "I'm alright, I guess. What happened?"

"Don't you remember? You were hit by the overhead mirror. Darling, you were so lucky. You could have been killed." She stroked Kate's free hand, the one without the IV drip needle taped to the back.

Kate tried to raise her head off the pillow and groaned. Something hurt terribly. She wasn't sure where.

Maureen said, "Use the pump. Here." She took Kate's free hand and placed in it a small object. "There, push the button. It'll release Demerol. You won't feel the pain—you can do it anytime it hurts." She watched, open-mouthed, nodding as Kate pressed the button. "That's right. You'll feel it in a second or two. It's going straight through that tube, right into your vein."

"Wow! Mainlining. This is terrific." Kate giggled.

"She must be getting it," Maureen said to somebody, a man, standing on the other side of the bed.

"Mommy, I saw Avi. And DeeDee and Joel and Gran. Where is everybody?"

"Darling, it's alright. Just use the pump." To the man Maureen said, "She's hallucinating. Avi's her husband. He was killed nearly two years ago. DeeDee and Joel are her two children. They're both going to college out of the country. I'm not going to call them. The Doctor says she'll be okay. No reason to bring them back all the way from Ireland and Israel."

"Her kids are in Ireland and Israel?" It was the man's voice.

"Yes, DeeDee, that's her daughter, is going to Trinity and her son Joel—he's my older grandchild—he's studying in Tel Aviv. His grandfather was a professor there before he was killed too."

"What do you mean, too?" The man spoke softly.

"It was years ago, before she even met Avi. I don't think we ought to be talking about all that. She can hear us."

Kate moaned softly. "I think this must be a hospital." She turned her head, the only movement she could make comfortably. To the man she said, "Who are you?"

"Lieutenant Quinn, homicide, NYPD. Here's my card." He held it close to Kate's face since both her hands were occupied. She read his name, squinting to focus.

"Lieutenant Irving Quinn, Homicide, NYPD. Just like you said." She was getting sleepy, but she giggled again, Irving?

"Yeah, My Mother's Jewish and my Father's Irish, so it had to be Irving, after my maternal grandfather."

"You must meet my daughter Deirdre Ginzburg. In her case, it's the other way around." She was asleep.

She woke up an hour later. Maureen was gone, but Lieutenant Quinn was still there. Kate looked at him. "Hi Irving. I'm back."

He uncoiled himself from the small armchair in which he had been looking over his notes. "How are you feeling now?"

"I don't know," Kate said honestly. She felt numb and out of touch with her body. Some drug, that Demerol, she thought. No wonder the junkies were so keen on it. "Isn't this stuff the same as heroin? I never tried heroin, even back in college, when I checked out everything else."

"No, not quite, but very similar." Irving Quinn, opened a notebook, his pen at the ready. "How much do you remember about this morning.?"

"You mean when the mirror fell down? Not much. I saw Jim Vandersagen—let's see, the mirror came crashing down and hit him. Then he was coming toward me. He had chocolate sauce on his chin."

"Yeah, I have that. He was hit first. That's probably what killed him and saved your life."

Kate was fully awake now and aware of throbbing pain in her chest and arm, but she didn't touch the Demerol dispenser button. "Did you say 'killed him'?" Jim's dead?"

"Yes, he died almost instantly. The overhead mirror struck him edgewise, crushed his skull and snapped his neck before breaking into hundreds of pieces. You got only a glancing blow. You have some broken ribs and a bruised shoulder. Of course, you've got a bunch of stitches in your left arm where the broken mirror hit you, but nothing life-threatening. You're pretty lucky. When this stuff heals up you're going to be alright. You'll be out of here in a few days."

Kate was too drugged to react. All pain, including emotional pain, was dulled by the Demerol. But she was able to think, if somewhat more slowly than normal.

"But what happened? The last thing I remember is we were setting up to tape the show. I'd walked to the back of the set for a minute and then I headed for the counter under the mirror. Let's see; Jim, I mean Mr. Vandersagen was standing there. He always likes to taste stuff if we're doing a cooking show. I remember, he dipped his finger in the chocolate sauce and raised his hand to put of it into his mouth. Next thing? Oh, yeah. I saw the mirror—it was just coming down, straight on top of him. Oh, and just before that, there was a little puff of smoke, maybe more than one. Right then I could see the mirror starting to fall. It was so fast!. I got that feeling—like when you're going to trip or something. You see it coming but there's nothing you can do. Jim went down and then there was this sensation. It was like being in an automobile accident. It seems slow, but suddenly there's this feeling inside your head—a gigantic rattling. The last thing I actually could see was Jim falling toward me. Did you say he's dead?"

Irving Quinn consulted his notes. He reconstructed the events as they were described by a number of witnesses. Kate Cassidy lay flat on the pillow as the Lieutenant told her what he knew about the case. Or, as he put it, the "homicide."

"That means murder, doesn't it?" Kate wanted to know. "Me too? Not just Jim? Did somebody want to kill me too?"

"We don't know for sure. But it's quite possible. You see, not only was the overhead mirror rigged to fall on whoever, or is it whomever? Anyway the person standing in front of the demonstration counter. Oh, and the chocolate sauce was poisoned, as well."

"You've got to be kidding!" Kate wanted to laugh, but her ribs hurt too much. She pushed the Demerol button instead and heard Inspector

Quinn saying something about cyanide or a similar poison in the chocolate sauce, "thiophosphate" he called it, "the kind of thing they use in insecticides and garden chemicals."

Her eyes closed again. Hmm, he thought, I must be boring her. After making sure Kate was asleep and, in any case, that she had told him all she could, Lieutenant Quinn went out into the hallway where he spotted Maureen who was leaving the nurses station. She had been conferring with someone, then waved as she turned toward the corridor where Irving Quinn stood, watching and waiting until she came close enough to hear him say, "Was that your daughter's Doc?" He pointed with his chin to the retreating back of a man entering the elevator.

"Yes, he's one of the best plastic surgeons in New York. He said there would be very faint scars on her arm after it heals. I hope he's right." Maureen fell into step as the two walked toward a small lounge at the end of the corridor. "I think we can talk in there. Is she asleep?"

"Like a baby. Ms. Kate Cassidy sure is one lucky lady. Plate glass mirror that size. Must weigh more than a coupla hundred pounds. Looks like whoever set the thing up knew exactly where and how it would fall when the charges went off."

"What are you talking about? Charges? I don't understand"

Quinn said, "It's okay, I'll explain in a minute. Though I don't know too much about it myself. The important thing is somebody wanted to kill the person, or maybe persons, standing at that kitchen setup. The mirror was rigged properly, we understand, but apparently, somebody hit a remote that fired off explosive charges that tore the fastenings. There were pops, your daughter said, little puffs of smoke. Next thing you know the mirror is coming down on somebody's head. It was made to look like an accident, but believe me, there was nothing accidental about this. Somebody wanted either your daughter or James Vandersagen dead. Maybe both of them. And if the mirror failed, the murderer was going to make doubly sure by poisoning the chocolate sauce."

"You think the same person who rigged the mirror also poisoned the chocolate sauce?"

"Can't say for sure. Can't say anything for sure. Um, Miss Cassidy."

"Call me Maureen, please Lieutenant." She smiled the smile that had kept her a star in one of the longest-running daytime soap operas until last month, when her character was killed off. Maureen was out of a job for the first time in more than twenty-five years.

"Well, okay. Maureen. Now, you were in the studio this morning, is that right? You were off to one side on the set. Do you normally visit your daughter's show, what's it called?"

"Come Home With Kate. It's a great title, don't you think? It's from when Kate was a little girl and she'd be playing with a special friend and it was time to leave. She'd always say that, 'Come home with Kate'—she was such a darling little thing."

The homicide detective was an experienced interviewer and he knew he'd make more headway with Maureen Cassidy if he just let her talk. She was no longer upset, but the grueling day had taken its toll. Now, she needed to ventilate. And Irving Quinn knew the best way to get information from a crime witness is simply to listen carefully.

Quinn left to get some coffee. When he returned to the lounge where Maureen waited, he handed her the Styrofoam cup and sat in the chair facing her. Then he said softly, "Just tell me everything, right from the beginning."

"I can't imagine why anyone would want to hurt my daughter. And I don't know anything about the kind of poison you're talking about. But, the mirror. Well, I've got my suspicions about that."

Maureen had combed her hair and refreshed her makeup. Then she had cleared her eyes of red streaks with drops of Visine which she always carried in her purse. Quinn thought it remarkable that she had recovered so quickly. Must be because she's an actress, he told himself.

Maureen seemed eager to talk. "It had to be that Rudy Macklin. He and Kate have been battling ever since the show started. She says she wants lights here, Rudy says there. She wants the set to look like an empty living room, he makes it look like a warehouse. They seem to fight all the time, these days."

"Do you know why? I mean, do they have a history or anything like that?"

"History? Yeah, you could say that. You could say our whole family has a history with Rudy Macklin." Rudy and Kate were toddlers when Maureen worked on her first TV soap opera with Larry Macklin, Rudy's father. "And before that," she explained, "Larry Macklin was in partnership with Jim Vandersagen at the Summer theater on Cape Cod where I had my first professional acting job."

It had not been a happy partnership, considering that by Summer's end, Larry Macklin had lost all the money he had invested, including the ramshackle building housing the theater and quarters for the cast and crew. Maureen recounted what, at the time, was rumored in the theater community—that Jim Vandersagen had run off with the profits, such as they were, and left Macklin to pay the debts.

Ten years later, Larry Macklin was producing live TV plays in the format they called anthology, a new, complete play each week. It was grueling, demanding work and at the end of one season, when he was still in his mid-forties, Larry collapsed on the set and died of a massive heart attack. Rudy was in high school.

At Larry's funeral, Rudy's mother, an actress called Sue Mackay, swore her husband had died because of what Jim Vandersagen had done to him in the early years. She alluded to misdeeds and sinister behavior that were part of Jim's meteoric rise in the world of radio, television and newspaper publishing. In fact, Jim Vandersagen had not yet founded the JGV network and Larry Macklin had little or no contact with his ex-partner except for those occasions when they met at industry functions.

There had been a persistent rumor that Sue Mackay had once had an affair with Vandersagen and that he had dumped her. But then, the world was full of women for whom being dumped by Jim was beyond rumor. His reputation for seducing and abandoning actresses made him the Don Juan of Videoville.

To Rudy Macklin, then a teenager, his father's death was a tragedy, but one in which he could identify no villains. He knew only that his father was gone and that, if he could, he wanted to work in television. He got his first job before he was twenty.

In recent years, about the time Jim Vandersagen's network was reaching its current magnitude, Rudy Macklin's reputation in television was at its peak. When there was a job opening for producer of the new Home show, Rudy was the logical choice. Vandersagen okayed the appointment without looking at a great many other candidates. The fact that Rudy and Kate were old friends made the appointment particularly attractive. Maureen told Lieutenant Quinn, by way of clarification, "It was a good way for Jim to keep an eye on Rudy too."

Quinn said, "Why would he want to do that?"

"I told you, Rudy has been sort of courting Kate since Avi died, and if Jim did, have any ideas...I'm not saying there was something going on between Kate and Jim...well, you know how it is with gossip, especially in this business."

"Do you think," Irving Quinn wanted to know, "Rudy might have had a more concrete reason for wanting Vandersagen dead?"

"Well, I don't know. You mean, Rudy might still be thinking about his father and what his mother said, blaming him for Larry's death?"

Quinn nodded.

"I haven't really thought about that. At least, not until now. Yes, I suppose you could say so, but, murder? I can't believe such a thing. Rudy could never—he's just not the murderous type. Rudy is simply not mean enough."

Irving Quinn knew better than to refute Maureen though, in his experience, there had been plenty of murders committed by people who appeared to be the very essence of kindness and humility.

"Tell me more about this Rudy guy. You say he's the producer? He'd know about the mirror and all?"

"Of course. The crews all report to him. He makes all the decisions about the sets and the lights."

The detective gently stopped Maureen from giving him a full account of how television shows are organized. He wanted to know about Rudy.

Rudy had gone to Columbia University with Avi and Kate, but dropped out before getting his degree. He was anxious to work full-time in television broadcasting where his father's contemporaries had made a place for him.

Later, Rudy worked on the Boston news show where Avi had been one of four reporters, then moderator, on a Friday wrap-up. Avi and Kate and the Macklins were a foursome, very friendly until Rudy and his wife split up.

The following year, when Avi went to New York to work on the *Times* as well as a weekly news roundup on JGV, it was only natural that Rudy should come along. Then, as Avi's career headed for the top, Rudy seemed to withdraw. He felt they were no longer equals. Avi was becoming a star while Rudy, as he described himself, was, "still just a glorified stagehand."

Maureen explained, "But I remember Avi saying it was all in Rudy's head—the difference in their status. Of course, you know how these things happen. Especially where there's such a big gap between incomes. But it wasn't Avi who snubbed Rudy. It was the other way 'round."

After Avi's death, when Kate managed to pull herself together and was reconciled to permitting Joel and DeeDee to go back to college, she was deeply depressed, though she functioned, somehow. Everyone, Maureen, Tom, Avi's mother, Jeanne, and her friends did their best, but Kate was working on a private timetable and handling her grief and loneliness in ways not all of them understood. Except for Rudy.

Rudy would go to her apartment and watch hours of old, classic movies with her. Sometimes Rudy would arrive with the ingredients for an exotic meal in the style of one of the food fads that come and go in New York. Once, after searching the markets, he arrived with a partridge and Italian truffles which he used in a dressing under the skin. "Fantastic!" Kate had announced as she tasted it. "Now, I'm going to need an entirely new wardrobe. Rudy, you should have been a chef."

"Oh, no," said Rudy, "that's Laurie's domain." Laurie, Rudy's ex-wife and once, a close friend to Kate and Avi, was now an innkeeper in Vermont. Rudy was lonely. Kate was lonely. It seemed the perfect climate in which to nurture a romance.

But Rudy was hesitant, perhaps because Kate signaled her unreadiness. Perhaps it was because of her new job and the fact that Kate suddenly focused her energy on it—and on her new boss, as well.

Maureen explained. "You see, Rudy had been trying to step in, you know, play the consoling lover. Rudy is a very sweet man and he and Avi were once very close. But Kate wasn't ready for another man in her life at that point. Rudy was hurt. He was probably furious at being rejected. And then, when he suspected that Kate and Jim..."

"What about Kate and Jim? You mean Vandersagen?"

Maureen nodded.

"Was there something going on between them? Was Kate having an affair with Vandersagen?"

Maureen stood. "How can you even imply such a thing about my daughter! My God, what kind of a question is that? Jim's old enough to be her father. And besides, he's a married man; he was her boss! He runs the—I mean ran, the network!"

"Well, your daughter is a grown woman and she's been a widow for a couple a years. Nobody'd be surprised if such a thing happened."

"But, Jim Vandersagen? He's old enough to be her father! Really, Inspector."

"No, I'm a lieutenant."

"Well, anyway, there couldn't have been anything between them, not with him. They just worked together. My God, Kate and Jim Vandersagen!" Maureen said it as if she were describing a particularly weird-looking, green-slime specimen that had just stepped off a rocket vehicle from Mars.

"That usually has very little to do with whether or not a man has an affair with a younger woman. And working together—that's a classic beginning for love affairs."

"Well, my daughter is not that kind of younger woman, I can assure you. She's hardly finished mourning her husband. How could she possibly be involved in a sordid affair with her boss?"

Irving Quinn declined to cite any of the hundreds of cases in which young widows sought to console themselves with affairs, liaison, dates,—or whatever they were called—with their bosses.

"But, what about my daughter? That mirror could have killed her too, couldn't it? In fact, how do you know it wasn't really meant for her and that Jim just got killed by accident."

"I don't know. I don't know much more than you do. I know that somebody wanted to kill either your daughter or Jim Vandersagen and if the mirror wasn't going to do it, then poisoned chocolate sauce would."

"But...." Maureen paused, afraid to voice her fears. Then, she plunged ahead. "You've got to protect her! You can't just let the killer run around loose. He might very well try again. Lieutenant, don't let anything happen to my daughter." It was more a plea than a demand and Quinn took Maureen's hand to let her know he understood.

The interview was over. Quinn stood first an helped Maureen to her feet. "Thank you for being so helpful. I know how upset you are about your daughter. But this kind of thing is absolutely essential if we're going to get to the bottom of the case. With a carefully planned homicide like this, the best chance we've got is to talk to everyone we can, especially witnesses, like yourself. And, don't worry, we'll keep an eye on Kate." He didn't explain further.

"You mean, I can go now?" Maureen had seen and played in enough cop shows to know that was the right question.

"Of course." Lieutenant Quinn actually gave Maureen the slightest bow from the waist. She nearly laughed. It didn't suit his rough-looking cop's face—a mug, her mother would have called it—nor his off-the-rack, wrinkled suit that had seen too many trips to the dry cleaners. Then she chided herself. Maureen Cassidy, she said silently, you've become a snob in your old age. A fine one you are, coming from Deirdre O'Hearn's cold-water flat under the El and over a saloon.

Maureen wanted to take another peek at her daughter before leaving, but she hesitated when she spotted Tom softly opening the door to Kate's room. Another meeting with him would surely cause her dormant ulcer to act up. She turned and took the stairs to the floor below before taking the elevator to the lobby.

Now, drifting in and out of Demerol-induced sleep, Kate dreamed of the events in her life. Not surprisingly, the show, and some of her guests appeared most clearly. Perhaps it was because, for Kate Cassidy Ginzburg, the show, her first in New York, was anodyne and distraction after the violent death of her husband of twenty-one years. And most helpful of all was the kindness and attention paid her by her new boss, Jim Vandersagen.

Media mogul, Yale graduate, blue-water sailor, scion of a seventeenth century Dutch family that had settled in the Hudson River Valley, James Gardner Vandersagen, chairman of the TV network, liked to look in on the magazine show that got its name during Kate's first lunch with her prospective boss. The working relationship began quickly and the chemistry between Kate and Jim was powerful from the start. They lunched, they dined, they walked the Avenues and went to the galleries. And, always, they had a great deal to talk about.

If anyone had seen them, their heads together over a drink or dinner, after a tape session, the assumption that an affair had begun would have been natural. And Jim made no effort to conceal his growing affection for the young widow. This, despite the difference in their ages; he was twenty-five years older.

Overhearing Jim and Kate, one might have been surprised to learn that, often, the subject of conversation was Kate, her children and her late husband, rather than something more romantic.

Kate and Avi had met, fallen in love and married while they were students, majoring in journalism, at Columbia University. She was in the eighth month of her first pregnancy when she waddled across the platform to receive her diploma.

Avi got a job at the *Boston Globe*. Kate stayed at home, mothering Joel and soon was pregnant with her second baby, DeeDee.

It was several years before Kate even thought about the career for which she had prepared at Columbia, but eventually, she found part-time work as an editor for a woman's magazine which led to her debut in television at a Boston station. She did a five-minute spot every evening about good buys on fresh produce in Boston markets. It wasn't the foreign desk at the *Globe*, as in Avi's case, but it was a sort of journalism and it kept her loneliness at bay when, during the next fifteen years, Avi traveled on overseas assignments which kept him away for weeks at a stretch.

Later, when the Ginzburgs left Boston to settle into a large, airy apartment in a great building on Central Park West, it was for Avi, a peak moment in his career. For Kate it meant she could, with the clear conscience of a mother whose children are grown, try for her own bit of spotlight in what to her, was the only city that really mattered, New York.

Only a decade before, the JGV network had evolved to cover a mass of TV, print and ultimately, movie distribution and production. Inevitably, Jim would cast an eye toward ownership of related acquisitions like motion picture studios with full-scale production of films for theater and television. At his death, Jim Vandersagen's dream was all but realized. In a last public statement, several days earlier, Jim had said of JGV, "We're commercial but not pandering and you don't have to be ashamed to admit that you watch the network at any hour of the day or night."

Avi became a star on JGV's weekly news roundup, when he was at home, broadcast from New York or—more likely—beamed by satellite-remote from some exotic place where events were moving. In fact, where there was news and possible danger, there Avi went; the hotter the spot, the better he liked it.

As the Ginzburgs became part of Jim Vandersagen's universe, their lives would change as well. The news reporter was to become, in his own right, as much a star as the figures whom he interviewed. People were often heard to say "So-and-So was on the Ginzburg Show yesterday." or "I wonder who's going to be on Ginzburg tonight." And when he wasn't doing his news show, he was doing what he loved best, visiting the places where the news was made.

Always deeply interested in the Middle East, Avi made several trips a year to the country of his father's birth. Just before he was killed, he had been planning to moderate a large meeting of all parties, including Muslim fundamentalists and moderates, from every one of the countries with which Israel had once been at war.

Their father's death, when Joel and DeeDee were in college, desolated them and their mother. For their paternal grandmother, Jeanne Rosen Ginzburg, herself a journalist, it was a grim irony. Avi died in much the same way as his father—gunned down by terrorists—while touring the West Bank of the Jordan River.

Now Kate woke again and looked around the austere hospital room. Moments before, as the drugs spun her mind, reeling through the labyrinth of memories, she had seen them all;, everyone whose life had touched hers; Avi, her children, her mother and Deirdre. But most vividly she had seen Jim Vandersagen. She was confused when she realized where she was and why. She lay still, too drugged for panic; she was sad instead. She felt as if she might cry if only she had the energy. Jim was dead. And, worse, his death may have been a mistake. Someone may have been trying to kill her instead. Then, with chilling lucidity, and a jolt of fear-triggered adrenaline, her mind focused. She was afraid. Suddenly, Kate was more afraid than she ever had been in her entire life, including the heart-stopping moment when, during labor with Joel, the doctor came into the room and announced that she required an emergency Cesarean section to save the life of her baby.

"Where's Avi?" she had screamed.

"I think he went out for a sandwich." said the nurse who had been monitoring her labor.

"How the hell can he go out for a sandwich at a time like this?"

The doctor was injecting something into her arm. "Oh men usually get very hungry during lengthy labors."

Just before relaxing into a lovely stupor, she had thought, if I ever get through this, I'm going to kill him.

But now, there was nobody. The person who was quite possibly trying to murder Kate was still out there. For all she knew, he could be waiting just on the other side of the door to the corridor. Frankly terrified, she whimpered, "Oh, Avi, why did you go away? It's just like you to be someplace else whenever something goes wrong."

Finally Kate wept openly, crying aloud like an injured and frightened child, wailing for Avi, for her mother, for her father and at last, when she was spent, she gave herself another shot of Demerol.

There were the usual noises one hears in a hospital, loudspeakers calling cryptic messages, voices outside her door, the rattle of lunch trays being collected. Kate was oblivious to them all. But somewhere, in that small part of her brain that refused to succumb to the drug, she tried to figure out why someone would kill Jim Vandersagen or, possibly, kill Jim by mistake while trying to kill her. If the killer had indeed been mistaken, that meant he'd certainly try again.

Would it be here, as she lay helpless in a hospital bed? Or would the killer wait until she got home and find his way to her apartment where she lived alone while the children were gone. Oh yes, the rational part of Kate's mind argued, your building has excellent security. But that hadn't stopped Evelyn Hingham's crazed ex-husband from getting past the doorman and breaking into her apartment to nearly murder her with a baseball bat.

More dreams followed, then Kate woke again. This time she pondered the likes of that policeman, what was his name? Irving something? How much help was he going to be in protecting her from a would-be murderer? Relaxing a bit now, she drifted into a daydream.

Irving something-the-cop. He wasn't bad looking. Stop it, Kate, she told herself. You've been doing that a lot lately. You've got to stop thinking about men as possible sex objects. She allowed herself a small smile. Well, maybe not sex, so much, it was cuddling she missed. The cop didn't seem like the cuddly type, too tall and stringy.

CHAPTER TWO

THE MORNING AFTER Jim Vandersagen's "accident" Lieutenant Irving Quinn was in his cramped office, talking with the detectives who were assisting him in the investigation.

Jonah Smith, whom people sometimes called Joannie, was tall, chocolate brown, bulky and very male. He did not mind the feminization of his name. He had been a college football player once considered by the pros until his father expressed a dying wish that Jonah follow him into the New York Police Department, upholding a family tradition. Jonah hated football anyway. He liked being a detective in today's high tech police world; he loved computers and the magical functions they could perform.

Smith's partner, Alexander Karalopoulis, liked to compare himself with the Kojak persona of the late Telly Sevalas, though his light but sinewy stature and luxuriant wavy hair hardly suggested the role model. The one thing Alex had in common with Kojak was his love of Greek dancing, something Jonah Smith never got the hang of. However, Alex was the ideal partner for Smith; they had been working together since their rookie days. Irving Quinn encouraged such bonding. As for himself, having made Lieutenant, he sometimes felt that working alone, if not burdensome, meant he must forego a certain comradely warmth. He was having to adjust to being called Boss or Lieutenant by those who had only recently called him Irv.

During their first quiet moment after the Vandersagen murder, the lieutenant and the two sergeants sat around the boss's littered desk with their cups of coffee. Leading off, Quinn said, "What do we know about this guy Vandersagen?" Jonah Smith pointed to the pages of printouts he had culled from the data banks of the city's newspaper morgues. It wasn't the drudgery of the old days when one had to paw through crumbling paper files, and more important, today, the information was infinitely more detailed.

Beginning with a major news story about James G. Vandersagen, Senior, in the late thirties, when young Jim was thirteen, Alex and Jonah told Quinn what they had discovered.

Long after the Great Depression had eased, when the war in Europe was about to erupt, James G. Vandersagen, Senior realized that he was not only broke, but that his attempts to recoup investments had soured. His next move then, had led him into New York State politics.

Using his position as a Senator in Albany, Vandersagen had, apparently, made more than one accommodation which the *New York Daily News* described on the front page: STATE SENATOR MADE SHADY DEALS.

Quinn said, "That's the kind of headline that made my mother insist we never take any paper except the Times. She had a fit whenever we read the others."

"Yeah, well, it gets better," said Alex. "It says he blew his brains out and his debts were paid by the wife's family. The fact is, if you believe the newspaper stories, the guy was a crook. But it all happens suddenly. One day he's a respected member of an old family; the next day he's a bum."

"Yeah," said Jonah, "we all have days like that."

For thirteen year-old James G. Vandersagen, Jr. it was the day which he always thought of as his initiation into the world of adults. He once told his first wife, "At thirteen, Jewish kids get a *Bar Mitzvah.*

When I was thirteen, I got to find out that my old man was a swindler and a thief."

His father had been upstairs in the study of the Vandersagen house on its private island in Long Island Sound, within view of Westchester County and its yacht club-studded shoreline. Jimmy, as he was then called, thought his father wanted to have the usual father-son chat about what the boys at his school called, "The F of F.", code for "The facts of fucking." The key word, if overheard by a master, might be grounds for expulsion from the prep school that educated the sons of Yale men before they went to their fathers' college.

The talk had begun simply enough. Vandersagen Senior asked, "Well, Jimmy, how's it going at school? The masters still as tough as they used to be when I went there?"

"I guess so, sir." Jimmy really didn't know his father very well, except for Summer vacations on The Sound or Narragansett Bay, when he was allowed to crew on the family's twelve-meter yacht. And then they talked only about the boat, the races and related matters. Their passion for the *Sea Lancer* was the only thing father and son had ever shared.

"Oh, come off it, kid. You don't have to 'sir' me. I'm your father. For Christ's sake. Why don't you just call me Pop or something."

Jimmy realized his father had been drinking. In fact, he was nearly incoherent. The boy stood in front of the large, mahogany desk, feeling foolish and wanting to be gone, but he didn't know how to withdraw gracefully, so he listened.

"You know, kid, this family has always been rich. I mean really rich. But we were just like everybody else when the crash came. Oh, we didn't lose it all, but we lost enough so my old man went nuts. Did'ya know he died in a fancy mental hospital? Well, not me; I'm not going to go like that. Not your old man. Listen, Jimmy, I jus' wanna tell you one thing. Don't try to get it back. Jus' don't try to get it back. Okay?"

"Okay, uh, sir. Is that all, uh, Pop? Can, I mean, may I go now?"

"Sure you can. G'wan. But, remember, you can't get it back. You gotta make it all over again."

Trying not to be appear too anxious to leave, Jimmy retreated and, very gently, closed the door behind him. He had walked about twelve feet down the hall toward the staircase, when he heard a single shot.

His mother, who had been in the bedroom next door, was the first to reach her husband. By the time Jimmy raced back into the study, his father had slipped out of his chair onto the floor where a pool of blood from his temple was beginning to stain the pale gray carpet. The small caliber pistol was still clutched in his hand.

There was enough money for Jim Vandersagen to go to Yale, and, during the war, when everyone was expected to live simply, the grand yacht stayed moored at the Larchmont Club. But Diana Vandersagen told her son, "There will be enough to keep up appearances so that when Vicki gets married, we won't have to hang our heads. But you'd better either plan on a career in the Navy or turn your hand to making a dollar, if you hope to even try to live the way we used to in the old days."

Jim went into the Navy after Yale and the NROTC, but within a year, he was discharged with bleeding ulcers. No great loss, he thought. Now, he could get on with fulfilling his father's advice—to make it all over again.

For Vandersagen, Yale had been a foundation. But not for the kinds of enterprises most of his classmates chose. They went into the stock and bond markets, they went to law school and joined old, established firms and they took low-level but promising jobs in family businesses. Most of them prospered. But, in light of his father's betrayal of his class—fraud plus suicide, many of these traditional avenues to success were closed to Jim. Even in the nineteen fifties, when many of the old standards had been abandoned, a crook and a coward remained poor currency when it came to the value of one's father's standing in the community.

At mid-century society stood precariously in the ever-widening gap between Victorian rectitude and late-century permissiveness. There was no place for the son of James Vandersagen, Senior in the world of people with good names and good connections. There was nothing for young Jimmy to do but carve out a new name and new connections.

Advertising was one career for which a Yale education was of some value and nobody gave a damn about what a man's father had done. In 1950 Vandersagen managed to get a job in one of New York's better advertising agencies. He was utterly bored by the client end of the business, but was genuinely fascinated by the tools of the trade, radio, television, newspapers and magazines.

The following year, while visiting the radio studio where a client's soap opera was being aired, Jim ran into his ex-classmate, Larry Macklin. Larry, had fooled around at the Yale Drama School and was now calling himself a director. Anyway, he was telling actors what to do and nobody laughed at him. Jim was impressed.

Larry had earned much of the cost of tuition at Yale by managing one of New Haven's pre-Broadway tryout theaters. Now, he was building a career in radio, off-Broadway, and increasingly, in live television drama.

Larry introduced Jim to some friends in the theater, who offered Vandersagen a chance to invest in a new musical comedy. Macklin said, "This is the big time, Broadway." It may have been little more than hype, but Jim Vandersagen had the soul of a gambler and the very idea of a Broadway show was too seductive to resist. He put up five thousand dollars, cash from the sale of his old Cord and some antique, diamond-studded cuff links.

Not only did Jim's small stake quintuple when the show was a hit, he decided that show business was infinitely more exciting than advertising. The theater was fun, and, if he could have fun and make money too—well his old man certainly wouldn't have quarreled with that idea.

That Spring, Freddy Sherwood was putting together a company to do three, maybe four shows in a place near Chathamtown on Cape Cod. Freddy, together with Larry Macklin, had conceived a dream. All they needed was a bankroll, or, in the vernacular, an angel. They already had the location.

In 1949 Larry had inherited an old building, a barn, really, and a large frame house. As Larry described the place, "on the outer elbow of the Cape—perfect; the ocean on one side and the bay on the other."

Together, Larry and Freddy had the know-how for turning the place into a theater and, with Jim Vandersagen and his Broadway winnings, they were certain they had the perfect threesome for a Summer theater to rival anything on the Cape, except maybe, Provincetown. As for Jim, he had fantasies about making considerable profit out of the playhouse project, but he dreamed too about putting the Sea Lancer back into its pre-war condition of splendor. He even dared dream about the Americas Cup.

The Chathamtown Playhouse was conceived one boozy Winter evening in Greenwich Village among three people who would give it a life full of action, drama and pathos. They toasted their creation and planned the Summer—from early June through Labor Day.

Larry Macklin, Jim Vandersagen and Freddy Sherwood called themselves the producers and director. The stars were to be professional actors. The second leads and supporting players would be selected from among the dozens of actors who had passed through Freddy Sherwood's classes. Nobody, except the stars would be paid much, if anything. Money was not why young people joined a Summer theater company. At least, not at first.

The two most promising members of Freddy's acting classes were a girl named Maureen O'Hearn and a young man from Bridgeport, named Tom Cassidy. Tom and Maureen too dreamed in the bitter cold, long Winter nights of New York, warming themselves with images of Cape Cod and the magic of the theater that was to be.

For most of that year Maureen O'Hearn and Tom Cassidy were an on-again, off-again couple. They quarreled, broke up and then made up. Maureen wavered between loving him and wishing for someone different. But Tom never went out with other girls. He said he would always love Maureen and made no secret of his wish to marry her. He kept asking, but she told him they were too financially insecure, to name but one compelling reason to stay single.

Maureen wanted to concentrate on her career, afraid that marriage would arrest her progress. She didn't want to be sidetracked by having a family, To make matters worse, she was beset by her mother, Deirdre's constant harping. "You should marry him, I tell ya. He's good lookin' and he's from a nice family."

"For God's sake, Ma, you never met his family. His mother's drinking herself to death, and his father's trying to become a saint. He's taking care of her and working twelve hours a day at that helicopter factory. Besides, I don't want to get married. So will you shut up, please, just once, shut up about marrying Tom Cassidy."

If Deirdre was hurt she kept it to herself. She was tired. She was tired of working as a cleaning woman, even if it was at the fanciest office in Midtown. If Maureen would just get married, get hold of some money...and maybe there'd be a baby to look after. Ah, how she'd love the luxury of being a real grandmother.

Tom Cassidy rarely went home to Bridgeport. He couldn't bear to see his mother lying in bed with the single glass on the table. He knew, and she didn't care that he knew, about the gin bottles under the bed. God, he thought, I'm not ever going to let booze destroy my life like that. He could smell the stuff through the pores of her skin, so he stopped kissing her, even on the cheek.

Pete Cassidy had once yelled at him. "Why do you have to do that fairy work, acting? You could take Engineering right here at Bridgeport U. You have any idea of what those guys get paid at Sikorsky? You'd be rich, boy. Instead, you're runnin' around the stage in your underwear, sayin' stuff like 'methinks' and 'thou doth' and shit like that."

Tom laughed. He loved his old man. "It's not underwear. Those are tights. And that 'shit' is Shakespeare. Besides, I don't want to be an engineer, except maybe for building scenery and stuff. And I don't need an engineering degree to hang lights and paint flats."

"You're not one a them queers, are ya, lad? It'd break my heart if you was—you know that, don't you?"

"My God, is that what you're worrying about?" Tom had never thought his choice of work in the theater might worry Pete. He wasn't even sure Pete had ever met a homosexual. They were starting to call themselves "gay."

"Don't worry, Pop, I love girls. In fact, I'm trying to get one of them to marry me. Maybe we can get married and I can get her pregnant in a hurry. I'm beginning to worry about this draft business. My number's gonna come up pretty soon.

"You ain't makin' enough money to get married, much less have a kid." Then he added, "You don't have to worry, boy. There ain't gonna be another war. Least I don't think so. Anyway, if you went back to school to study engineering, at least you could be an officer and not get shot at if there is a war." Sometimes, Tom Cassidy found his father's logic baffling.

After quitting classes at Bridgeport in his sophomore year, Tom got a full-time job as a bellhop at the Waldorf Astoria. It was the perfect arrangement for a young student actor, and a long tradition among the Waldorf house staff. Hours could be arranged if someone got lucky enough to get a job and there was always time for acting classes which were paid for out of earnings of tips and wages.

Tom had never told anyone, but he loved working at the Waldorf where he could observe the comings and goings of not just the very rich, but star-actors and as well as directors and producers. There were other, more expensive, more subdued, fine hotels in New York, but for Tom, none had the cachet, the style, the sense of opulence of the Waldorf.

That Spring, he had nearly danced around the locker room in his neat bellhop's uniform; he was going to be in Summer stock! His boss said he could have his job back at the end of the season.

They were to arrive at what Larry Macklin was now calling the Chathamtown Playhouse the first week in June; rehearsals to begin immediately for The Taming of the Shrew, Life with Father and Our Town. The stars, Quentin Price and Leona Fairleigh, would work for scale because they needed the exposure. Everyone would benefit from working with seasoned old hands like these, though Leona might scratch out the eyes of anyone whom she heard describing her as "old."

The rest of the crew, actors from Freddy's studio, local kids and Yale classmates of Jim Vandersagen and Larry Macklin made up the rest of the company. Macklin was in charge of set-building and lighting; Freddy and John MacDonald, who was expected to come after school closed in New York, would help to direct and stage-manage. Jim Vandersagen was in charge of financial affairs.

Two days before everyone was to leave for the Cape, Vandersagen appeared at Freddy's to give people their bus tickets and small cash advances for meals until they got settled. A cook had been hired but she wouldn't arrive until the following week. And, the last night before going to the Cape, everyone was invited to the yacht club in Larchmont, for a cocktail party. "Wear your prettiest dresses ladies. And you guys. Try not to look like the bums you are."

That night, Tom and Maureen walked uptown toward Chelsea where Tom had a room in a brownstone house run by a German couple who had been letting rooms to actors since before the war. They had assured Tom that his room would be waiting for him after the season on the Cape.

Tom and Maureen were in high spirits. They had eaten spaghetti and drunk cheap red wine at the Italian joint near Freddy's and now, they were looking forward to a few hours alone together in Tom's room.

Making love was still a bit strange for Maureen, but Tom was a careful, gentle partner and he would not press her if, on occasion, she was a bit reluctant. Nor was he without sympathy for her terror of pregnancy. At his urging, she had gone to a clinic and been fitted for a diaphragm. Using it seemed to dampen the spontaneous nature of lovemaking, but, Maureen thought, better that than pregnancy. She always said a Hail Mary whenever she slid the little rubber cap in place and added an extra dollop of Ortho cream. Then she promised herself she'd go to confession very soon.

She was shy and Tom tried to bring her in and out of the house without having to meet the other roomers. But Hilda, the landlady, made Maureen feel that there was nothing sordid in the affair. Seeing a young, good-looking couple reminded her of her youth in the early thirties before she and her Jewish husband had fled Hamburg. "Zo nize, young kits. I like to see zem." And she would pinch the ample pouch of fat that hung over her husband's belt.

Tonight, Hilda handed Tom a letter. From the look on his face as he tore it open and read it, she and Maureen both knew it was his draft notice. He was to report for induction and basic training in the Army the very day everyone else was to leave for Cape Cod.

Another actor named Ned Randal took Tom's place. He tried to sound sorry that Tom had been drafted, but Maureen wanted to slap him. "Yeah, I'll bet you're sorry. All I've got to say is, you'll have your work cut out for you, trying to be half as good as Tom Cassidy."

Though she missed Tom after he left and she went to Chathamtown, Maureen wasn't morose. With rehearsals and building a theater out of little more than four walls and a roof, the whole company was in a fever of activity.

The highly visible Jim Vandersagen worked as hard as everyone else and was especially kind to the actors.

He was there the day Maureen experienced her first, not her last, verbal attack by Leona Fairleigh.

To Freddy, Leona said, "If you let that little snip step on my lines one more time, I'm going to get on the first bus out of here and you can see how well your pushy Irish Rose does then. Somebody ought to let her know that Bianca is a supporting role. And you ought to teach her how to act before expecting a real professional, like me, to go on stage with her." Leona was certain that Maureen had heard every word. As the cast stood, open-mouthed, Leona turned upstage with a satisfied look on her face. In tears, Maureen fled and Freddy called an end to the rehearsal.

Flying down the steps toward the weed-filled back yard, Maureen almost collided with Jim Vandersagen. "Here, what's this? That bitch make you cry?"

Maureen took his proffered handkerchief and nodded, still sobbing.

Jim put his arms around her and patted her shoulder, making soothing noises. When she got control, he said, "Better?"

"Yes, thanks, Jim. God, I've made a mess of your hanky." She held it limply.

He covered her hand and then took the handkerchief and put it into his pocket. "Isn't rehearsal over for today? You got something to do tonight?"

"Learn lines for Our Town, that's all."

"Don't you know them by now?"

"Of course, but...."

"No buts. I'm going to drive you over to Hyannis and buy you the biggest lobster in the State of Massachusetts. Would you like that?"

It had been a grueling three weeks and she had not had time to talk with the big, fair-haired man. She knew that few girls were indifferent to his appeal. It was not just the Yale-old-family-yacht club-air of self assurance that made Jim Vandersagen attractive. He was nice. John MacDonald had taught Maureen that the word nice was weak and should never be used to describe anything, much less a person. But, in the case of Jim Vandersagen, Maureen was convinced there could not be a more perfect word.

The evening in Hyannis, at the big, old fashioned hotel was the sort of thing that had been seducing lovers since the beginning of Cape Cod's reign as a premiere Summer resort.

Jim and Maureen walked the beach and, when she admitted to being sleepy, he took her to a quiet motel.

Jim's lovemaking was electrifying. Unlike Tom, Jim never asked if this or that was alright. He just took her smoothly from restful stroking to a raging, clawing orgasmic height she had never achieved with Tom. Nor had she known herself to contain so much sheer greed for sex. Again and again, that night and nights to follow, Jim Vandersagen and Maureen tore from each other a kind of desperate pleasure.

Toward the end of the season, they went, once more, to Hyannis. How could she, she thought, ever go back to making love with Tom after this? Sobbing again, but this time, for having spent herself in the delirium of her sixth orgasm in less than an hour. Maureen kept her wits about her just enough to avoid saying, "I love you."

The following night, after the show, she couldn't sleep in the hot little room she was lucky enough not to have to share with another girl. Barefoot, she walked to the bathroom, then to a small balcony that overlooked the side porch of the house. She heard voices. Macklin? She wasn't sure.

Then she heard Jim Vandersagen say, quite clearly, "You really ought to try that little Irish piece. I'm telling you, she's a wildcat."

Three

IRVING QUINN, leafing through sheets of computer-generated profiles of the cast and company at the Chathamtown Playhouse in 1951, said what everyone else was thinking.

"It looks like every one of these people back then on Cape Cod could tell us a lot about our Mr. Vandersagen. I wonder how many of them are still around."

"That's the whole point." Jonah said. I hear the theater company was full of people who still have connections to this guy. And, as far as I can see, quite a few of them have, or have had motives, for knocking off the big V."

Quinn agreed. "Okay then. Those people at that Cape Cod theater— I think it's essential that we talk to everybody who was up there."

Alex said, "Not everybody. Some of them are dead."

"Very funny." Irving Quinn stayed on track. "What about this guy Tom Cassidy? Didn't the producer, Rudy Macklin say his father once told him that Maureen and Vandersagen had a wild affair just before she married Tom? I know it's ancient history, but a guy can nurse a lot of resentment for years after his girl climbs into the sack with another man while he's at Fort Dix, sweating through basic training."

"Yeah," said Jonah, "but I think you're better off looking at the people in his life now. I mean, in his life until yesterday."

"Like who?" Quinn liked to let his men think for themselves.

"Well, for starters, how about her?" He was pointing to a poor reproduction of the wedding picture, in formal cutaway and designer gown, of James G. Vandersagen and Sally-Ann Peterson. This was in the Spring of 1952 and the story told of the alliance of the Peterson newspaper and radio heiress with "the new owner of local television station WJGV."

Quinn peered at the blurry picture and said, "I'll bet that wedding cost more than my old man made that whole year after making sergeant and being on the force for half his life."

Alex nodded. "Yeah, those society weddings, my father's a caterer—and let me tell you—just the booze alone...."

"What about her? Weren't they divorced in a big way about twenty years ago?" Quinn flipped through the sheets. "Yeah, here it is."

It was another reprint from the Daily News. The headline screamed, I FOUND HIM IN ANOTHER WOMAN'S BED!.

"Where else," Jonah laughed, "In another woman's kitchen?"

"Here she is, the other woman." Alex pulled up a glamorous portrait of Adele Vandersagen.

Quinn took the picture and squinted. He was soon going to have to get reading glasses. "I've got an appointment to see her this afternoon. She was in the studio yesterday. I wonder if there's a reason she'd want to kill Kate or, for that matter, her husband?"

In an initial interview, yesterday, Rudy Macklin had told Lieutenant Quinn that several crew members had overheard the loud quarrel between Adele and Jim Vandersagen. Another man's voice was heard too. He was identified as Adele's half-brother, Gil Kenyon.

Though nobody could pinpoint the exact time the voices were heard, it was within half an hour before the crash. And Gil Kenyon was definitely in the studio when the mirror fell. Quinn assigned Jonah to locate and interview him.

After the pandemonium in which Jim's death was determined and Kate was taken to Roosevelt hospital, Rudy Macklin was in his small office near studio C. He poured coffee for himself and Quinn.

"Well, I wasn't in the studio when it all happened. In fact, until fifteen minutes ago, when I walked in, I had been sitting in a chair at the endodontist's"

"What's that?"

"Not somebody you'd want to spend a whole lot of time with. He's a dentist who specializes in root canal work." He pointed to a molar. "It's this one here. Been giving me pure hell for weeks now. The tooth fairy says one more visit and he'll be finished with me."

"How long was your appointment?"

"Let's see. I got there a few minutes early, but I had to wait nearly half an hour. And then, actual time in the chair? I'd say forty-five minutes. Then, down the elevator and out onto 96th Street. It took at least ten more minutes to get a cab; you know how it is at that time of the morning. I got here," he looked at his watch, "ten o'clock, not a minute earlier."

"What about last night? Tell me about that mirror. Who rigs things like that? Were you here? What time did you leave? Who's in charge of the studio when you're not here?"

"Whoa, Lieutenant. Let me give it to you one step at a time. He poured more coffee and said, "Okay, starting with setting up the studio, last night, here's what you ought to know."

The studio in which Kate's show was taped had about a hundred, fifty seats configured as an amphitheater. The set was large enough to accommodate anything from a kitchen arrangement, like the one for which the mirror was rigged, to a round table for conversation. Sometimes the setup was quite elaborate like the one the previous week.

The guest was a famous city and town planner, who, using scale models, built an entire city, complete with tiny cars, an interurban railway and houses arranged on spoke-like streets that led to shopping, schools and transportation hubs.

On this set too, overhead mirrors were rigged so that cameras could shoot the reflections of the model town, as the designer placed various elements on a large table-like surface.

"Who rigs those mirrors?" Quinn asked.

"Usually, it's the carpenter, though the electricians and cameramen get involved too because of the lighting, you know, angles and reflections and stuff like that."

"And the mirrors are always a single piece?"

"No, usually, there are several, each one serving a different camera. Today, for example, we had two. One over the stove area and the other above the counter. It was the counter mirror that fell."

"Just what made it fall?"

"Oh, that's easy. Each set of lashing was blown by a squib."

"A squib? Sounds like something you clean your ears with."

"Yeah. It's an old standby in movies and stuff. A squib is just a small explosive charge that releases key sections of a structure so that gravity does the rest."

Quinn was not sure he understood.

"Look," Rudy got a videotape and started it. "I'll show you." The monitor on his desk showed the opening credits for a Western. Then Rudy fast-forwarded the tape to a particular scene. In the foreground, a mounted man rode toward the camera, while behind him, what appeared to be a solid adobe wall, collapsed. It was as if it had been struck by shellfire from a distant canon. "See that? What happens is, the wall is wired and the squibs are fired by a remote. Just like this one." He turned off the monitor with a hand-held control.

"So you mean, someone who had rigged that mirror to fall, just picked the right moment to fire the remote and, boom! One or maybe two dead people under it when it drops?"

"That's right. I think that's what happened."

"Any chance it was rigged with a self-timer? You know, like a bomb?"

"I don't know. Your people wouldn't let me near the thing. They're all over the place. But I don't think there was a timer. The usual squib isn't set up that way."

"Where does somebody get those things?"

"In New York? My God, man, the city's full of people making movies and television shows. There must be fifty places that make and sell stuff like squibs and other special effects paraphernalia."

"Did you say the studio is set up the night before and then locked until the following morning when the taping starts?"

"Yes, usually. The later crews work on it because the studio is empty and they have all night, if necessary, to build the sets."

"And then?"

"What do you mean?"

"I mean, what happens when the crew finishes a set? Can anybody just walk in here and do something like rig these squibs?"

"No, especially not these days. The crews generally finish before six o'clock to prep a studio for taping the following day. Later, if it's a complicated set. When they finish, the place is secured and locked. Nobody gets in without a key."

"Who's got a key?"

"Well, let me see. I've got keys, so does the head electrician, Steve Chomko. And Andy Rubin, he's the carpenter. But, hey, I know where both of those guys were last night. I was with them. We were at our regular Tuesday night poker game. Last night it was at my house. We locked up here about six-thirty and all three of us went directly to Riverdale. Andy had his car so it wasn't too bad, going up the West Side Highway. The five other regulars got to my place before eight o'clock. We sent out for Chinese. I've got a big rec room, perfect for poker, and I um, I live there alone now. I'm divorced, you see."

Quinn saw perfectly. He said, "I grew up in Riverdale. My folks still live there, Riverside Avenue. Later on I lived in Great Neck, but I've got an apartment in midtown now. I'm divorced too."

"She left or you left?"

"I did. She's still there. My boys are in college and she's not at the house a whole lot. I miss the kids. But, God, I hated commuting from Long Island." Then Quinn was all cop again. "Did you see the mirror after it was rigged?"

"I sure did. In fact, we were a little short-handed last night, so I helped Steve and Andy. I can tell you this. When we left the studio last night and locked the door, that mirror was rigged perfectly—not a squib in sight."

"Were either of these guys...," Quinn looked at the notes he'd been making, "Andy or Steve, in the studio this morning when the mirror fell?"

"I think only Steve was. Andy said he was going to work again tonight, not come to the studio until about four o'clock. I think he's doing something for the big fashion show they're having here tomorrow afternoon—lots of stuff to do—a runway, bandstand—stuff like that."

"So, whoever fired those squibs, uhm, how close would he have to be with his remote?"

"That depends on how strong a signal you wanted to send. Could be anywhere from a couple of feet to 'way in the back of the studio. But the kind of remote I was talking about is probably like your garage door opener."

"Now you're saying you were at an all-night poker game?"

Rudy rubbed his jaw where the Novocain was wearing off. "Yeah, I lost a couple of hundred, but it took until seven o'clock in the morning."

Quinn accepted more coffee, thinking, this stuff is probably as bad for your liver as booze. "What did you do before you went to the fancy dentist?"

"The usual. I threw everybody out of the house, grabbed a hot shower and some food. Then I drove to the parking lot at the end of the subway line—you know where that is?"

Quinn nodded.

"I waited forever for the train and rode down to 96th Street to keep my appointment at the endodontist's"

"No sleep?"

"Nobody sleeps on poker nights, except the married guys. They have to go home eventually, or there's trouble."

"What about Andy, didn't you say he left early? Could he have stopped at the studio before going home?"

"Oh, no, not Andy, man. He lives out in the boonies, Rockaway, for God's sake. He's gotta leave no later than one o'clock. Andy's not what you'd call a hard-core poker player." Rudy's jaw was beginning to ache. He shook two aspirin directly into his mouth from the small bottle on his desk.

"Anyway, why would Andy want to hurt Vandersagen, or Kate, for that matter? I don't think they ever even saw one another until a month ago. Andy just got this job. Used to work for NBC up in Boston."

"And, what about Steve, the electrician? Wouldn't he know how to rig a squib?"

"Sure, we all do. But Steve's new here too. He's been working on Broadway for years. The show he was on closed about ten days ago and our old chief electrician, Bob Friend, well, he retired and I wanted somebody I could work with. I've known Steve for years. But that's it. I don't think Steve has ever had anything to do with either Vandersagen or Kate, except to say hello of course. Anyway, he was at the poker game until six this morning. He said he went home, grabbed some breakfast and got an hour's sleep before showing up here at eight o'clock. Steve wouldn't have had time to mess with the mirror. He was working with the light board ever since he got here. The camera crew too—they work together, you see."

"No, I don't see, for sure. But what you're saying is that both these guys and yourself can account for your time between last night at six-thirty, when you locked the studio, and this morning at—what time was the door unlocked?"

"Steve said he and the camera crew got here on the stroke of eight. And they can all vouch for one another."

"One more question, Rudy, then I'll let you go. The room, what do you call it, the Green Room?"

Rudy nodded.

"If somebody in the Green Room had a remote, could it send a signal through the walls into the studio here?"

"I'm not an engineer, but I'd guess if you had a transmitter strong enough, or it were wired to trigger another transmitter, maybe you could do it. But, from what I know about these things, you usually have to beam straight to the receiver—just like your TV control."

"But it's a thought, isn't it?"

Rudy shook his head. "Anything's possible, especially in this business. I gotta go. There's a taping in Studio B. No mirrors, this time."

"Just one more thing," Quinn sighed. "I've heard it said that you and Kate have differences from time to time. What I mean is...well, do you two ever fight?"

"Fight, Me and Kate? No, we don't fight. We sometimes have words about how the set or the lights should be, but, God, I've known Kate since we were kids. She was three years behind me at Columbia. I was best man at her wedding. Avi and I were so close...." He shook his head.

"I guess there's a difference between two professionals discussing their work and what you'd call a 'fight', right?"

"Right. And don't let Maureen Cassidy tell you anymore bullshit stories about me and her daughter. She used to drive my old man nuts—now she's doing the same to me." Privately, he wondered how he'd, get along with Maureen if he could persuade Kate to marry him. She may have the face of an angel, Rudy thought, but as a mother-in-law, well—if I had a choice, I'd take root canal work.

CHAPTER FOUR

LEAVING KATE IN the hospital after having been reassured by Irving Quinn that her daughter would be safe, Maureen got a cab to the garage where she had parked her car. And, as always when under stress, she could not help but think of Deirdre. She was grateful that her mother had been spared the sight of her granddaughter in so sorry a state.

Deirdre. Whenever there was trouble. Who knew more about trouble than she? Never for a moment had she allowed Maureen to forget a past which was not hers to remember. The poverty and the terror of being the other, Catholic in Protestant-dominated Belfast.

It had been different for Maureen growing up in New York, where everyone she knew was Catholic. Protestants were the other, like the tall blond girls in her high school or the totally beyond-reach lanky, handsome boys from private schools and colleges who crowded into Schrafft's after Saturday matinees at the theater. And there were dark-haired, confident Jewish girls whose fathers, Maureen was certain, were all furriers, providing their pampered daughters with little white fur shrugs to wear over their chiffon dresses. The Jews all seemed to live on Central Park West, while the Protestants lived on Park and Fifth. Uptown, in Harlem, when Maureen went for the first time to the Apollo Theater, she encountered blacks and Puerto Ricans as fellow New Yorkers. Though they were in her Manhattan school, she regarded them as so exotic they might as well have lived on another continent. As for the other boroughs, in time she learned just how big the city really was and she learned too, that people of every ethnicity tended to be somewhat self-absorbed and provincial, each group in its own fashion.

It had seemed so simple to Deirdre. There were themselves, Irish and Catholic, misunderstood, persecuted, forever among the least favored of God's creatures. Though yes, she did acknowledge the Eye-talians, for after all, weren't they too of the same Mother Church? This despite their tendency to be somewhat weird and forever, in her opinion, smelling of garlic.

For the moment, Maureen had to put thoughts of her mother on hold. There was the traffic to navigate first. In New York, traffic is like an evil deity with the power to destroy at a whim. One prays to it—oh please, don't be too crazy on the Triborough, just let me get up First Avenue with the synchronized lights really working this time. And please, please, no lunatic East Indian cab driver swiping my fender and claiming it's my fault!

As she emerged from the garage in the city's waning daylight, Maureen continued her prayers for a trouble-free trip North toward Larchmont, hoping to beat the worst rush-hour traffic. But, by the time she waited to get into line onto the FDR Drive, the early commuters were already choking the roads out of the city.

There was an endless ribbon of red tail lights which she knew meant she would become a part of a long, slow-moving river of cars that oozed, rather than flowed, towards Westchester County. There was nothing to do but wait and think about the things that had happened this morning.

Finally in the pattern, the car warmed against the chilling Autumn air, Maureen relaxed and went over the interview with Irving Quinn

He had said to tell him everything. Well, she had told him as much as she could—but everything? Where, she wondered, should one draw the line between what must be told and what must, forever, remain secret?

It was true, she had talked herself hoarse while Quinn kept refilling the coffee cups—as if she weren't nervous enough already, but she was too polite to refuse. The cop had wanted her to start at the beginning. Where was that? Perhaps she should not have talked so much about her mother. But then who would she be without Deirdre? Dead now nearly fifteen years, her mother made her presence known to fight, to cajole, to advise, to be available for consultation when life grew complicated.

Deirdre surely had been no stranger to complications. In 1928 she had stood, the infant Maureen in her arms, as she watched her young husband, Danny O'Hearn, gunned down by thug-like police, the British Royal Ulster Constabulary, the RUC. They were looking for a rumored cache of guns and ammunition, which an informer had told them were hidden in the O'Hearn's flat. But, in spite of turning the place over inch by inch, there was nothing.

In fact, Danny had been an anti-British activist since he was eleven years old in Dublin, the day of the Easter Rising, when he was witness to his father's death in O'Connell Street. Then he was sent to Belfast to live with relatives who, themselves, nurtured a fiery hatred for British rule.

Each day in Danny's life was dedicated to his primary role in the struggle to rid Ireland of her British rulers. He lived and ate and breathed the cause. But, for all that, he was a young man with a merry way about him. Then he met and married Deirdre Connors who had come to Belfast with her widowed father after her mother and three younger brothers had, one by one, died in the flu epidemic of 1920.

Living in a tiny flat, Deirdre had played kitchen canary to her father and watched him die too, after a fall from a scaffold where he had been steam-cleaning the city hall. Marriage to Danny and then having the tiny, red-haired Maureen a year later, made life for the O'Hearns, the nearest thing to paradise either of them had dared to hope for on this earth.

Though Maureen remembered nothing of the event, she could, even today, repeat, nearly word for word, Deirdre's description of the RUC horror. The armed thugs were screaming, shaking Danny, "Where are the guns, you fucking Irish sod! You've got them, we know it." Two of them kept their rifles pointed at Danny's head while a third put the bayonet point of his gun against Deirdre's throat

The RUC in Northern Ireland, during the years following the Great War, was a dumping ground of sorts for the jobless, disaffected and bitter ex-officers and men who had survived the war only to find poverty and defeat in an utterly exhausted England that was trying desperately to bring order into the cities of Northern Ireland after the partition. The RUC went about the job with all their rage and fury directed at the Catholic minorities wanting passionately to add the six counties of Northern Ireland to what had become the Republic of Ireland.

Rebellion, sedition, revolution—these were the words the British used in describing the objectives of Belfast's Catholics who lived in the reeking ghettos of the city. That there were caches of guns and ammunition, the RUC had no doubt. The question was, where were they, and who had hidden them?

"Leave me wife and baby alone, you stinking cowards! There's nothin' an innocent woman with a child can tell ya. If it's blood ya want, go ahead and shoot. But it's me you'll shoot or the Lord will rain such destruction down on yer head, you'll never again see the light of day!"

"The guns!" Their leader yelled. "Where have you got them?" And he motioned to the bayonet pointer to lower his weapon. With that Deirdre walked away, hearing Danny's curse, "You'll burn in hell before I tell you anything you...."She turned at the sound of gunfire and saw the blood spring from Danny's face as bone and tissue gave way under the impact of rifle bullets. The RUC officers bolted and ran through the open door to the hallway and she heard only the sound of the their clattering boots on the stairs. Danny O'Hearn made no sound.

Deirdre cradled her baby in one arm and with the other she tried to hold the lifeless head of Danny, one month short of his twenty-third birthday. He hadn't said a word about where the guns and ammunition were hidden, so he had died a hero. And the Organization was very caring and careful too about the widows of their heroes. For who knew how much a youngster like Danny O'Hearn might confide, in private moments, to his adored wife?

In time, the Organization arranged for Deirdre O'Hearn and her infant daughter to be sent to New York. In 1928, it was a good place for a young Irishwoman and her child to disappear into one of the teaming immigrant communities of the city.

There was enough money for the first few years, but soon it was gone and Deirdre, still mourning and as Maureen recalled, eternally sad, went to work. She found a job, cleaning offices after regular work hours and arranged for someone to look after Maureen while she was gone.

It wasn't prams in the park for Maureen O'Hearn. It was more like another toddler in a crowded flat full of stairstep children belonging to the Gerritys. And instead of birdsong, the children were lulled to sleep by the sound of the Third Avenue El trains as they rumbled by the window.

Maureen grew up quickly in the forced draught of Third Avenue and Sixty-Second Street. By the time Deirdre got a better job cleaning elegant offices in the new Empire State Building, Maureen was in school, going to and fro in her crisp pleated Catholic school uniform, clutching a pile of books to her still-unformed breast.

Mother and daughter rarely saw one another on school days because Deirdre left for work well before Maureen returned home. But Maureen, as early as age ten, was more than able to manage in her mother's absence.

After school, she sometimes stopped at Gerrity's saloon before entering the door leading to the hallway and stairs to the flats directly above. Often, if she was lucky, there was an envelope that Deirdre had left.

Now, with a new millennium in view and she, so far from her childhood, Maureen could still recall the gloomy interior of Gerrity's, with its perpetual odor of spilled beer, rancid corned beef and cabbage with an overtone of something sour and unpleasant, most likely, wet bar towels that were so grey with use and no laundering, one would be hard-pressed to guess their original color.

Tell him everything, she thought of Lieutenant Quinn—that's what he had asked her. No, there were some things Maureen never told, the ugly secrets remembered only when circumstances forced down the barriers her mind had constructed against them. Some things were so private she had kept them to herself, even in the confessional. For though the memory was shameful, she knew, somehow, there was no sin on her part. Only a sense of having been soiled, like the sour-smelling towels in Gerrity's.

Now, the car's heater was on High. She turned it down but could not wipe away the memory of that blistering June day. She was eleven years old, and she was hoping that her mother had left an envelope containing a few coins, maybe a quarter, so she could go to a movie where the air-cooled theater provided the only respite from the afternoon of early-Summer heat. She would often see the double feature twice plus the news and cartoons because movie theaters had continuous showings. She had been known to sometimes see the main feature three times, especially if Clark Gable was starring.

That year, the country's economy was still in the grip of depression and her mother's hours had been cut back. Deirdre was lucky enough to have a job at all. Many of the families in the neighborhood were on relief, a shameful condition into which, Deirdre was proud to say, they had not fallen. Somehow, there was always money enough for Maureen's favorite activity—going to the movies. That day, she desperately wanted to see the picture at the Loew's theater or was it RKO? She did not remember for certain. But she never would forget Bette Davis in Jezebel.

Stopping in the doorway to Gerrity's, she called, "Hello, Mr. Gerrity?" From the darkness where she could barely see him, Gerrity boomed in a voice coarsened by whiskey. "C'mon in, girl. Don't stand out there and fry in the heat. C'mon."

"No. I was just wondering. Did my mother leave an envelope for me? It's for the movies. She doesn't like to leave money in the flat. Did she? The money, I mean." Gerrity made her nervous. She didn't know why.

"Ya mean money to go to the fillums? Ya like the fillums do ye? Well, let's see. I t'ink we c'n manage a quarter or two. C'mon in then, girl, it's blinded I am lookin' at ya in that doorway there."

Her heart pounding now, Maureen stepped into the open vestibule, a small, square space with a dirty floor of cracked black and white tiles. To one side was another door, open for a breath of air, leading directly into the saloon. In the dim light she could make out Gerrity himself, sitting on the bar, dangling his feet. He wore a pair of dusty, badly worn, high-cut boots with elastic inserts. The boots were huge and sinister-looking

Come closer, girl. I can't see nuttin' widout me specs." Maureen edged forward, wary, like an animal sensing danger. "Com'ere. I said. I can't hardly see." Suddenly his arm shot out and grabbed her wrist, the one not clutching her books. He pulled her toward him. At her eye level she could see his filthy trousers which barely contained his huge belly. And straining against the cloth was a bulge that Maureen knew from having diapered little boys for the neighbors, was what she and her friends called the thing. They knew the thing grew large—they had experimented with the babies. And they also knew that the thing on a grown man was not something interesting and amusing—it spelled mortal danger.

Now Gerrity had her wrist in a choking grip and he was pulling her forward. As she resisted and pulled back he jerked her arm, twisting her body so that her left arm lost their hold on the books and they fell to the floor. Gerrity managed to put her hand directly on the bulge, holding it there and using it to stroke it as if he were holding a brush. Maureen screamed and shrieked and used her now-free left hand to flail at him. She twisted her body and, with all her strength she punched at the bulge. Gerrity let go of her wrist and before he could get down from the bar, Maureen scooped up her books and ran, still screaming from the saloon.

She didn't go upstairs to the flat. She knew Gerrity had a key—he was their landlord. Instead, she walked down to Carla Rodino's flat on sixty-first. Mrs. Rodino, who spoke little English, took one look at Maureen's flushed face and fell to her knees, embracing the child. Mrs. Rodino didn't ask what happened, exactly. She murmured, "Che Cosa?, Che Cosa?" Maureen waited until she knew her mother would be coming home. Only then did she return to the flat. As she met Deirdre in the doorway, Maureen made the first of hundreds of pleas for them to move to another place.

"But I don't see any way we c'n move. How could we? I can't find rooms this cheap any other place in the city. Gerrity lets us have the flat for next to nuttin'". Maureen assumed their low rent had something to do with the Organization which continued to take care of Danny O'Hearn's widow and orphan. Maureen's pleading and begging went on for years until after the end of World War Two, when she had finished high school and waited tables at Schrafft's.

Now, she recalled the precipitating moment that had given her the courage to defy Deirdre and present an ultimatum, "Either we find new rooms and move, or I go by myself and live without you."

One afternoon, having finished a busy day shift at Schrafft's, Maureen decided to go directly home after work, instead of going to the acting class she normally attended between five and eight in the evening. Her head and body ached and she was sure she was coming down with the flu.

Climbing the stairs to the second floor flat in front, she heard Ellen Gerrity's shrieking, "Ya disgustin' shit! Y're fit for nuttin' but flushin' down the toilet. That's what I'd do to ya, if I could move yer stinkin' body. You and herself. Yeah! You, Deirdre O'Hearn, ya shittin' piece of Belfast trash, you're nuttin' but his fancy New York City whore." Ellen liked the sound of that. She repeated it, "Gerrity's New York City whore." Then there was the smack of Ellen's large, black leather purse, as she swung it again and again to strike the face and head of Gerrity, who sprawled, semi-conscious in a chair at the kitchen table, directly facing the open door to the flat.

Maureen recoiled at the smell of urine that had soaked Gerrity's trousers and she stared, unbelieving, at Ellen swinging the leather bag with all her might to strike the face that was now bloodied by the impact of its brass clasp. "I oughtta let yer whore take care a ya. Let her clean up the pukin' mess ya made, drinking and shaggin' up here all afternoon, while I'm downstairs tendin' the brats ya forced on me." Smash! Again, the purse flung Gerrity's head aside. Smash! Ellen hit him again.

Finally, Deirdre screamed. "Enough! Stop before you kill him. Let 'im alone until he can stand. Then I'll send him back to you. And he's yours to keep. I never wanted him, the good Lord knows that, even if you don't. Now get out. Go home and wait until he can stand. Then he's all yours."

Deirdre's face was bright red and slick with tears she didn't try to wipe away. She barely noticed her daughter who had turned to run back down the stairs to the street. Then, hardly aware of her destination, Maureen walked South on Third Avenue.

She turned West on 60th Street and then South again when she reached Fifth Avenue. After passing the Sherry Netherland and Central

Park, there were distractions in every shop window. Just before she reached Saks she stopped in front of Saint Patrick's and hesitated. Should she go in, light a candle and say a prayer for her mother's soul and Gerrity's? To Hell with them both, she thought.

At this moment she had no kind thoughts even of her mother, for whom she usually felt great compassion. And, she asked herself the first questions she had ever entertained about her faith. Was she about to lose it? As she fought back tears, standing in the middle of Fifth Avenue in the early evening, Maureen wondered if this was the kind of thing that made you lose your faith. And, if that were to happen, what would she be? She would then no longer be able to call herself a Catholic. Please God, she prayed, without much conviction, don't let me lose my faith.

She and Carla Rodino had been discussing this problem since they were in the sixth grade at Saint Anne's when the girls were given an assignment. They were to write an essay entitled What my Faith Means to Me.

Neither Maureen nor Carla was declared to be a budding Saint Theresa of Avila, but Maureen got an A. Now, confronting the issue as a young woman, it was much more difficult than it had been in sixth grade.

Maureen swallowed her tears, wiped her eyes and walked a block to Saks. There, in the meticulously-dressed windows with their arrogant-looking mannequins, was something she could consider objectively. It was 1947, the New Look was all the rage, skirts were long, waistlines impossibly narrow and drapery and flaring silks were being shown in deep, dramatic colors, all of which would look smashing on Maureen. If she only had some money.

She walked up and down the Avenue, looking at more clothes in the windows at Bergdorf's, Lord and Taylor and Altman's. She slavered over the jewels at Tiffany's and Black, Starr and Gorham. Then, her feet killing her, she boarded a bus and went to Greenwich Village, where if she hurried, she'd be just in time for tonight's acting class at Freddy Sherwood's studio.

Maureen, having apparently regained her composure, ignored her aching head and fever. She swept her mind free of the scene played by the Gerritys and her mother. Now, she was an actress and would concentrate on an altogether different scene. She took her place among the half-dozen girls whom Freddy had invited to read for a showcase he was planning at a small local theater. She read for the part of Antigone with all the passion and sorrow hidden in her own soul. Sophocles might have written his tragedy specifically for Maureen, so perfectly did she reflect the play's pathos and nobility in her reading. Freddy said she was terrific, but he never got enough money together to put on the show.

Maureen never talked to her mother about what she had seen and heard. But Deirdre knew that Maureen understood what Ellen had meant when she called her Gerrity's New York whore. And now, Maureen understood why Deirdre had resisted moving to more costly rooms elsewhere. But, the waitress job at Schrafft's paid well—the tips were very generous, what with the city full of returning service men—there was no longer a need to stay in the Third Avenue flat.

Given a post-war shortage of cheap apartments, Deirdre was easily persuaded when Freddy Sherwood was willing to sub-let his three-room flat on Columbus Avenue at little more than the official rental. What Deirdre didn't know was that Freddy was moving into John MacDonald's brownstone house near Waverly Place in Greenwich Village, a place that was to become one of Maureen's retreats when things became too difficult with her mother.

The West side was a considerable improvement, over Third Avenue, and they loved the apartment; it was blissfully quiet without the sound of El trains rumbling by.

Whatever arrangement Deirdre had with Gerrity in the past was never revealed to Maureen for she was too ashamed to ask. Nor did she ever tell her mother about Gerrity's atrocious assault when she was a schoolgirl. Somehow, both mother and daughter had entered into a silent pact. Gerrity's name was rarely mentioned and Maureen never went back to the old neighborhood, except for the occasional wedding or funeral. Mother and daughter rarely talked about the Third Avenue flat. It was as if they had never lived there. They had put something dark and threatening into an out-of-the-way closet with a door that must never be opened again.

With World War Two over, and the Cold War about to begin, Deirdre was busier than ever. She took a second job, waiting tables at

Longchamp's, replacing the last of the elderly waiters who had stayed on after the younger men went to war. She reasoned, "The restaurant's in the same building, right there on the ground floor of the Empire State. All I gotta do is take the elevator down and I c'n make a pretty penny until closin' time."

The money was good and Deirdre brought home luxurious food from time to time. Certainly, in the past, during the depression and then the war, the O'Hearn's had never dined so well.

Pivotal to all was the war, or as Maureen thought of it, The War, though she had been a schoolgirl and remembered little before VJ Day when all New York celebrated with gaudy exuberance. She would always think of it as the point at which she and her mother had made the transition from a life of poverty to one in which they began to enjoy a relatively decent standard of living.

Maureen wondered if the war in Viet Nam had been, for Kate's generation, the same kind of defining period. She supposed not since it seemed to have had no beginning and no definitive end. Kate herself had devoted years of passionate energy trying to stop it. Maureen, thought, trying to stop a war is just as important as fighting in one. She wondered if her grandchildren, Joel and DeeDee would be spared having to fight in or against some massive war during their young adult years.

As for her own adulthood, her career, her life had been nearly magical in its blessings, despite the divorce from Tom. After that, everything had seemed to simply fall into place. But here was Kate. First her husband, dead of a senseless act of violence. And now this; was Kate really the target of that mirror? She shuddered again thinking of how close it had been. Who? Who? Why would anyone want Kate dead? Or Jim Vandersagen?—well, that, she could understand...

She went back to thinking of her own beginnings. It was easier than to trying to unravel the problems of the present.

The post-war boom had made it possible for Maureen to be hired as a seventeen year-old waitress at Schrafft's. Normally, a girl had to be eighteen. But, everywhere, jobs were plentiful. There was a sense of optimism in the air despite the doomsayers who predicted that an appalling confrontation with the Russians was threatening the peace.

Schrafft's had always hired pretty Irish girls to wear their crisp black uniforms with starched white aprons. Maureen, with her red hair and green-eyed beauty, combined with a sturdy, fully-fleshed figure, easily passed for twenty. Good looks, as every waitress knows, is as much of an asset as knowing when to smile and how to set a plate before a customer.

Freddy had taught Maureen how to smile beguilingly but not flirtatiously. He said that worked best with the elderly ladies who frequented Schrafft's. He had spent a whole evening teaching the young women in the class the subtle differences between flirtation and friendship.

One day, Maureen tried to teach Deirdre what she had learned. "Ya mean ya pay good money to a feller who teaches ya how to smile? I know how to smile, and t'ank you very much."

At first, Maureen worked after school, part-time, while finishing her Senior year at Hudson River High. But immediately after graduation, she worked full, eight-hour shifts. For the next three years her life was defined by two activities: Waiting tables and making money was the first. The second, and raison d'être, was made possible by the first. Waiting tables paid for acting lessons. Freddy Sherwood's studio was Maureen's university, her finishing school and, ultimately, the key that unlocked the door to a world in which one gets paid to pretend to be somebody else.

That senior year at high school which she called, "My wonderful year," she fell in love with her English teacher, John MacDonald and, naturally, kept her feelings secret. And MacDonald discovered something in Maureen, something she wasn't sure she had, nor dared to hope for, a talent for acting.

It was after she had read the sleepwalking scene from Macbeth. He told her he was impressed with her fire and the depth of her passion. Later, when she told him how desperately she wanted to become a professional actress, he told her, as gently as possible:

"Maureen, dear. I think you have real talent. With your beauty—you are beautiful you know, with that hair and your eyes the color of an English meadow—you'll be sure to make your way." She was in ecstasy. John Robert MacDonald thought she was beautiful! She thought he was too. Later, she told Carla Rodino, "I really thought he was going to kiss me, the way he looked at me an' all." For only a moment she lived in that mystical world where incredibly handsome men and beautiful girls find each other and pledge eternal love with a kiss.

Then he spoke again. "But you have the most terrible New York accent. It's pure Hell's Kitchen, at best. If you're serious about acting, you'll have to get some training and you'll have to learn to speak properly."

She hid the pain well. "You mean, I have to find a Pygmalion? Why can't you teach me? You speak beautifully."

"Thanks, that's very kind. But I'm not the one you need. I have a friend. His name is Frederick Shervitz, but he's calling himself Sherwood these days." He grabbed a sheet of paper and started to write. "He gives acting and speech lessons. He's got a studio in Greenwich Village. Here's his address. I'll arrange everything. Freddy'll have you speaking like Wendy Hiller in no time."

In no time, Maureen realized that her beloved Mr. MacDonald and Freddy Sherwood were lovers and that her teacher's interest in her was purely professional. Freddy made no pretense about his homosexuality, which Maureen found thoroughly exciting and, of course, shocking. "Queers," she and her friends had called them. There was nothing queer about Freddy Sherwood. He had the eye of an artist and the soul of a romantic sixteen year-old girl. Maureen and Freddy understood one another perfectly.

"Darling" Freddy had said, the first time she went to his studio, his hand on her shoulder, turning her round and round as if she were a large doll, "You're really too short to be a great actress, but with very high heels and a better set to your head, I think I can pull it off. Do you want an English accent, or an all-purpose high-class American one?"

"Whatever you think, Mr. Sherwood."

"For God sake, don't mumble. And look me straight in the eye. We don't want any of this poor working-class humility. If you're going to be an actress, you'd better start sounding like an aristocrat—they're the only parts worth playing. And for Christ's sake don't call me Mr. My name is Freddy."

Deirdre thought it was madness to spend hard-earned money on lessons for acting. "Everybody knows ya can't make any money at it. Lookit all them poor, starving actors used to work at Longchamp's.

Ain't none of 'em gonna get work as actors and pretty soon they'll be comin' back and takin' my job, you watch."

Deirdre was always so full of negativism. That's what Freddy Sherwood called it. He told Maureen that negativism is an actor's worst enemy and that she must guard against it constantly. Her one defense against her mother's carping was to concentrate on what Freddy was teaching her.

How she loved the lessons, listening to records of vowel and consonant pronunciations. She learned how not to dentalize her Ts and Ds. and to lengthen vowel sounds And Freddy trained her to listen to her own vocal level, to avoid the harsh pitch of an unmodulated voice. And, forever after, Maureen was never heard to say "Noo Yawk."

John MacDonald had her read everything, made her understand, not just the grammar, but the logic that makes language work the way it does. And when he had her read great books, he designed exercises that were, in effect, mini-courses in dialogue-writing. Her particular favorite was Anna Karenina, that headstrong, passionate heroine of Tolstoy's who would die so dramatically.

From Freddy she learned the technicalities of how certain facial expressions are made, exactly where to place her tongue in making particular sounds. She developed an ear for the difference between written and spoken English. In fewer than three years, Maureen learned so eagerly that John MacDonald and Freddy both agreed that very soon she'd be ready to work in Summer stock on Cape Cod.

By 1951 she was indeed ready. "Cape Cod?" Deirdre had said as she watched Maureen prancing around the living room in their tiny apartment, "Where in God's name is t'at? And what t'e hell is Summer stock?"

"It's where they do shows up in Massachusetts; they put them on for the Summer visitors. Every good actor gets a start in Summer stock." She stopped short of explaining that a season on the Cape would qualify her for membership in the union; she'd have her Actors' Equity card. Membership in the union was the magic key that might unlock the doors of theaters. Of course, it was only a first step in the upward climb of an acting career, one where most new Equity members either get stuck or get out.

That year, Maureen's confidence was boundless. She would know an optimism of youthful euphoria never again to be equaled in her lifetime. The only hint of doubt came from her mother.

Deirdre worried at her. "But will ya get paid? You know I can't handle t'e rent here all by meself. Ya gotta help out widda rent. You can't be 'tinkin' to leave me here all alone the whole Summer, can ya?"

It had been a long day on her feet at Schrafft's and Maureen was tired. "For the love of God, the sound is TH!" she said, exaggerating the pronunciation. You've been in America forever. It's not 'tinkin'. The word is think! For the sake of sweet Jesus, Ma, speak English!"

"English is it! You want me to speak the language of them bastards as killed me Danny. It's Gaelic I'd speak if I could remember any of it. I'd never again, 'til I take me last breath an' die, speak the tongue of the devil himself—those English murderers!."

It was pitch dark when Maureen paid the toll at New Rochelle. God! how she hated Autumn. The days not only grew short and cold, they forever reminded her of the September that the Chathamtown Playhouse closed for the season.

That late Summer of 1951 on Cape Cod had been more than a young actress's preparation for her profession. It was another experience in which Maureen learned how to mask her emotions, replacing the real with the socially acceptable. She learned too that her life, though she fervently believed it to be overall, ordered by God, was hers to shape, even to change, in minute, but important ways.

Maureen learned that though she could do little about the tempests of fortune, there were countless forms of shelter where she might wait for sunnier weather. Or, she thought, maybe the rains'll fall gently, like the quality of mercy, hah!

Whoever had rigged the mirror that killed Jim Vandersagen wasn't much given to mercy, was he? Or, she thought, maybe she. Probably not a woman, she reasoned. It was true that there were some women working backstage on sets, doing what were traditionally men's jobs. But they were still a rarity. And she knew of no women who worked with the kind of explosives used in special effects. Somehow, dynamite was a male thing. Then, of course, there was poisoned chocolate sauce. That's the kind of thing a woman does. Hadn't Lieutenant Quinn suggested that there might be two people involved? Two? Maureen laughed. She could think of a dozen people right here in New York who were probably delighted that the son of a bitch was dead.

Now, so many decades later, she could still hear the words through the Cape Cod Summer darkness, "Irish Piece."

The morning after she had overheard the slur, Vandersagen was finishing breakfast in the large room that served as a combination mess and recreation hall for the Chathamtown Playhouse cast and crew. When she walked in he had greeted her with a huge smile and a sweeping gesture. "Here's my red rose o' the morning and there's your chair, darling."

She swept by him as if he were invisible. He raised his eyebrows, leaned forward to make sure she saw him and then watched her retreating back. With a shrug of incomprehension he picked up his cup and drank the last of his coffee.

Later that day Jim had tried once again to speak to her but Maureen gave him a steely look and said nothing. She did not see him again. It was several days before she was able to appear casual, asking Larry Macklin "Have you seen Jim anywhere?"

Larry, as usual, harried and running late for the opening scene of a matinee, said only, "Jim's gone sailing. Bermuda. Not coming back. Told me he'd see me in New York next month.

Maureen was relieved. Now she could get on with her life without distraction. She reached into the pocket of her shorts and pulled out Tom's letter that had come the morning before.

....So we could get married the day after the last show and even have a few days for a short—really short—honeymoon, right there on the Cape. How about Provincetown? Let me know as soon as you can ....Honey, I can hardly wait to see you!....

It wasn't so much a proposal—he had been proposing to her for years. Tom's letter was more of a detailed plan. He had applied for and been accepted for training as a medical corpsman. He was to have ten days of leave before going to Letterman General Hospital at the Presidio in San Francisco. Sadly, there wasn't enough money for Maureen to follow him to California, but he understood, she would want to go back to New York immediately after the season, in any case. He knew how anxious she was to start making the rounds as a professional.

The letter that Maureen wrote to Private Cassidy at Fort Dix was full of happy determination. ....What a wonderful idea. Everybody says Provincetown is perfect in September, after all the tourists have gone. We can be married at the little church right here. I know the priest and he says all we need is a few papers. Don't forget your baptismal certificate! I'll do the rest....

The short notice would allow for little in the way of planning—there was neither time nor money for an elaborate wedding. But it was virtually wartime and the Church looked with compassion upon a soldier about to go far away, to Korea, where all that fighting was going on.

Tom thought of himself as a coward. At least he had been so labeled by the schoolyard bullies when he was a child. In the World War just past, he had been too young to be drafted and felt both relieved and cheated. For, like most young men, Tom had looked with awe upon the uniformed men who came and went while he was still in school. Now, it would be his turn. The medical corps wasn't a place to become a decorated hero, but it was an honorable calling and he knew he could do the job without fear or shame. He also had no idea of what he would experience. In that sense, he was the equal of any young man going off to a far-away country where a war was being waged in the name of principles which he understood not at all.

Years after The Korean War, watching M*A*S*H. on television, Tom thought of the real horrors he had witnessed. In his recollection, there was nothing funny about the unit where he spent nearly two years. Even today, he remembered moments during which he nearly wept, seeing the victims of the carnage. And there were times, after a particularly grueling triage and endless hours, assisting surgeries, when he would find a quiet spot where he allowed himself what had become a luxury, sobbing like a child, not caring if anyone heard. If anyone did hear, it was never mentioned.

The day Tom got Maureen's letter he had just learned that the transfer to the medics was confirmed. Life was promising and, more than anything, including marriage to Maureen, the world was about to open for him to have a good look at it. He was excited. He made feverish plans. He was going to see San Francisco. He knew he would probably have no more than a day or two of leave during the advanced training at Letterman He decided he would cram into forty-eight hours every sight and experience the city might offer.

He was too excited to sleep much the night before he went to the Cape. Marrying Maureen was wonderful—he was drowning in happiness. But his delight carried a germ of something he realized later was fear. Of course there wasn't much time for fear. The wedding day was arranged for day one of the ten-day furlough following the end of basic training.

Deirdre complained about the short notice. Her letter, written painstakingly on the cheap, ruled paper she bought a few sheets at a time, made clear what she thought of the idea.

....There's no time for a proper wedding. And you're expecting me to get on a bus and go all the way up there by myself. It's bad enough, you've been gone all Summer, now you are going to get married, but not in a proper church. Please send bus fare and money for me to buy a dress.

Your loving Mother,
Deirdre O'Hearn

Maureen complied and reassured her mother that the marriage would not go unblessed by the Church. And Deirdre's fears about the long trip were no problem since Tom's Father, Pete, widowed now, gallantly volunteered to drive Deirdre to Chathamtown in his brand-new Plymouth.

The Summer ended with the Bride and Groom being feted by the entire company of the Chathamtown Playhouse except, of course for Jim Vandersagen whose picture had appeared in the Boston paper, with the rest of the crew of *Sea Lancer*. CAPE COD THEATER OWNER WINS. Larry Macklin was heard to say, "I thought I owned the place."

Later, the wedding guests, particularly Freddy's group from New York, trudged back into the City, some hopeful, others disillusioned.

Maureen was in a frenzy to get her Equity card and look for work in the real theater. When she gave her name, the secretary said, "Are you sure you want to be Maureen O'Hearn? That's an awful lot like the movie actress, you know the one, O'Hara? I suggest you try something more distinctive."

She had only been Maureen Cassidy for a couple of weeks and the name didn't seem to fit, but she tried it. "Well, I've just gotten married. My name's Cassidy now. How would that be?"

After checking her list and not finding another Maureen Cassidy, the secretary said, "Perfect." Then she typed the two sections of the official card, took Maureen's money and said, "Welcome to Actors' Equity. You're a real professional now."

Maureen felt neither professional nor well. In fact, she nearly fainted once, getting off the cross-town bus and then began throwing up regularly every morning before going on rounds. Some actress, she thought. Unless I can find a part for a very pregnant lady, I'm out of luck.

She went to a radio show and auditioned for Larry Macklin who had landed the producer's job. He gave her a script, neatly typed, and fully annotated with pauses and accents. He asked her to read. "Pretend this is live, and an audience is listening to you. You've got to read and act and not lose your place. Think you can manage?"

She said yes, but she wasn't sure. The show was called The Wandering Ones. Maureen read the part of Jeanine, a young girl traveling with a troupe of acrobats and clowns. The meandering story covered plots and sub-plots with plenty of tears and laughter.

Maureen was perfect. Larry was surprised that, without his instructions, Maureen used the technique essential to live-from-script acting, the ability to read two or three lines below the one that was actually being spoken. She was silently grateful for the hours of drilling at Freddy's studio. He said there were some very good actors, but they'd never work on live radio shows because they couldn't master the trick. He had warned his students about sometimes getting fresh copy minutes before air time. "And," he warned, "you'd better be ready."

Freddy had told Maureen she was a natural, and today, she heard Larry Macklin say the same thing. She was so grateful she nearly yodeled, but recovered her decorum and thanked him. Yippee! she said to herself, no more carrying armloads of dishes at Schrafft's. Getting the radio job meant she could work right up to the last minute before her baby was due. And, she was allowed to join the radio actors guild too—that meant scale; possibly twice the money she could earn as a waitress.

Except for being pregnant, Maureen loved that year. Her skills were developing, she acquired an agent, and there was plenty of work—everything from soaps to commercials.

The following year, when she made the transition to television she had become a solid professional. It would be years before leading roles were offered her. But her good looks, combined with genuine acting ability brought her steady work and, eventually, a permanent place on the roster of working actors and actresses who are always in demand, but who do not make headlines. Some might have described Maureen's career as uninteresting, but she knew how lucky she was to have found so cozy a niche when most of her contemporaries were still carrying the blue-plate special.

The year Maureen got her first major TV role in a daytime soap on a national network, Jim Vandersagen bought a local radio station and an affiliated television station. Bought was rather a euphemism, however. The fact was, his wife, Sally Anne Peterson, went with the package. It was true that Vandersagen was forced to mortgage the Sea Lancer and other assets, but without Sally Anne the call letters WJGV would never have come into existence.

Maureen remembered the day she saw the wedding pictures in The Times. The bride was resplendent in a gown of reembroidered lace with an obscenely large spray of calla lilies, trailing yards of white ribbon. And the groom stood beside her, stiff and somewhat haughty in cutaway and striped pants, with a beautifully draped cravat. She thought of her wedding to Tom in the only Catholic church in Chathamtown, with its weathered shingles and bare, utilitarian interior.

As for her dress, it was the borrowed wedding gown—a simple one, to keep the cost down—from the wardrobe of The Taming of the Shrew. Tom wore his uniform. There was a small snapshot, her only memento, that showed Tom smiling broadly, while Maureen grinned as the sunlight made dark shadows of her dimples.

That year, as Maureen's acting skills improved and her pregnancy became ever more irksome, Deirdre busied herself with preparing for Maureen's baby as if it were her own. She knitted, she crocheted, she went to Bloomingdale's basement and bought everything the sales clerks told her she would need. A second-hand crib was donated by

Carla Rodino's mother. She had been saving it, she said, "in case I had another one."

The Rodinos had five children, clothed and fed on the proceeds of a tiny shoe repair shop. All were grown or nearly so. Carla was fulfilling the girlhood dream she had shared with Maureen in which they would become nuns and dedicate themselves to God. Carla was a novitiate in a convent on Long Island. God, how Maureen missed her friend and confidante.

During working hours there was enough to distract her, but in the evening, as Deirdre worked on baby clothes and chattered, there were times when Maureen thought she would lose control.

Toward the end of what had to be the longest pregnancy in the history of the human race, with her back aching, her legs swelling and her skin a mask of red rashes, Maureen felt ugly, both inside and outside. One night, after once again listening to the saga of Danny O'Hearn witnessing his father's death in O'Connell Street the day of the Easter Rising in Dublin, 1916, Maureen finally gave way.

"Shut up, Ma. I mean it. If I hear another word about Danny O'Hearn I'm going to scream. Scream! I'm going to yell so loud the people in the old neighborhood are going to hear me. I don't give a good goddamn about O'Connell Street. And I don't give another goddamn about Danny O'Hearn." Now she was whipping herself into a fine frenzy. "If you knew how sick to death I am of hearing about Danny this, and Danny that. Or maybe I should say Saint Danny. For Chissake, if Danny had lived, he'd probably turn out no better than that bum, Liam Gerrity."

Deirdre's slap across Maureen's face was sudden and it stung, leaving red patches. She lowered her eyes to hide the tears. Her mother had never struck her before, not even so much as a whack on the behind. Now, for what seemed like an eternity, the two women stood, face to face, each panting for breath, recovering as after a sudden disaster, assessing the damage. Then Deirdre turned and went into the single bedroom in the apartment. Maureen, tired beyond endurance, skipped her nightly ritual of removing makeup and brushing her teeth. The hell with it, she thought, and stretched out on the sofa-bed where she normally slept in the tiny living room

It was nearly three o'clock and Deirdre had fallen into an uneasy sleep when she heard Maureen's voice, muffling a groan. Barefoot, her hair matted with sleep, Deirdre went to her daughter, all anger forgotten. The mattress was soaking wet. Maureen sat cross-legged at the foot of the bed, moaning as the cramping began. Soon she was making deep-throated animal sounds in rhythm with the labor pains that tore across her back.

Twenty hours later, the sister at St. Vincent's hospital showed Maureen her new daughter. Exhausted, she took the baby, looked at her and smiled. "She's bald. She hasn't got any hair."

"Of course she does." The Sister of Charity took the sleeping infant and held her close to the light. "See that golden down? She's going to be a flaxen-haired little princess with blue eyes. Too bad she doesn't have your red top. Well, you'll just have to have another one, won't you?"

Won't you! she thought. If nuns had to have babies, they wouldn't be so goddamned cheerful about the whole thing. And then, after handing the baby back to be returned to the nursery, Maureen began to cry. She wept until she fell into a profound sleep from which she woke an hour later, having absolutely no idea of what it was that had made her so sad. "Kathleen," she said aloud to the woman who sat, reading in the next bed. "We're going to call her Kathleen."

CHAPTER FIVE

TOM WOULD NOT see Kathleen until she was well into her second year. She took an inordinately long time to fall in love with her Daddy. But once begun, the father-daughter bond remained unbroken through everything from divorce to teenage rebellion to a drug bust in a West Side establishment where Columbia students were believed to gather for plotting to overthrow the university staff, if not the government of the United States.

Though the Cassidy marriage had been officially sundered twenty years earlier, nothing had diminished Tom's affection for his daughter. He was always there when Kate needed him.

It was Tom who had encouraged her to go after the job that had opened up shortly after Avi's death. The JGV network was planning a new magazine show and they were looking for a new face, "Someone," Jim Vandersagen had said, "not associated with creeps and freaks," that would appeal to the crowd that spends money on food, furnishings and everything else evoked by the word home. Jim Vandersagen had seen the demographics indicating that people were fed up with excess and wanted to snuggle into something cozy. What could be cozier than a show called *Come Home with Kate*?

Vandersagen, despite a reputation that made Donald Trump look like a cloistered seminarian, was reworking his image and that of his network. One columnist suggested it was perhaps a good businessman's anticipation of a trend, rather than an elevation of purpose. The observation was essentially true and, in a recent interview, confirming he was after a different market, Jim had been quoted as saying, "We're commercial but not pandering and you don't have to be ashamed to admit that you watch JGV, no matter what hour of the day or night."

Fulfilling a promise he had made at a national conference on improving the quality of prime-time television, moving away from sex, violence and sensationalism, JGV was forcing other networks to take notice. JGV advertising ran in major magazine and newspaper outlets, billing itself as The Network for Discriminating Viewers.

"Yeah," one wag put it, "Vandersagen's getting himself sanforized and simonized before the government steps in and does it for him. I suppose now we all have to go back to where married couples always sleep in separate beds and everybody wears pajamas."

Whatever his motives were for restructuring the network's content policy, Jim's campaign for cleaning up commercial television was already beginning to pay dividends. And ...Come Home...was among the major shows to prove that there was a substantial audience for programming that eschewed the shocking and the sleazy.

Kate's show got good ratings from the start. She seemed born to the role of gracious hostess, without Martha Stewart's saccharine sweetness, nor a news hen's tartness. Instead, she came across as a good listener who was as fascinated by what her guests had to say as were the home and studio audiences.

By the end of its first season, the show was a hit and it was predicted to become the model for several others fashioned in the same low-key, homey style.

Vandersagen—"the ubiquitous", some people called him—liked to look in on Kate Cassidy's show. He had a deep personal interest in everything bearing his signature. His boyish enthusiasm was both part of his charm and his ability to irritate. In Kate's case, she liked her new boss. And she sensed he liked her too. Romance had nothing to do with it, she told herself. And anyway, it was still too soon after Avi. Much too soon, she told herself. Besides, people don't go around having affairs with their bosses no matter what one read in the papers. Not smart, Kate Cassidy told herself. Avi certainly would not approve.

And now, Jim was dead. Why? Oh, she answered herself, Jim had enemies everywhere. She knew very little, really. But even a casual look at the man's life would reveal a path littered with signposts telling of careers destroyed, women's hearts shattered, an ex-spouse and a current wife, both of whom had been quoted in the press as everything from utterly devastated to just-plain pissed-off at their Jim.

One thing was sure, if she had heard the cop correctly, the person who rigged that mirror was familiar with studio operations. Big help, that. Everybody who came in contact with Jim Vandersagen was, one way or another, involved in studio operations.

But, finally, Kate's concern was a straightforward question. Was the killer, or killers—there might be more than one—still out there, somewhere, trying to kill her too?

She drowsed trying to remember the name of the cop—Irving something. God, she hoped he was as smart as he looked, and that he'd find the guy—maybe not a guy—maybe a woman. Nah, she told herself, women use poison. They don't rig mirrors. Poison! She was asleep before the panic set in once again.

The gentle knock on the door and the streak of light from the hallway, woke her from the light sleep during which she had dreamed about the first time she and Avi had gone to Mexico and spent two weeks smoking pot, eating enchiladas and realizing that if two people share a room in a hotel in rural Latin America, they have to give up all modesty about using the toilet. That was when Kate first realized that intimacy can be established in ways that have nothing to do with sex.

She opened her eyes to see Tom, her father.

"Hi, Dad. I didn't know you were in town. How come you didn't call?" Kate was shocked by Tom's appearance, so she used her goody two-shoes voice to cover up, hoping he would not read her thoughts as he had when she was a child, before acquiring enough skill to dissemble.

He walked toward her, closing the door to the corridor. Then he took her hand and leaned over the bed's metal barrier to kiss her.

"How're you feeling? Are you okay? Need anything?" He moved his head from side to side as if to deny what he was seeing. "You sure gave us a scare. Another step forward and that mirror would have been on your head too. God! Katy, you just appeared out of nowhere."

"I know, I went to the back to put in my contact lenses. Were you in the studio? How come you didn't let me know you were going to be there?"

"Well, I got in late last night, went directly to the Waldorf. I slept like a log until nearly seven this morning. I've got an interview and some meetings. Then I was supposed to go right back to the Coast. So before that, I figured I'd sneak onto your set and see what you're up to. But now, after this, well, I think I'll stay in town until I'm sure you're alright. I only planned to stay a couple of days, but I won't have any problem; I'm in my regular suite." Tom always stayed at the Waldorf Astoria when he was in New York. He said it was the only hotel in the city that hadn't changed since he'd moved to California.

Tom's face looked like a death's head, the skin pulled tautly over the bones. His color was pallid with a yellow tinge. Oh, damn, Kate thought, he's gone back to drinking again. She wanted to hug him and tell him it was alright; he could go to the AA meeting right there at Roosevelt Hospital. They had a walk-in clinic too. But she was silent, both of them embarrassed because Tom knew what she was thinking.

It was after a particularly unpleasant binge that her mother finally decided she'd had enough of Tom Cassidy. She wanted a divorce. He was about to go to California to shoot a picture and Maureen had filed in New York State on grounds of adultery, of which there was plentiful evidence.

That was long ago, before booze and age had taken their tolls of Tom's handsome face. How long had it been since his eyes had been clear blue and his now-sparse, dirty-grey hair still reflected yellow light? Kate had last seen him on television two years before as he accepted an Oscar for Best Director for his remake of Justine, the first of Lawrence Durrell's Alexandria Quartet. Now Kate wondered if he'd live long enough to work on the remaining three pictures.

Still drugged against pain, she thought back to the day Tom had left the house in Larchmont. It was the last of her life in what she considered a normal family until she created her own with Avi, Joel and Dee Dee.

As if she were replaying a tape, she recalled overhearing the last angry words between Maureen and Tom the afternoon he was leaving for Hollywood.

"I want her to come to the Coast with me, at least for the Summer. You've got to let me take her."

Maureen was trying to keep her voice down so Kate wouldn't hear from upstairs where she was supposedly in her room, doing homework. She was twelve.

I've told you before, she's signed up to go to a very prestigious girls' riding camp. She's been looking forward to it all year. I just can't yank her out of that because you've got a job in Hollywood. Tom, I've told you a thousand times, I'm not going to let my daughter be turned into one of those Hollywood brats. Besides, what would you be doing anyway? You're going to work on a picture. What's she supposed to do while you're shooting? I'm sorry, but the answer is no."

Deirdre, from her room at the top of the stairs, could hardly avoid overhearing Maureen's quarrels with Tom. And she always made sure her door was ajar so she could understand every word.

Tom said, "Don't expect me to give up without a fight. I'm not going to be satisfied with just visiting rights. She's my daughter, and I want, at the very least, to have joint custody."

"The only way you're going to get custody is after I'm dead and even then, I'd rise out of my grave to keep her from living with a drunken, broken-down..." She stopped. She would not get sucked into the whirlpool of trading insults with Tom. In many ways, his tongue was far sharper than hers and she had the emotional scars to prove it.

"This isn't finished, Maureen, I'm warning you." His bags were packed and he heard the taxi honking discretely in front. He would be flying out of White Plains to Chicago, then on to L.A. "I'm going up to say goodbye to Kate. You can consider that I've said as much to you—permanently."

He had taken the stairs, two-at-a-time. In the hall, Deirdre was standing outside the door to her room. She put her finger to her lips for silence, then stepped inside, inviting Tom to follow her. He wasn't there for more than a few minutes.

When he put his head into Kate's room, there were tears in his eyes. She leapt up from the desk where she had been sitting, unable to work. "Oh, Daddy, I'm going to miss you so much. Promise you'll come back as soon as you finish the picture, promise!"

He held her for a second, then kissed her still-perfect little girl's cheek. "I can't promise when I'll be back, but don't you worry. You haven't seen the last of your old man. I'll write and you'll write and we'll talk on the phone. And don't worry, you'll always be my baby."

Kate wrinkled her nose. "Dad, I'm almost thirteen. I wish you wouldn't call me your baby."

Tom didn't trust his voice, so he just hugged her harder than he had ever done before. "I'll call you this weekend." He threw her a kiss and left.

Maureen heard the front door slam. She stood, not looking out the window, but alert for the sound of the taxi door's closing followed by the acceleration as the driver pulled away.

Maureen thought, is it really over? Fourteen years with Tom Cassidy. Really, more like sixteen if she counted the two years during which they had an on-again, off-again relationship, both as lovers and fellow students at Freddy Sherwood's acting classes.

After Tom's taxi left, Maureen had gone into her mother's room and, whispering, she demanded, "What did you tell him?" But Deirdre said nothing. Maureen was too exhausted to get into a fight with her mother too, so she let it drop.

Now, in the small hospital room, father and daughter were silent as twilight turned the sky beyond the window to a meltingly beautiful shade of blue. Below, the city lights began to appear.

Tom's Adam's apple moved in his scrawny neck. He held Kate's hand rather too firmly, then he kissed her again. Finally, he spoke.

"Look Katy, the sky. Do you remember when you were taking French at Larchmont Country Day School, and I told you what they call it in France?"

"Sure, *L'heure bleu*. And, I remember, when you went to Europe, you brought me a bottle of the Guerlain perfume. It was gorgeous, blue perfume. You know, I can't find it anymore. I wonder if they're still making it."

The Cassidy's made their first trip to Europe together the first year they realized they were no longer starving would-be actors. By any standards, they were successful and, for the first time in their lives, they had money to spend.

Tom and Maureen had been quarreling; their fights were becoming harsher and meaner. The apartment was too small for all four of them and it was time to look for a house. Maureen wanted Kate out of the City, and Deirdre had been wishfuly thinking aloud about having a little garden.

When he had suggested they look in nearby Long Island, Maureen sneered. "Oh, Tom, Long Island is full of Jews and Shanty Irish." She had her heart set on Larchmont or Mamaroneck or even Rye.

Tom's response was no more than Maureen expected. "And you think you'll do better in Westchester? Christ, Maureen, you're such a snob. There are Jews everywhere, in case you hadn't noticed. And as for the Irish, up there, they're Lace Curtain—not much of an improvement over Shanty."

Ultimately they agreed on Larchmont because they found the perfect house. It was two blocks from the railroad station, thirty minutes to Grand Central Station. And, since Deirdre would probably never learn to drive, another great advantage was its proximity to a Catholic church, only a block away. "Great!" Tom had complained, "Now she'll be all over us every goddamned Sunday morning, dragging everybody to Mass. Let's get one thing straight right now. She can make you go, she can make Kate go, but there's no way your mother is going to take charge of my lapsed Catholic ass. As long as she continues to understand that, we'll get along just fine."

"Shsh, she'll hear you." It was a constant in their lives, trying not to be overheard by Deirdre.

When they moved to Larchmont, and allocated the bedrooms, little had changed, for Deirdre had claimed the bedroom nearest the top of the stairs. When someone warned, "She'll hear you," Deirdre knew another fight loomed and made sure she didn't miss a word.

By Spring, when they finished decorating the house the Cassidy's had become leaders among the top ten television soap opera stars. They were both tired and grateful that it was the end of the season for their show. Happily, they would have most of the Summer off. Tom was planning to ease out of soap opera to work in motion pictures, and had begun directing low-budget films.

But now it was time to stop and rest. Tom and Maureen were exhausted, burned-out, and they hoped to get away from the years of routine that had frayed their nerves, leading to more and more quarreling. He thought a vacation in Europe might help. And it would coincide with the Cannes Film Festival.

Maureen had never been out of the States and sometimes felt a perfect idiot when she overheard people chatting about Italy or France, the London theater, shopping in Paris. And Tom really wanted to make the trip. It seemed perfect—the timing was right, and if the Cassidy marriage could be salvaged, the trip would be worth more than the sum of its parts.

Deirdre was delighted to have the house and Kate all to herself, though she swore there was nobody who could fully take charge of Kate. At the age of nine, she was becoming a handful. But Deirdre didn't really complain because she secretly believed that with her mother and father out of the way, the child would be much happier. With Maureen especially, there were so many rigid rules that both Kate and Deirdre were always on edge. A few weeks with just the two of them, Deirdre was convinced, would be a tonic for everyone's nerves.

Tom and Maureen took the classic grand tour. As always, it was Tom who decided which museums and cultural activities were best. They saw hundreds of paintings and sculptures and went to the theater every night when they were in London. In France, they went to the opera. They went to the Louvre and saw the Mona Lisa.

Maureen was not impressed. "It's not much is it? It's so small. And what an ugly color her dress is."

Tom spoke almost automatically. "There you go again. You do that all the time. All you ever want to look at are pretty things. But art isn't always pretty."

Before Tom could deliver what Maureen called his regular art lecture, she walked away, crossing the gallery to look at Louis David's huge canvas. Napoleon crowning Josephine was much more interesting even if Tom declared it to be little better than magazine art.

Early on, Tom had made himself responsible for developing Maureen's taste in art and music. Sometimes he would sigh in exasperation when she rejected the Picassos and Henry Moores at the Museum of Modern Art, saying she preferred the Fragonards in the Frick collection.

"But they're simply beautiful. They have nothing else to offer." Tom had protested.

Maureen tried not to sound petulant. "But I like them because they're beautiful. What's wrong with that?"

"Nothing. There's nothing wrong with beauty for its own sake. But that has nothing to do with art."

And so they wrangled. Tom, the analyst of everything, insisting that Maureen see things from his point of view. It was hopeless, though, at first, she tried. Later, she began to fight back, saying she had a right to like the kind of art that made her feel good. It was a mistake. She had yet to learn how not to give Tom the kind of opening he relished.

"You sound just like the Irish kid from Third Avenue who never learned anything. For God's sake, Maureen, I've asked you to take a couple of courses at The New School—at least, get your eyes opened."

"What's wrong with my eyes?" She blazed, "You think the only person who can see is Tom Cassidy. Considering how you're half in the bag most of the time, it's a wonder you can see anything!"

They would say nasty, hurtful things to one another until Maureen was in tears and Tom went grimly silent. At times, days would go by before one said a word to the other. The Larchmont house had a spare room, an office really. But there was a sofa-bed in it, and Tom often went there to sleep. And, sometimes, except when he arrived at the studio for his work on the soap opera, Maureen didn't see him for weeks. Shacked up with one of the younger actresses, she supposed. Moreover, she didn't care.

But the trip to Europe had been his peace-offering and they managed to quarrel less. Probably because Tom had made a solemn promise to himself that he would try not to be so critical of Maureen's taste in art.

Florence was the one place where Tom, for a time, found no fault with his wife's taste. They spent whole days in the Uffizi Gallery, drunk with color and, for once, when Maureen murmured "Beautiful!" at something or gasped at the splendor of Titian or Botticelli—beauty for its own sake—he was mercifully silent. They walked the narrow, ancient streets and shopped wildly for things neither of them had been able to afford until now. In the Medici chapel, the scale and depth of Michelangelo's work was so overwhelming, Tom didn't give a thought to how Maureen saw it. He realized that words were superfluous. The visual riches enveloped them like a coating of honey, sweetening everything.

And, that night, for the first time in months, they made love. Tom became, once more, the tender, sensitive lover he had been when they were students at Freddy's. And she, now mature and fully able to respond, gave herself to the voluptuous. If that was what could happen when they looked at great art, maybe Tom wasn't so crazy after all.

By the time they got back to Larchmont, Maureen knew she was pregnant. She was furious.

"How can I be pregnant now, when I've finally got the romantic lead? This is impossible. I can't do it. I wont do it!"

"What choice do you have?" Tom was being reasonable.

They were in the car, driving into Manhattan to shoot the day's episode of the show in which they both had been working for the past three years, The Grand Design.

Maureen was angrily mopping her eyes. They'd be bloodshot and Sunderland, the makeup chief, would have a fit trying to clean them up. "Goddammit! I'm not going to carry this baby. I don't care what you say or what my mother says or even what the holy Pope in Rome says. I'm not having this baby!"

Tom was silent for a moment as he maneuvered the car into the right lane on the Triborough Bridge for the exit to the East Side Drive. Then he said, "I think I ought to have something to say about that. After all, you can't even think about abortion, the Church…"

Maureen whipped around in her seat, jerking her lap belt so it bit into her thighs. "You? What do you mean? You're not trying to tell me you've suddenly decided to go back to the bosom of Holy Mother Church? When was the last time you went near a church that didn't have a Michelangelo inside?" Her tongue dripped acid enough to erode the marble of The Pieta.

"Well, you're right. I'm not terribly religious. You could even say I'm not even a Catholic."

"Not Catholic! Don't be ridiculous. People don't just stop being Catholic unless they've been excommunicated. Of course, you're

Catholic. Anyway, this is news to me." Still angry, she sneered, "Since when have you decided you're not Catholic?"

"Since the day I looked through the Rectory window and saw my mother fucking the priest!" Tom had eased into the right lane on the Drive now and was anticipating the exit ramp. "Being or not being Catholic has nothing to do with it. I want this baby and I'm not going to let you abort my child."

"Let me! Who are you to let or not let me? This is my decision and I'll be the one who makes it." But it was a futile argument, for Maureen herself knew she could never have an abortion. It was simply not possible to swim against the tide of Tom and Deirdre and a church which had been, for most of her life, as much hers as the color of her eyes or her hair. In the very cells of the organism that called itself Maureen Cassidy, she was Catholic and she would carry this baby, conceived in the passion aroused by the beauties of centuries of great art. She hoped for another girl.

She was pleased when the producer persuaded the writers to alter the scripts, hurriedly marrying her character to the leading man, so she could have her pregnancy as part of the show. It was hugely successful, one of the few on-screen pregnancies since Lucille Ball had done it so gracefully and funnily on I Love Lucy.

Maureen found nothing funny about it. She was horribly sick every morning, she hated the way her face bloated, half-concealing her eyes, and her back ached. Oh, how her back ached. This baby had better be something really special, she thought, pushing away the truth—she didn't want this child—and she was afraid it would grow up unhappy and unloved.

Maureen's dilemma was resolved when the baby, a boy, was stillborn, in the eighth month of her term. She was silent, plunged into the depths of guilt and sorrow, so profound that she hardly noticed Tom, Deirdre and ten year-old Kate in their own suffering.

CHAPTER SIX

IN KATE'S HOSPITAL room, as darkness enveloped the city beyond the window, she gave herself another dose of Demerol and began to relax as the pain receded. Her voice was soft as she drowsed.

"Daddy, you think I ought to be worried about Adele Vandersagen?"

"What do you mean, worried about her?" He was patting her hand.

"Well, I think she hates me. I'm willing to bet she'll drop the guillotine at the board meeting next month. She's got all Jim's shares now, so that probably makes her a major stockholder. My contract's up for option next month and I'll be out on my ear. Damn! I love doing it. It's so much fun. And where's she going to find a replacement for me? Oh, Daddy, I'm so sleepy...."

Tom straightened his back to relieve the cramp brought on by leaning over the bed. There was a soft knock on the door as it opened.

Rudy Macklin came in holding a huge bouquet of red roses. He doesn't know, thought Tom, that Katy hates red roses. She thinks they're vulgar.

"Hi, Mr. Cassidy," Rudy was whispering.

"Hey, it's Tom. And you don't have to whisper, our Katy is out cold, you might say."

"Yeah?" Rudy looked at the serene face of Kate as she slept, her head and shoulders slightly elevated. "God, she's gorgeous, isn't she?"

Tom nodded. "Yeah, she looks like one of those Canova marbles in the Santa Croce Church in Florence. Except," he laughed, "the one I'm thinking about was a man, a cardinal. I don't remember." He was rambling. He needed a drink.

"Look, Rudy, why don't you get those flowers put in water and wait a couple of minutes. She's been drifting in and out of sleep so she'll probably wake up in a little while. I know she'll be glad to see you. Tell her I had to leave, okay?"

"Sure, Tom. I'll tell her." My God, Rudy thought, Kate's old man. He looks terrible. He guessed that the stories coming out of California were true, that Tom Cassidy was letting himself go straight to hell, helped along by the bottle.

How many years had it been since he had given up acting altogether to put his energies into directing? Tom had produced a considerable body of work, gaining a name for films that were works of art. One critic had written, "Cassidy's films are so beautiful, they can stand alone, frame-by-frame, like so many still photographs." Rudy couldn't understand why Maureen always laughed out loud when he or somebody said how gorgeous Tom Cassidy's movies were. She sometimes added something like, "Yes, but is it art?" Then she'd laugh again.

The next morning was clear and brisk with a hint of the Winter to come. Irving Quinn was glad he had worn the Burberry over his tweed jacket and slacks. It wasn't classy, but at least he wouldn't look like a cop in a cheap suit when he called on Adele Vandersagen in her Waldorf Towers apartment, the place she called her camp away from her real home in Texas.

She had always hated the place she called "the mausoleum" in Westchester which was the official residence of James G. Vandersagen.

It overlooked Long Island Sound from a hillock in Rye and was, Adele thought, the very essence of old money. After Vandersagen Island had been sold, it was all that was left of the original family holdings and Jim refused to let it go. Now that he had remade the family fortune, so to speak, he was determined to hold on, as if it were something with which to redeem the name that his father had sullied. But Adele hated the place, and, when she couldn't live on the ranch she had inherited in Texas, she "camped out" in the six-room Towers suite.

Her buzzer permitted Quinn to enter the private elevator but she, herself answered the apartment door in the modest vestibule. "Come on in, Inspector or Lieutenant or whatever they call you. Here, let me take your coat." She put Quinn's raincoat in a small closet and, with her hand, gestured toward a large living room beyond the entry area.

"Sit anywhere." She said. "I've got a bad back, so if you don't mind, I'll tuck up on this sofa. Do you want some coffee? It's a pretty chilly morning, isn't it? A nice hot cup of java?"

"No, thanks, I'm all coffeed up already. You know we cops use coffee like a car uses gasoline."

"Some tea then? I'll ring for it." And she reached behind her to a table and touched a button. A uniformed maid appeared and Adele said, "Mina, would you bring us some of that jasmine tea, please?" Then, looking at Quinn, she said, "This'll be lots better than coffee. Want anything with it?" He smiled and shook his head.

Jesus, he thought, it's like Masterpiece Theater. Then, reaching into his breast pocket for the ever-necessary notebook and pen, he paused.

"Is that a Donna Quinn you're wearing?"

Adele's hand reached to her shoulder where the toga-like garment hung from a knot and flowed in graceful curves to her knees. Beneath, her entire body was enclosed in a soft, clinging fabric. The effect was sexy, but in a very understated way, given the rich texture of the fabric and its muted color, a dark, almost black, purple, like a ripe eggplant. Her only jewelry was a pair of cabochon amethyst earrings.

"I would never have expected a policeman to recognize a Donna Quinn...but, of course! Is she related?"

"My wife, ah, ex-wife."

"I just love her clothes. They're so intelligently designed. I think she's a genius."

"I do too." That was the trouble with Donna, he thought. Living with a genius is tough on everybody, even a cop. He cleared his throat to indicate a change of subject.

Adele smiled. "Of course, you want to get on with your questions." She grew sad-looking, genuinely, Quinn thought. "I guess I have to talk about poor Jimmy. Did his secretary give you the official biography?"

Quinn nodded and he said, "Mrs. Vandersagen, that's not why I'm here. I know this has been a horrible experience for you, but I have to ask you about yesterday."

The tea tray was brought in and Adele used the moment to collect her thoughts. She poured and handed him the steaming cup. The she said, "I guess everybody at the studio heard me yellin' at him, didn't they?"

Her voice was relaxing and picking up a bit more of the Texas drawl that two decades in New York had not obliterated.

Quinn nodded. "Did you quarrel often with your husband?"

"No, I wouldn't say often. But, I'll have to admit, the last couple of years, things haven't been too great for us. And, no matter what you've heard, Lieutenant, I loved my husband. I guess that's why that girl, Kate Cassidy was the only girl of his—and believe me, Jim Vandersagen always had some girl stashed away—the only girl that worried me. In the past, when I found out about some girl, it didn't used to bother me. I loved him, and I know enough to let a man be what a man wants to be. It could've been golf or art collecting, anything, I wouldn't have minded."

Quinn wasn't sure where this was leading, so he sipped the surprisingly good jasmine tea and waited.

"You see, when Jim was married to the cucumber princess...." She paused. "You know, Sally-Anne Peterson? That's his first wife. I call her that because I swear, no matter what happened, she was always cool as a cucumber. Damn! A house could fall on her, and she'd just shake out those good bones of hers and walk away like nothin' happened. Well, I'm not like that. When I get mad I get loud. My Daddy spent a fortune sending me to fancy girls' schools, but, after all, I'm just a cowboy's daughter and, as they say, blood will tell.

"Well, when I met Jim, I knew he wasn't just fallin' in love with my luscious curves and baby-blue eyes." She moved her hand vaguely across her body which, though she was nearer forty than thirty, revealed Adele Vandersagen as an attractive, if slightly overweight woman, who had been exquisitely beautiful in her youth.

"No," she continued. "Jim had taken old man Peterson's radio stations and newspapers and then he was movin' into the big time. He had WJGV in New York, but because of the way the law was, he couldn't get himself a newspaper. He wasn't about to tackle the Gannetts in Westchester; and anyway, he didn't want to mess around the edges of New York. No, what he wanted was something much bigger—something that would take the JGV network everywhere. Not just geographically, across the whole country, the whole world. He wanted into the future as he saw it. That meant cable, and cyberspace—big time. He wanted the means to be everywhere, in every market, in every medium. Just last week, he was makin' deals about this interactive stuff.

"Well, anyway, even twenty years ago, Jim Vandersagen was thinkin' big and he went lookin' around. When he got to Fort Worth, where my Daddy was doin' the same thing, it was like a marriage made in heaven. Except Jim and my Daddy couldn't get married and I could. No only that, I fell for that big feller like a baby fallin' off its first pony. So, I did what a girl does at a time like that. I got my Daddy to buy him for me."

Adele laughed. "Oh, I read the papers. They didn't say it in so many words, but it was all there. The difference was, I wasn't just some spoiled little rich girl, and my Daddy wasn't about to give me away to some dude who's all hat and no cattle. No, he worked out a deal that made both Jim and me bigger and richer together than we ever could have been separately."

"There was talk of divorce, though, wasn't there?" Quinn had been looking at his notes.

"Oh, hell, the papers are always yellin' divorce. Look at those Trumps. I'll bet, if she'd have just let him run out his string with that Marla Maples, they'd be all patched up again. But, to answer your question, no, I never filed for divorce and neither did Jim. We used to fight, sure, but it was nothing. That is, until Kate Cassidy came along."

"What about Kate Cassidy? How did she make things different?"

"I can't say exactly. It was just this feeling I had. When he hired her to do the Come Home show it was like he'd been bewitched. Hell, I don't know if he was having an affair with her. If that were the only thing, I could live with that. I told you, girls were a kind of hobby with

Jim; he used them, that's the only word, used them the way a man plays golf or shoots skeet. No, there was something else. Suddenly, he developed this fascination for her. It was "Kate" this and "Kate" that, until I got so I couldn't stand the sound of her name."

"You were in the Green Room yesterday morning, weren't you? The crew said they heard you and your husband quarreling."

"That's true. I'd been wanting us to go away somewhere, but he said he couldn't get away right now that there was this big shakeup coming what with all the new technology. Why, they're writing the rules as they go along, and Jim didn't want to be out in the cold when the deals were going down. I'll admit, I was pushin' him because I wanted to put a whole bunch of miles between Jim and his new plaything."

"So, would you think I'd be exaggerating if I said you were extremely jealous and thought of Kate as your rival? You know, in a court of law, that kind of thing can be considered a motive for murder."

"Murder?" Adele looked as if she never had heard the word. Why would I want to murder my husband? I just told you I loved him. Jesus, Inspector." Suddenly Adele Vandersagen began to cry.

Quinn leaned over the low table on which the tea service sat, poured himself some jasmine tea and waited.

"Sorry," said Adele. She wiped her tears quickly with the back of her hand. "I don't usually do this kind of thing, but I'm still upset. I just can't accept the idea of Jim's being dead. Every couple of minutes it hits me and then I've got to get back on track. But, whatever do you mean, murder? Jim died in an accident, didn't he? Some stupid stagehand not doin' his job right? Tell me that's what happened."

"That's not what happened." Then Quinn explained the details. He did not mention the poisoned chocolate sauce.

Adele Vandersagen sat, wordlessly. Quinn could see that she understood perfectly the implication that her husband may or may not have been the target of the rigged mirror. "You're sayin' that mirror could have been set to fall on Kate? Or on both of them? And you think I could have done that?"

"No, I haven't said what I think. I'm just telling you what the District Attorney might think. I will tell you this. You'll be expected to remain available for further questioning. You understand?"

She nodded. "What about Jim? My lawyers tell me you won't release his body. We have to arrange a funeral, you know."

"Yes, I know. The Coroner should be releasing his body within a few days. You can go ahead and make your arrangements." He rose to go, putting down his cup. "Oh, by the way, do you have any idea of what a squib is?"

"A what?"

"A squib."

Adele laughed. "I just know that's a trick question, but honestly, Inspector, I haven't the faintest idea of what you're talkin' about. Sounds like something you read at the bottom of a newspaper column, you know when they run out of story before they run out of space?"

"Lieutenant, I'm not an inspector. And about the squib—that sounds like a pretty good definition."

As Irving Quinn rose, he set down his cup and turned toward a large French door facing uptown. The autumn colors of Central Park, ten blocks away, made a lovely backdrop. He walked to the door, peered through to a small terrace and saw a table and four chairs with a large potted tree in one corner. The tree was bare. "Nice view from up here. Do you ever do any gardening out on that terrace?"

"Gardening? Well, I guess you just don't understand Texas. Out there, what we call a garden is what you grow vegetables in. It's not like here in the East where gardens are for flowers and you get your vegetables at Gristedes. I assume you're asking about if I grow flowers, right?"

"Something like that."

"I don't know what growing flowers has to do with my husband's death, but the answer is no, I wouldn't know a zinnia from a heliotrope. The only flowers I know about come from the shop downstairs. They send a couple of arrangements every other day and put them on the bill."

"So you never have planted flowers out on that roof-garden?"

"Well, if you want to call that itty bitty terrace out there," she gestured toward the door, "a roof-garden, it's okay with me. But that tree thing in the pot that's lost all its leaves—well that hardly makes it a garden, does it?"

"Do you ever do anything with it, spray it or fertilizer, maybe?"

"Not me. Maybe Mina or her husband—he's kind of a butler, valet, whatever Jim wants him to be, and the chauffeur too, of course. Maybe Schultz, that's his name, maybe Schultz gives the thing a sprinkle of something once in a while. But I haven't noticed, because, as I said, when I want the country, I go home to Texas."

"Just curious," Quinn said. "Oh, and thanks for the tea. You're pretty sure I'll be able to find it at Zabar's on the West Side?"

"If you can't find it at Zabar's on the West Side, then it'll be a bonanza for the fancy grocers on Madison Avenue. They just love it when Zabar's can't come up with something they sell over on this side of town."

She had walked him toward the apartment door and was about to get his coat. He said, "Oh, one more question, and then I'm out of here. Was your brother with you and your husband yesterday? Was that the third voice the crew said they heard?"

Adele nodded, "Yeah, my baby brother, Gil Kenyon."

"They tell me the conversation was pretty loud, almost like an argument. Do you and your brother get along alright?"

"Well, Gil, he's my half-brother. And as for whether or not we get along, that depends."

"On what?"

"Depends on whether or not he wants something from me. You see, brother Gil is from my Daddy's second marriage, after my poor Mamma was killed?" Quinn nodded. He had interviewed women from Texas before and knew the question indicated that there was more to follow.

"Well, Gil sort of had an idea that he'd like to give Jim Vandersagen some business advice. Like this time, Gil has his eye on buying into a movie studio. Sort of like what Ted Turner did when he bought those three hundred old Paramount movies, and then bid on Castle Rock Entertainment. Well, Gil, he was insisting that Jim and I put up our shares in JGV so he could buy some on-its-butt studio in Hollywood. Jim told him to take a hike and I agreed. You see, Gil really doesn't have the kind of head for this business that Jim and my Daddy had. All Gil's got is a large chunk of stock and he's itchin' to do something with it."

"Something as serious as murdering Jim?"

"Wha...Gil? What earthly good would it do him to murder Jim? He doesn't benefit by Jim's death. I do, of course. But if you think I'm going to let little Gil get his hands on the company my Daddy and Jim Vandersagen built, you're workin' the wrong street. Anyway, Gil Kenyon's not that kind of kid. Well, I guess I should stop calling him a kid. He's got to be twenty-six or thereabouts. He's more interested in girls and fast cars than real business."

"You and Jim Vandersagen had no children, is that right?"

"No. It's really sad too. I wanted kids, but just couldn't do it. Jim's got a couple of sons, though. They're about my age, maybe a little younger. He left them very well provided for. And so did old Peterson and that guy, what'sisname that the cucumber princess married—-oh, yeah, real money. I can never remember if he's Schlumberger or Rothschild. One of those. You know, Eurotrash."

Quinn shouldered into his Burberry. "Yeah, Eurotrash. We don't get to see much of them at our precinct."

The elevator operated smoothly. Standing in the tasteful walnut-paneled cubicle as it descended, Irving Quinn decided he liked Adele Vandersagen. He hoped he was right in his hunch about her not being a killer. Though, after more than twenty years as a cop, he had learned never to put much faith in hunches.

Quinn was mildly annoyed that he had to ride all the way down to the lobby to board an entirely different elevator to the eighteenth-floor suite where Tom Cassidy was staying. He hoped it was early enough in the day to find the famous director sober and able to answer questions.

Chapter Seven

LIEUTENANT QUINN WAS reviewing the case *The Daily News* called "The TV Mogul Murder." The papers were speculating about Kate Cassidy as a possible intended victim. Apparently, they knew nothing of the poisoned chocolate sauce—just fine with Irving Quinn.

As a matter of principle, Quinn avoided telling news reporters anything he could conceivably conceal from them. After twenty years on the force and years of combat duty as an army officer in Viet Nam, he had learned never to volunteer any information to the press. They rarely got the facts straight, and he was convinced, they had few scruples about inventing information when it suited them.

"Okay, Alex, you went up to the Cassidy house with a search warrant. What did you find?"

"Well, I'll tell you, Boss, I didn't find much. And none of that stuff, uh, whadya callit?" He looked at his notes. "Oh, here it is, thiophosphate. There were all kinds of garden things, you know, chemicals and like that. They have a shed out back, but I wouldn't say the place looks like one a them English gardens or anything in a picture book. It's pretty ordinary, you know, a few hedges...."

Quinn prompted, "The chemicals, Alex. What did you find?"

"Well, there's rose stuff and flea spray and here's one I like, aphids and beetle killer. I musta looked at twenty different bottles and cans, read all the fine print too. Not once did that thiophosphate word show up. But you know something? Most of them bottles have gotta be pretty old. They're mostly empty or there's just a tiny bit of dried-up old gunk left in the bottom. Looks to me like the lady who lives there doesn't fool around with gardening much, or maybe she's one a them environmentalists, you know, the ones who don't use chemicals anymore. Maybe even that stuff was left there by another person, you know, before they sold the house to this one?"

Quinn liked to affirm his detectives whenever possible. "Those are all good points, Alex. Maureen Cassidy told me she had no idea what kind of chemicals were in her garden shed."

Alex went on, "She told me the only work she has done these days is just the lawn and cutting the hedges, front and back. And a few rose bushes. But she's got a man comes in once a week in the Summer and she don't know nothin' about that chemical stuff. Says it was her mother was the one liked gardening, but she's been dead for a long time. Maybe that's why there's no fresh stuff out there."

"Okay, for the moment, we'll say the poison in the chocolate sauce didn't come from the Cassidy house. Anybody else check for that stuff? Jonah, you come up with anything?"

"Nobody on my list's got a garden except Rudy Macklin. He lives up in Riverdale. Nice house, but man, the outside—it's going to hell. Weeds up to here." He put a hand under his chin. "I didn't see any chemicals anywhere. I don't think the place has been touched all year. And with the leaves starting to fall it looks like a haunted house."

"Yeah," Quinn said, "that's what happens when people get divorced." He thought of the immaculate, white colonial in Great Neck, with its gleaming black shutters and crimson door. The garden was Donna's pride where she spent hours in the Spring and Summer, planting color-coordinated beds of flowers. The house had been showcased on one of the town's charity tours. The year before Donna had been ecstatic when the interior was featured in a slick magazine with classy color photographs. Too bad, he thought, Donna couldn't spare some of that creative energy for making our marriage work. Then he remembered that the counselor had told him to stop blaming his wife for the failure and accept some of the responsibility himself.

"Okay, who else was in the studio that day who might have a motive for killing Jim Vandersagen and/or Kate Cassidy?" He was writing names on a white board with a thick crayon-like object. The first were Maureen and Tom Cassidy:

As he wrote he shook his head, "But they were not together, so we have to think of them individually."

Adele Vandersagen "She says she never left the Green Room, but she can't prove she wasn't in the studio when the mirror went down."

Rudy Macklin "He was having root canal work done, but there was a period after the poker game when he could have come downtown from Riverdale, rigged the squibs, then hightailed it up to the dentist—nah, too much. Let's scratch him for a minute."

Quinn peered at a note. "This guy, Warren Dix. It says here he's a producer too. How many producers they got on this show?"

Jonah said, "I talked to him. He was here, but he says he was in his office down the hall, near the green room. He's the guy who keeps tabs on the money. You see, they've got a budget for each show, and he's like, you know what they call them...."

"Bean counters?" Irving Quinn remembered his own father, a real, old-fashioned street cop who once, in an unguarded moment, had described his father-in-law as a bean counter.

His mother, a schoolteacher, was incensed. She said, "My father is a CPA!" The title had been her father's hard-won entree into the middle class. Charlie Quinn, abashed at having caused even a whisper of pain to a wife he worshipped, put his arm around her and said. Oh, I'm sorry my dear; you've all the right in the world to be proud of your old dad." Then to dispel any further tension, he pranced around the room. "And don't you forget, I'm an NYPD cop, an I got the badge to prove it" He was relieved when his wife rewarded him with a smile. Irving and his sister thought their parents acted goofy, but they laughed a lot.

Quinn had a fleeting thought—if he and Donna had laughed more... Quickly, he made the mental shift back to the subject at hand. "So, you interviewed him and you think he's in the clear?"

Jonah nodded.

Alex wondered, "Could this Dix guy have any reason to kill his boss?" I mean, doesn't the money guy, the producer have to keep the boss happy about the budget?"

"Sure, but why kill him?" Quinn said, "No, I don't think so."

Another name on Quinn's list was Gil Kenyon. "He's Adele's half-brother and he's got a chunk of stock in JGV. She's got the idea he's after her to help him get hold of a movie studio or something like that. Maybe getting all the stock into his sister's hands would make her an easier touch than Jim. She says she's not susceptible to her baby brother's pleading, but who knows? Has anybody talked to this guy?"

Alex said, "I left messages both at his house and his office. It's not a real office, just a rented cubby. It's downtown, with a phone and voice mail. Nobody's seen the guy. Do we want to bring him in?"

"Not now. I'm not sure we could get a warrant and, even if we could, we have nothing to hold him for. Better to just let him be. If something turns up later, we can always track him down." The Lieutenant looked at his watch. "I think we're almost done here. But one of you ought to follow up on the ME's toxicology report. I want to find out how much of that thiophosphate they found in his body."

It had been two weeks since Jim Vandersagen's death. Kate Cassidy was recovering rapidly from her injuries. Quinn had telephoned her a number of times, and he sensed she was having a struggle with the idea that someone she had cared about was dead. That sense of sadness had not come through in the early interviews, while she was still unable to leave the hospital. The drugs, he thought; Demerol sure takes the edge off all kinds of pain, including the emotional. One reason, he kept telling himself, that he wanted to speak to her again, now that she was in better shape. That, and the fact that he liked talking to her.

Kate said she had been getting ready to tape a number of new shows for the following weeks. "No, I'm afraid we won't be seeing anymore of Glenda Russo," she told him The terrified guest, who was to have appeared on the show about eating cake and staying thin, had not been heard from again. When the mirror fell, she was lucky enough to have been nervously pacing backstage. Immediately afterward, she fled, and was now holed-up in Vermont somewhere, presumably, writing another cookbook. Quinn and his staff had done enough background-checking on the woman to rule her out as a suspect. She had never met either Jim Vandersagen or Kate Cassidy until her agent booked her for the show some five months earlier.

Quinn was hoping that Kate might shed further light on the people who were known to be in the studio that day: He looked at a note on his desk and quickly reviewed the list he had been working on with Alex and Jonah. He wanted to make sure nothing was overlooked.

Kate's parents, Tom and Maureen Cassidy? Would either of them want to murder Vandersagen? Maybe, but certainly, neither of them wanted to murder their daughter.

Again, he reviewed Rudy Macklin's story and his alibi, the poker game and the dentist appointment. No holes there, he thought. And no new ideas, either.

Quinn then took an exhaustive second look at what they had learned about the regular crew, including the chief electrician and carpenter, neither of whom had any apparent motives for harming Kate or Vandersagen, He eliminated them all. Besides, they each had an alibi for their whereabouts before the official opening of the studio at eight o'clock that morning. And everyone agreed that the squibs must have been rigged on the mirror before the studio opened, but after it had closed the evening before. The job was done by someone who knew how to get around in the complex of studios and offices But, he looked at his notes again. "It's hard to believe that nobody we talked to—maintenance people, watchmen—nobody saw anything."

"Yeah," Alex said, "it's like that wherever you go. If people had any idea of just how bad their regular security is, they'd have a fit. What about the guy's wife? Wasn't she there before the studio officially opened? Nobody remembers what time she showed up."

Quinn looked again at his notes. "No, she arrived a few minutes after the electrician got there. He said she watched him make coffee and waited so she could take a cup back to the Green Room."

He was still reserving judgment about Adele Vandersagen. Several people confirmed having heard her in a quarrel not only with her husband, but with her younger brother. If not a quarrel, at least, there were some pretty loud voices heard coming from the Green Room. And, of course, she had admitted to being jealous of Kate.

Finally, there was Gil Kenyon, whom nobody remembered having seen in the studio at the moment the crash occurred. Though, of course, all eyes were directed toward the stage, as the sound of smashing glass was heard.

Tom Cassidy had been sitting in the last row of audience seats, obscured in shadow, the house lights still off. He told Irving Quinn he was sure there was another person in the same last row in which he was sitting, but that he could not identify anyone, even as to gender.

"It could have been a man or a woman in that seat, is that what you're saying?" Quinn had asked. "Right." Tom said. Then the Lieutenant showed him a picture of Gil Kenyon. Tom said he did not recognize the face.

Irving Quinn sipped some tea. He had found the jasmine tea at Zabar's and made it in the small drip pot he had bought for the purpose. He motioned with his cup, as if to offer some, but Alex and Jonah exchanged glances and politely refused. Then he said, "Oh go ahead, get a cup of that black battery acid from the pot. I'll wait until you get back."

The two detectives sat again with their Styrofoam cups while Quinn stirred his tea, thinking aloud, "Kate Cassidy herself. Yeah, I know," he argued, "she says she went back to put in her contact lenses and Vandersagen's body fell on her. But why couldn't she have rigged the mirror to fall? She has a key to the studio. She could have gone back, hit the remote and miscalculated by walking forward too soon. My only problem is why? Why would she want to kill him? Why would any of them want to kill the guy? Who benefits from his death?"

"That's easy," said Alex, "Adele. She gets all his stock and control of the company."

"No, not quite." Quinn said. "There are a number of shares outstanding. Her brother has some, so does Kate Cassidy, for that matter. But maybe Adele's the one after all. She might have wanted to get rid of a woman she was jealous of and, at the same time kill her husband for control of JGV. You know, the old two-birds-with-one-stone; two for the price of one. She could get rid of both of them and take over the whole network. There's nothing like getting rid of your rival, your husband and, to sweeten the bargain, you become head honcho of the guy's business. Except, I don't think Adele knows thing one about using explosives, whatchamacallits, squibs. She has no idea of what they are. Now, Kate, on the other hand—she's been in TV studios for years. No, she's always done news shows. They don't go around blowing up things." He absently snapped his pencil in two, the second one since starting to work on the case. "How much stock does Kate have, anybody know?"

"No but why would that make a difference? Kate's got kids," Jonah said. "Wouldn't they inherit their mother's shares if she died?"

"You'd have made a good lawyer, Joannie," said Alex.

"I'd rather be a good detective, but thanks."

"Kate, somehow, this has to do with Kate," Quinn shook his head. I guess I'll have to talk to her again."

He thought to himself, I really don't have any reason to question her again. He thought of the last time he had seen her. He had a precise mental picture of what he had seen, as she led him into the living room of the upper West Side-apartment.

It was spacious without being grandiose, with good, but not distinguished furniture, none of it new and some of it showing signs of wear. The colors were soft shades of green and peach with a bit of bright print here and there. Quinn had enough knowledge to recognize a good-sized, authentic Kilim rug on the floor. Between his mother and Donna, his taste had been shaped almost by osmosis. Women with good Kilims and well-used, but good furniture don't usually go around killing people.

He realized that Kate's blond, blunt-cut, shoulder-length hair, with just a touch of silver and her clear, blue eyes tended to distract him from his work. But he decided to call her again, and this time, he'd invite her to something, a movie? Maybe the opera. He hadn't asked her if she liked opera.

"I said, Lieutenant, could I put you down for a couple a tickets?" It was Alex whose question Quinn had not heard.

"What tickets?"

"You know, for the Annual Hellenic Society Festival. It's next weekend, just like last year, at the Armory."

"That's it!" Quinn reached for his wallet. "Yeah, I'll take two. Thirty bucks? More than last year isn't it?"

"Yeah," Alex was unapologetic. "The food's terrific and there's all that dancing. The show alone..."

"Okay, okay. Gimme two tickets." He thought, yeah, Kate would probably still be a little too stiff for the real jumping around, but the band played slow numbers too. He remembered how miserable he had been the last time, when he had gone alone. Months from a nasty divorce, he was desolate, trying not to stare at all those apparently blissful couples, doing the measured dance routines they had been rehearsing all year. He had courteously asked Alex's mother to dance. Then, after a marvelous Greek dinner, excused himself, pleading neglected police work. Greek dancing. Alex always said it was the most exciting, much better than disco and rock and roll. Yeah, he was sure Kate would love it.

He made the call soon after the two detectives left his office. He almost forgot that his office wall was glass and he was visible to a number of people in the room beyond. Everyone who cared to look, could see the Lieutenant with a broad grin on his face as he spoke on the phone.

"Not only is the food terrific, you'll get to see some sensational dancing."

"I know Greek dancing is wonderful. We toured the Greek Islands once and we danced like crazy. It's like that all over the Mediterranean. Alex would probably have a ball on an Israeli kibbutz with those kids, dancing by firelight. I couldn't do much fancy stepping right now—I'm still pretty sore. But just watching would be fun. Yeah, of course, I'd love to go. These days I've had a choice between my mother and going out to see doctors. Believe me, I'm ready for anything."

Maureen had insisted upon accompanying Kate home from the hospital and staying with her, stubbornly refusing the pointed suggestion that she return to Larchmont. Then Maureen took charge of Kate's recovery with all the zeal of a woman who, for too long, has had nobody about whom to be concerned, or, as Kate put it, "to push around."

The morning of her discharge, when Kate said, "I can manage, really I can," Maureen vehemently disagreed.

"No, you can't. You need somebody to look after you. And if you won't come home with me, I'm coming home with you. You can't be alone at a time like this."

As they left the hospital, Kate lost the first skirmish in this most recent battle of wills with Maureen. She was too tired to argue further. "Okay, but you can only stay for a little while. You've got to get on with your own life and I have to do the same. I want you back in Larchmont no later than next week, okay?"

Maureen said, "Okay, okay, next week." The cab pulled away from the hospital's main entrance and they settled back for the trip uptown. Kate was too tired to extract a solemn promise, figuring she would put her foot down later if her mother did not indeed leave at the agreed-upon time.

It wasn't so much that Kate objected to her mother's company. She had to be sure she could manage without her. Learning to be comfortable on her own after Avi's death was an achievement hard-won. She didn't want to retrogress, although Doctor Hoffmann had assured her that once she had met a challenge and conquered it, there was nothing more to fear. The psychiatrist had been very supportive—like a coach, in a sense.

After her children's clamoring to be free and away from the scene of mourning, she had reluctantly agreed to let Joel and Dee Dee go back to their colleges earlier than she might have wished. It was somewhat like the times she had taken daring chances; riding a horse too fast or rock-climbing. She was frightened but she was proving to herself that she was tough.

At one therapy session, she was wrestling with the idea while Doctor Hoffman waited in silence. Then Kate said, "It's like a kind of Olympic medal-event, in a way. You're saying I'm going to win the Gold for letting my kids go?"

Audrey Hoffmann nodded. "Yeah, life is full of those little competitions where the only one you have to win against is yourself. But you're the toughest competitor you'll ever meet." That had been more than a year ago.

At this point, in spite of being afraid of an unknown killer somewhere, Kate was determined not to give up and let Maureen turn her into a mewling infant. Then she thought, just because somebody killed Jim Vandersagen and maybe wants to kill me too, I must be nuts trying to show how brave I am. God, she thought, trying to shake off the gloom, I'll bet I wouldn't even lose points for going up to Larchmont and locking myself in my old room.

Even when she had begun to think clearly, she was especially frightened about the chocolate sauce and what might have happened. Anybody, the crew, her guest, even her mother, might have done exactly as Jim had done, swiping an index finger into the stuff for a quick taste.

Most of the samples of food, bought or made especially for use on camera, like the jar of chocolate sauce, were often subject to spoilage under hot lights. After a recent case of food poisoning, Rudy Macklin had requested that food which had been standing be discarded after the show. I guess, Kate thought, as usual, Jim paid no attention to Rudy's memo.

Then she reasoned, Jim Vandersagen, after all, was a law unto himself, and if he wanted to taste something on the kitchen counter, he was damned well going to. She remembered telling Maureen about that. Her mother had said, "Yeah, I know. Nobody in the whole world was ever able to tell Jim Vandersagen what he was and was not permitted to do."

Kate was so shaken by the events everyone called the accident, that she reestablished a series of therapy sessions with her psychiatrist. She explained, "I just don't think I can talk about any of this with my mother."

Audrey Hoffmann was about ten years older than Kate.

"Of course not. That's precisely why the science of psychiatry was developed. Nobody can talk things over with her mother. I haven't spoken to my mother about anything more personal than noodle pudding—you know, kugel—since I left medical school. And, to this day, she swears my kugel will never be as good as hers. Let's stop worrying about your mother and talk about your feelings This Jim, a great loss?"

"Not like that. It's worse, and it's so complicated," Kate wailed.

"That's what I'm here for."

Kate knew that Doctor Hoffman was there to help her deal with her feelings, but she said, "What I really wish is that you could write me a prescription for getting along with my mother. I swear, she's acting absolutely crazy. What am I supposed to do about that? The only thing she talks about is Jim Vandersagen. I know it was a terrible experience for her, being there and my getting hurt. And there's her history with him—she never shuts up. It's all I can do to not scream, enough!"

"You're a mother yourself. You know the best thing you can do is just let her deal with it any way she can. If it makes you crazy, I can help"

One day, as if a switch had been turned off, Maureen stopped talking about Jim Vandersagen. She had found something far more absorbing, though she wasn't behaving much differently. She was frantic and, Kate thought, even obsessed. One early evening, long after the promised departure date for Larchmont, Maureen arrived at Kate's apartment in a state bordering on hysteria. Recently she had learned that her soap opera character was to be killed off. At first it had seemed simple. Her agent would find a new role quickly, but the outlook was far from rosy. She was beginning to panic. It would be her first time in years without work on which to concentrate.

Kate knew her mother did not need money—she had been very careful to save and invest wisely. But like any actress who had not been without work for a quarter of a century, she was daunted by the idea of finding another role in a different show.

Maureen fretted; she said it felt like the old days when she had clawed and scraped, always afraid that her last job would be the end of a career which had barely begin. The old terror had not changed. Though she knew her anxiety was unfounded, there was nothing she could do to dispel the mounting terror—no job, no prospects and the utterly irrational fear that she would be forced to go back to carrying plates at Schrafft's. Ridiculous, she thought, Schrafft's went out of business years ago.

Kate reassured her. "There must be a thousand things you've always wanted to have enough time to do. This should be a welcome break for you."

"No, you don't understand." She felt it in her soul. How could Kate understand how it had been back then? The idea of not working was nothing less than inconceivable. There was genuine despair in her voice. "What am I supposed to do at this point? I'm too old to learn anything else. I don't even know how to cook!"

Kate refrained from comment—Dr. Hoffmann once told her that she should listen for the signal that calls for a remark instead of wading in just because someone stops for a breath.

Maureen went on, as if Kate were not there. "God, I'm so mad. I could have gotten out of my contract last January and gone to work for that new nighttime sci-fi serial. I sure hope it's not too late. They're still casting for the pilot. Of course, it's on another network." That triggered more talk of Jim Vandersagen.

"I can't say I'm sorry to be leaving JGV. It's been, how many years? More than half your lifetime, and a whole lot of mine. But I hardly ever saw Jim after he married Adele and got the brass-ring, big-time. Did you ever see him outside of work or the studio? I mean, socially"

Kate was instantly wary. Her mother had to know that Jim Vandersagen had taken her out to dinner several times.

"Well, I did go to dinner with him. But it was nothing more than the boss being kind to one of his workers."

They both knew she was understating the case. One night, when Jim and Kate were having dinner at Sardi's before the theater, Maureen and Andy Feuerman came in and were seated at a table across the room. They hadn't been there for more than a few minutes when Maureen saw the way Jim and Kate were looking at one another.

At the time, Maureen thought, if ever there were two people on the brink of a love affair, or worse, in the opening stages of one, they were Kate Cassidy and Jim Vandersagen. Maureen was so upset, she excused herself from the table and went to the ladies' to splash cold water on her face. Andrew Feuerman was a famous investment banker, accustomed to swift changes of plan. While she was gone, he squared with the headwaiter and, having retrieved Maureen's coat, was ready to go out the door. It wasn't until they were in a cab, that he dared to ask, "What was that all about?"

"I can't exactly explain," Maureen said. Andy did not press. He simply put his arm around her and said, "Wanna go uptown and let me cook you something? Or do you really want to see that show for the third time?"

Andy. The first man in Maureen's life as a mature woman, that she had ever considered marrying. Well, she thought, I'll tell him about it later. "It's been running too long, anyway. They're walking through their parts by now. Let's give the tickets to him." She pointed to the cab driver.

"Hey, thanks." The driver said as they got out on Park Avenue, in front of Andy's building. "These tickets are worth seventy-five bucks apiece. If I get over there fast, maybe I can scalp them. I sure as hell ain't givin' up a nights work to go to a lousy show, when I can get better stuff on television."

Remembering the sentiments of the cab driver, Maureen wondered if it was true. Was live theater becoming obsolete?. The old yearning for work on the stage had never left her, but now, with her old job gone, she was forced to confront the facts. She was a television actress—to be declared dead presently, it was true—but she had a couple of Emmy Awards. Had it been enough to compensate for the sense of failure at not having been on Broadway?

There was no time to brood about unmet expectations. Some day her agent would find something. Now, she had a more important job to do.

As Kate recovered from her injuries, Her mother was doing what had nearly driven her mad through all her growing-up years—hovering. Under ordinary circumstances Maureen was, if not indifferent, a somewhat detached mother. She could afford to be—Deirdre was always on hand. But if Kate were ill or injured, or she seemed morose and troubled, Maureen quickly became overprotective to a point which, more than once, had made Kate wonder how much was real and how much was the actress playing a role.

Now out of the hospital, quite capable of being on her own, Kate was trying to shake Maureen. "Mom, you really ought to go home. I can manage with cabs to see doctors and I'm already thinking about starting back to work in a week or two. There really is no reason for you, or anyone else to stay here with me." Might just as well tell the rain to stop falling, she thought.

Saying no to Maureen was probably the most difficult part of being a daughter, Kate thought. She had begun her campaign immediately and now, two weeks later, Maureen was still here. But she knew she could not win against the *idea fixe* of her mother that she was needed. Maureen had taken charge and would remain in charge until Kate could wear her down. Or, Kate prayed, her agent calls and says Maureen has to go to work.

Nearly two weeks after leaving the hospital, Kate was comfortably snuggled in bed, pleading to be left alone with a good book, when her Mother-in-law, Jeanne Rosen, appeared.

My God, Kate said to herself, Avi would have made a lulu of a New Yorker sketch out of this: Two women, one, an actress playing the role of Mother McCree. And the other, a tough news woman trying to play a Yiddishe Mama. From Maureen it was "Darlin', you must get some rest." And Jeanne tried to top it with, "Sweetheart, I should make you a nice pot of chicken soup." Neither one of them could cook and both hated being around sick people.

Despite her still-sore ribs, Kate laughed. "Get out of here. Go into the kitchen and call Grossman's Deli on Broadway. The number is by the phone. Have them send up a half gallon of chicken soup and three orders of today's special for dinner." She lay back on the pillow and sighed as the two women retreated.

Maureen and Jeanne went into the kitchen, as ordered, then Jeanne said, "Where the hell do they keep the gin in this place? I think we need martinis." Maureen found the gin and vermouth and both went into the living room to catch up on their mutual grandchildren.

Joel, was finishing his senior year at the University in Tel Aviv and planning to stay in Israel for graduate work in archeology. His interest in the Middle East had been sparked both by his father and what he knew of his Sabra grandfather who had been born on an Israeli kibbutz. Joel was frantically learning Hebrew and Aramaic as well as everything he could about the Ginzburgs who had emigrated from Russia in the mid nineteenth century to pioneer in the inhospitable land then called Palestine.

He said being there made losing his father no less painful, but at least, he felt he might find something to account for the apparently meaningless death. His letters to Kate and his grandmothers were infrequent and, suspiciously, the descriptions and narratives were word-for-word duplicates, despite the handwritten salutations.

"Well," Jeanne Rosen was philosophical. "In this day and age, everything else is mass-produced, why not letters to your grandmothers."

Maureen agreed. "At least he writes. Not like Dee Dee. She thinks long distance, especially with reversed charges is the way to keep in touch."

"I've solved that problem, "Jeanne said. "I'm putting in one of those eight hundred numbers, so she can call anytime she wants. That should be a whole lot less than it's costing me now."

"Terrific idea." Maureen said. "I'll call the phone company as soon as I get back to Larchmont. You ought to see what it costs just between here in the city and up there, a half an hour away."

"More of this?" Jeanne rattled the ice in the all-but-empty martini pitcher.

"Not for me." Maureen said. "My name's not Tom Cassidy. He would go through three of those pitchers before the official cocktail hour began at our house."

"Yeah, I remember. The first time I ever saw your husband really drunk was the night before Kate and Avi got married. That was some wedding rehearsal wasn't it?"

Both women laughed.

Kate had designed her wedding as the prototypical flower-child affair. The ceremony was to be held on a beach at the East Hampton house of Avi's professor of journalism.

"What do you mean, you want to wear a red dress?" Maureen was mildly shocked. Deirdre was nearly apoplectic. "A red dress? For a Bride? Why it's a sacrilege!" Deirdre was a traditionalist where weddings and funerals were concerned.

"Why?" Kate had said. "White is the color of mourning for lots of people. Red—on the other hand—red is for celebration, excitement. Red is happy. I'm going to wear a red dress."

"But you're going to be a bride. White's for purity. For virginity." Deirdre was adamant.

In an aside, none too quiet, since Deirdre's hearing was failing a bit, Kate said, "Mom, I'm pregnant."

Maureen laughed and Kate laughed and Deirdre was indignant. "I don't see what's so damned funny." She went to the stairs and stopped at the bottom for dramatic effect. "We'll see what your father has to say about this."

That year, Tom was in Italy, filming spaghetti-westerns and had wired to say he would be back in time to give the bride away, but that he had to return immediately for the editing and dubbing. "Fine with me," said Maureen. She had grown accustomed to being in charge.

Avi got less opposition from Jeanne. Jeanne Rosen Ginzburg had been what used to be known as a red-diaper baby. Her father and mother were fiery trade unionist, card-carrying Communists during the thirties. The conventions of what they termed, "the ruling classes" were of no moment in their lives and they had given their blessing to Jeanne's city hall marriage to a visitor from Palestine whom Jeanne had met while they were both at New York University. If her son, Avi wanted to get married to a girl in a red dress, on a beach with breaking waves for wedding music, it was okay with her. She knew Yael would have approved. About the part where neither the bride nor the groom wore shoes, she was not so sure. Also, she had asked, "What's this business with a Unitarian minister? Couldn't you find a justice of the peace? And aren't the Cassidys Catholic? What about all that religious stuff?"

Avi reassured his mother that Kate had worked it all out with her mother. As for her father, "Tom Cassidy says he's lived enough of his life being forced to go through the motions of being Catholic. It should be refreshing, for once, to not be a hypocrite."

"But why Unitarian?" Jeanne had insisted on knowing.

"Because he's an ex-classmate of mine—Gary Sessions. Besides, he lives right nearby in Hampton Bays. Don't worry, it'll be okay. Everybody will love it. Gary may be a Unitarian minister, but at heart, he's a hippie just like us."

Jeanne had said, "Oh my God. You're going to make it another Woodstock!"

"No, Mom, don't worry. We're allowing for the older generation. We'll have champagne. Nobody's going to pass you a joint when it comes time to toast the bride and groom. And, oh yeah, I'm going to break a glass. I kinda like that idea. Where did that tradition come from anyway?"

"How the hell should I know?" Jeanne Rosen spent most of her days in or near the White House briefing room in Washington. She wasn't much for tradition herself.

When Kate and Avi were married, instead of being surrounded by siblings and cousins, they were enveloped in a crowd of their contemporaries, some of whom were dressed in an odd assortment of clothing, wearing beads and fetishes, while a group of musicians played guitars, drums and flutes. They sang, they danced, they chanted. They thought no old traditions were observed; they geuinely believed they were creating new ones. They would have been surprised to learn that their wedding was not unique. The rustic wedding, a staple the world over, had taken its place alongside the formal, white nuptials, as one of many choices for American couples.

"The wedding was fun, wasn't it?" Maureen asked Jeanne who was returning from Kate's kitchen with another pitcher, less full than the first one.

"Yeah, and look what happened. Kate got more conventional than we ever were. And Avi went out to slay dragons, while Kate stayed home with her babies. She's a better cook, better housekeeper, better everything than we were, isn't she?"

"I guess neither of us is ever going to be really domesticated, are we?" Maureen was stirring the olive in her martini and then eating it slowly, as if to savor the liquid in which it had been soaking.

"No, it's like that story you used to tell about your mother. She was the domesticated one wasn't she? You used to call her the homesteader. Diedre and her vegetable garden in Larchmont."

When the Cassidys and Deirdre O'Hearn moved into the house, in the late fifties, one of the first subjects of contention had been the back yard. Within a week, Maureen and her mother were arguing about what to do about the rear garden, which, at that point, was little more than a muddy field with a few forlorn roses in need of radical pruning.

Maureen remembered her mother's potatoes. Deirdre said being able to grow potatoes again made her feel like the girl she had been on the farm in Ireland before her own mother had died. How she loved that vegetable garden. "It's like being back in the old country. Now then, I'll dig us a little garden and we'll grow potatoes and some nice cabbages and greens. And I'll make colcannon like me Ma did in the Spring when the little green shoots come up."

Maureen said, "For God's sake, we don't need to grow potatoes. They've got perfectly good potatoes at the A&P. Just plant a few flowers and maybe a rose bush or two. Then let it go. Colcannon—Christ! you won't eat anything more interesting than potatoes and corned beef. I can't even get you to taste something as simple as broccoli."

"Well how c'n you expect me to eat food that you just know has got to be really weird. Only an Eyetalian'll eat a thing like that whaddya call it, broccoli."

That afternoon, Maureen was still fuming after having taken Deirdre to the A&P where her loud voice and brogue had made heads turn. Late in the day, the store was full of tennis-togged young matrons who would stop in after the games to pick up the makings of dinner for their commuter husbands who would arrive on the 6:14 from Grand Central. They pretended not to notice, but Maureen was sure they were wondering who this loud-mouthed old woman was. She made a mental note to take Deirdre to the A&P earlier, mornings, before the perky matrons appeared.

Tom had listened to Maureen's complaints about her mother's wish for a garden. God, he thought, she can be a mean bitch. All the old lady wants is a place to dig in the dirt like she did when she was young. He and his father had grown vegetables behind their old house in Bridgeport.

That weekend, while Maureen unpacked dishes and worried her way through upholstery sample books, Tom went out in the back yard and placed four stakes and strings in a rectangle. Then with a spade he had bought at the local hardware store, he dug up part of the back lawn. It would be two more weekends before he was satisfied that Deirdre's garden was ready to be planted with seed potatoes and cabbage. They would have to wait until the fifteenth of May before setting out tomato plants and squash the way Pete Cassidy did every Spring when Tom was a boy.

As for Maureen, she never went near the garden. Kate helped, weeding and gathering cabbage, zucchini and tomatoes. And Maureen, now and then, tried her hand at cooking them, making feeble attempts to duplicate the exotic meals she had eaten in New York's elegant restaurants. All her efforts were dismal failures.

Finally, it was understood that Maureen would visit the kitchen on rare occasions. Now and then she managed to make scrambled eggs and toast for her own breakfast, after everyone else had gone. Neither Tom nor Kate appreciated Maureen's eggs which they described as "yellow bullets."

Deirdre never criticized Maureen's cooking, and did not complain about the rare invasions of her kitchen. The garden, however, belonged to her alone. And the housekeeping too. She had made herself the sole arbiter of the physical management of the household. She planned meals, worried over cleaning, linen, laundry, marketing. Maureen hoped her mother was happy working for her own family instead of cleaning offices. She never asked Deirdre about that. In fact, Maureen hardly ever talked to Deirdre about much of anything beyond household matters.

The two women were not given to any real intimacy. It would have embarrassed them to speak of their inner lives. Especially Deirdre, for whom deep, personal feelings generally remained unspoken except when she retold details about the death of her Danny or gave advice, including detailed programs for the best ways to raise a child like Kate.

As long as Deirdre was alive, Kate was the common concern of both women. That they quarreled often was simply accepted—it was a primitive, if not terribly effective, form of crisis management. What was surprising was that Kate had turned out so well, with no more—and a whole lot less—rebelliousness than most of her contemporaries.

Those were the years when so much was happening; Maureen's concerns about Tom's drinking and infidelities; Tom's increasing disenchantment with Maureen; pre-adolescent Kate, on the brink of the emotional inferno daughters and parents must endure until adulthood arrives. This turbulence tore at the structure of their lives and occasionally, there would be an explosion as if the household were a small, dormant volcano that must release internal pressures in clamorous bursts, spewing fire, fury and, sometimes, destruction.

As for Deirdre's observations of the Cassidys as a family, she kept her own counsel. But in one sphere, at least, everyone acknowledged that it was Deirdre who made it possible for both Tom and Maureen to concentrate wholly on their careers. And Deirdre, "Gran" to Kate, fairly glowed with the pride she took in keeping the house and garden looking so perfect. Sometimes, when Maureen got home late, bone tired from shooting one, sometimes two episodes of the show, she would murmur, "House looks great Ma." Deirdre knew then she had been particularly blessed, and remarked, "God made women to keep houses, so you could say I was doin' the Lord's work." Most nights,

Maureen had the good sense to keep her mouth shut. Other times, she wanted to throttle her mother for such posturing. But, it was little enough to allow Deirdre to take pleasure in the role she played in the family. Without her, things would have been far more complex, if not utterly chaotic.

While Deirdre kept house and cared for Kate, Maureen and Tom saw to it that she had plenty of money, her own checking account and time to visit her friends in the City. Several times a month she walked to the railroad station and went to Grand Central. She rarely talked about the people she saw, but Maureen guessed that she called on the few families who continued to live in the remnants of tenements that still stood near Third Avenue after the El was torn down.

Except for places like P.J. Clark's, which had become a sort of museum piece, the old saloons that had once lined the Avenue, were giving way to slick, tinted-glass high rise office buildings. The apartments, once crawling with bugs and kids and screaming mothers, were gone. Sometimes Maureen wondered about the old neighbors; where in the city do all those people live these days?

CHAPTER EIGHT

THE ARMORY IN New York is a great mausoleum of a place with vast expanses of space, ideal for the kind of monster parties given annually for fund-raisers, art exhibits, affairs. The word *affair* is so much a part of the currency in New York, it gave rise to the famous old joke about two women gossiping. One says, "I hear Mary SoandSo is having an affair." The other woman asks, automatically, "Oh, who's catering?"

Tonight the Greeks of New York City were giving themselves a party, an affair. Though most of the Greeks came penniless to the city, they had, like other immigrant groups, managed to find places in every income and social class. For many in the Armory tonight, the only thing that bound them was the fact of being Greek. And being Greek, like being Irish or Jewish or Russian or Puerto Rican or Jamaican or Southern Black or Chinese or Korean or any of the scores of other groups and sub-groups that populate a major city, is something which, to date, has continued to defy the myth of the melting pot.

"Anyway," Kate said to Irving Quinn, during a lull in the loud music, "why would anybody want to melt in a pot. It's a horrible idea, like something my mother does when she tries to cook. She smiled at the group of dancers in costume that were ready to perform. "No, I like this idea much better." She drank from the glass in front of her. "Alex, what do you call this? It tastes like licorice."

"Ouzo," Alex said and poured another tot into her glass, making a milky swirl in the melting ice.

"Yeah, ouzo." Quinn said. "And you'd better go easy on that stuff. It's famous for the world's worst hangovers. I know, I had one last year."

"That's another thing you always hear." Kate said, clapping her hands with the crowd as the rhythm picked up, "Everybody thinks his ethnic liquor makes mythically horrible hangovers. And that an outsider will surely be deathly ill if he drinks too much. You drink too much of anything, you're gonna have a hangover." She tipped up her glass and drained it.

Alex shook his head. "Kate, believe me, it's true. There's nothing mythical about an ouzo hangover."

Irving Quinn nodded his agreement, shrugged his shoulders and clapped along with the rest of the crowd.

During dinner, when the orchestra played both traditional Greek music and more conventional dance numbers, the circle dancing proved too much for Kate's still-aching ribs. But she and Quinn managed several slow turns around the floor. At one point, after dessert and before the big show, the lights were lowered and the corny, mirrored palladium was pressed into service, with its flashing reflections making colored light dance around the room.

Kate's height, in medium heels brought her head level with Irving Quinn' jaw. For a moment, he wished she were shorter. He would have liked to feel her head in the curve of his shoulder. Cut it out, Quinn, he told himself. For all you know, this beautiful blonde may be a suspect in her boss's murder. But the music, borne on a wailing clarinet, was a song about somebody's lost love, so it was very hard to think clearly. He stopped bothering to think when Kate's hair brushed his face and he inhaled the fragrance of a sun-drenched garden of Summer flowers.

The party was far from over when he saw how tired Kate was. He assured her, "Don't worry, they'll understand." Alex and more than a dozen men were on one part of the dance floor, working out elaborate designs, steps that Alex said came from his grandfather's village in

Greece. Kate laughed when she saw one of them plaster a one-dollar bill to Alex's sweaty forehead. "If the money is still there when the music stops, he gets to keep it," Quinn explained.

In the taxi, on the way across town to Kate's apartment, he kissed her. It was as if they had been kissing like this forever. No fumbling, nothing tentative, just a sweet, firm, ouzo-flavored kiss that outlasted even the traffic light at 79th Street.

Kate didn't explain that she felt safe in asking him upstairs because Maureen was still with her, though, at this hour—it was past midnight—she would be fast asleep.

Quinn was uncertain of where this would lead, but he knew it didn't matter because whatever was happening was entirely out of his hands. Kate Cassidy might just as well have had him encased in a pair of handcuffs as she led him past the doorman, into the elevator and through the apartment door.

"Shsh, we have to be very quiet. My mother's been staying with me and I'm sure she's asleep."

Quinn didn't know whether to be disappointed or relieved. The next step, if any, in this relationship—though it was too soon to call it that—was not up to him, anyway. Where Kate was concerned, he realized he had no will. Nor did he care. Now, he understood that famous movie scene in which Gene Kelly runs around in the rain, jumping on garbage can lids.

Kate said, "I think we've both had an awful lot of that atrocious ouzo stuff. I'm going to make us some coffee. Go on, slip off your shoes. I'm out of mine. My feet are killing me. Here," she put a fat cushion on the coffee table. "Put your feet up on this. I'll be right back."

She disappeared and Quinn did as he was told. His black slip-ons came off, each with a little plop. Ah, he thought, nothing a cop likes better than to take off his shoes after a shift. He remembered his father's large, splayed feet in their black socks with the ankle holster just visible, as he put them on the footstool after a long day. Irving Quinn no longer wore an ankle holster and tonight, because it was a night off, he was wearing his one good suit, too fitted to allow for a shoulder holster. No matter. He would hardly need to be armed here.

They sat side-by-side in the dimmed lamplight, speaking softly, Kate's unshod feet folded beneath her on the sofa.

Like other people with grown children and marriages behind them, they exchanged enough information to fill in the blanks left by their odd meeting and their sudden affinity. Neither Irving Quinn nor Kate Cassidy would have acknowledged it, but inexorably, they were forming a take-no-prisoners synergy. The sheer implausibility made it impossible to acknowledge. Cops don't fall in love with witnesses to, and possible victims of, murder. They don't, Quinn told himself, they don't. To cover his consternation he looked around and stopped at a small table with a photograph of a very young woman.

Kate followed his eyes, explaining, "That's my daughter, Dee Dee. Deirdre Ginzburg." She laughed. "And you think Irving Quinn sounds silly? She's in Ireland right now, caught up in investigating her Irish roots. She found out last year that there's an O'Hearn scholarship, apparently established a century ago. Dee Dee was the first one to discover it and claim her right to it, so she switched to Trinity after her Freshman year at U. Conn."

Dee Dee had her grandmother Maureen's beauty, with the same animation in her face. Her hair was the dark mass of a Pre-Raphaelite heroine; it surrounded her head and fell to her shoulders in wild abandon. Her eyes were a strange shade of blue-green. "Doesn't look much like you," Quinn said.

"Oh, she got Avi's hair and my mother's eyes. Aren't genes the strangest things? My son, Joel is blonde and dark-eyed. Avi used to talk about his Jew-hair and thick black eyelashes that all the girls envied. He hated the way his hair curled and waved. It was this thick, shiny black mop but he wanted to have shoulder-length, straight hair like everybody else in the sixties and early seventies. Remember when girls were ironing their hair?"

Quinn laughed. "Yeah, Donna did that. The idea was to look like you didn't do a thing to it, but I remember that Donna said she spent a couple of hours every day, just making sure her hair was perfectly straight."

Once he had thought Donna Marino the most gorgeous woman in the world. He had felt about Donna the way he was feeling tonight. Except that tonight, he was more frightened than he had ever been in any wartime fire fight or New York City raid on a crack house against an arsenal of automatic weapons. Irving Quinn, who had a reputation for being glib, grew very quiet.

Kate sensed his wariness as she did her own. They were like strange dogs in an encounter on the Avenue, intensely drawn to one another, but safe on their masters' leashes. She was grateful for Maureen's unseen presence. An awkward moment of silence was covered quickly by Kate. "Well, we were terribly young in those days. I guess we were all a little crazy, weren't we?"

"Not about everything. Even though I wasn't really a part of all that, I knew what you were doing was right."

"You mean the war? You were in Viet Nam while we were raising hell against it. You thought we were right? How did you feel about that?" Oh my God, she thought, I'm beginning to sound like Doctor Hoffman.

But Quinn welcomed a chance to tell someone with whom it was safe to say what he had kept to himself for a long time. "I felt like somebody in one of those existentialist plays. I knew one thing—the war was insanity. But I was a part of it, doing what I was told to do. I was in the army, so I didn't have the luxury of going out and demonstrating."

"I'm glad we didn't meet then, Kate said. I don't think either of us would have given the other time to explain. We'd have just turned away."

Before he could stop himself, the words were out. "I'd sooner die than turn away from you, Kate." He put his hand out and she reached forward with her own.

Quinn finished the story of how he came to be in Viet Nam. While at Fordham where he was a pre-law student, the ROTC was one more building block in the financial package required to keep him in school. His father and mother, though secure in their jobs with the city, were really strapped by the mortgage in Riverdale and college costs for Irving and his younger sister, Bea.

"So, I sold my soul to Uncle Sugar and instead of giving me time for law school, they decided to commission me right after graduation and turn me into a professional killer."

Kate arched her brows at the rhetoric.

"Well, you know what I mean. Hell, I had no idea of what was going on. But down there in the jungle, I finally figured it out. Old men make political decisions and they expect young men, and these days, women, to execute those decisions and sometimes, die for them. You kids back in school in those days; you were telling them you didn't want to play by those old rules anymore. You had the nerve to tell the old politicians that in a real democracy, the people should be the ones to decide whether or not something is worth killing and dying for. They made it sound like treason—they had to. How the hell could they justify what they were doing otherwise?"

Kate smiled. "You know, I'll always regret not being old enough."

"Old enough for what?"

"Old enough to make a stink at Columbia like Avi did. He was there in '68, making lots of noise. And his mother wrote things in The Nation. God! It was exciting. But I was too young. I was still playing field hockey at Larchmont Country Day."

"What's a country day?"

"Just what it sounds like, a fancy, high-priced private school. My God, everybody there was in favor of the war. They thought the guys at Columbia were a bunch of red, commie traitors. I thought it was terribly exciting and that was when I made up my mind to go to Columbia and major in journalism. Christ! what a commotion it made. My Gran kept clutching her chest and saying how 'Tis a heartscald to see her going to school with all them Godless reds!'"

"I never knew my father's parents. They were Irish too. They died before I was born. Was she really like that?"

"Was she! You've got to picture this. There's my Irish grandmother, still got a brogue on her you can cut with a knife. And my oh, so elegant mother, with the upper class accent she learned in acting school. Well, my Gran, she gets the idea, she wants me to go to Manhattenville, you know, of the Sacred Heart? I can hear her now, 'Like the Kennedys. All them Kennedy girls go to Manhattenville.'"

"Mind you, my Gran had the equivalent of a sixth-grade education which was pretty good in Ireland, but she had no idea of what I had learned at Country Day, except she knew they taught good manners. She didn't know that we smoked pot, made out with boys, all that stuff. She just took my mother's word that I was being sent to the best school money could buy and my Dad had managed to convince her that it was Catholic, even if we didn't have nuns for teachers."

Kate stopped. "My Dad. I'm going to have lunch with him tomorrow. I'm trying to keep him in town so he can get into the dryout program at Roosevelt or New York Hospital while he waits for a place to open up at the Fletcher Clinic, you know the one? It's in Connecticut. I've heard their success-rate is even better than the one on the Coast, the Betty Ford. But my Dad—it's so hard. I've been pleading with him He's a tough case, insists on going back to California, so I'm trying to work something on that end too."

"I'm going to see your father tomorrow. Just routine stuff. I want to talk to him one more time if he's planning to go back to California. There are still some questions I need to clear up. So, uhm, about Columbia—you did finally go there—to college, I mean, didn't you?"

"Yeah, but by the time I got there, there wasn't much left to raise hell about. Avi had all the fun, even that sit-in when they were protesting the Christmas bombing of Cambodia. He used to talk about it a lot. Do you remember it?

Not any one thing except—I remember one of the guys near the end; it was an example of me on my best behavior. We were in the officers' club in Saigon. There was something on TV about how the war was a study in idiocy and what business did we have, killing fifty-thousand of our best young men. Well, somebody in the room agreed. I think he said something about this stupid war. And another guy, really self-righteous, yells, 'Yeah, but it's the only war we've got.' If I had done what I felt like doing, I'd have wound up in Leavenworth."

"So, you didn't say anything?"

"No, and neither did any of at least a dozen others I knew who felt the same way I did. That's what I mean when I try to explain to my own kids about those days. It brings up all sorts of questions about one's personal ethics, how you handle issues like that, and what do you tell your children who are old enough to understand?"

"It was so much easier for us in many ways. We were so disgustingly self-righteous. I know we must have been insufferable. Now that I'm a parent with grown kids, I can look at it more clearly. We thought we knew it all. And now look at us. We're still stumbling around trying to figure out what's right and wrong. At least you're doing something about it now, aren't you."

"How do you mean?"

"Well, you're a policeman. I guess you have to wade through some pretty ugly things from time to time. How do you keep it from breaking your heart?"

That was a question Donna had never asked him. True, she hated his job, but mostly because it was not well-paid and hampered her social ambitions. But he doubted she had ever questioned the state of his heart.

"What I mean is, being a cop in a place like New York has to be at least as difficult as it was in combat in Viet Nam. I know, I read the papers. Our policemen—and women. God! The pressure must be horrible."

He shook his head. "But didn't you anti-war kids hate cops, called us pigs and stuff like that?"

"That's right. I said we were insufferable. Partly, it was because the cops were pretty hostile. I knew a lot of people who had been gassed and beaten up. But some of us were deliberately provocative, and I think, for some, it was a kick—flirting with danger—and a sort of a badge of honor to have something to show for it, like a banged-up face.

"I wonder if there were any cops who felt the way you had when you were in the army. You said your father was a policeman. Does he ever talk about those years and what he really thought?"

"God no. He was very proud of me, off fighting for America and against the Commies. He never questioned it at all. If the government said we were the good guys and they were the bad guys, that was that. The only time I got into it with him was right after the Kent State killings—do you remember that?"

"Students demonstrating and the National Guard shot four of them. Of course, I remember."

"Four people were killed—four kids throwing stones! I was pretty shaken up about it and I tried to talk to my father. He wasn't haven't any. He was furious with the students and he kept talking about keeping the peace. I tried to make him understand: Fifty-five shots, M1, 30-caliber; pistol-shots, five, I think; a shotgun blast. There were twenty-eight shooters—twenty-eight guns against a bunch of kids throwing stones! That wasn't peacekeeping; it was an execution squad!. We're not supposed to do things like that in our country. But he just wouldn't listen, so I dropped it and never mentioned it to him again."

"Yeah, it's still a shock to think of us shooting at kids for throwing rocks, but, really, it happens in a lot of places. Think about Ireland or Israel." Kate paused. She didn't like where this was going. It was like the early days with Avi. Avi did have some blind spots about Israel as she had about Ireland. One day they declared a truce, agreeing that injustice abounded, and that journalists like Avi were doing their best to report events as evenhandedly as possible.

She explained, "For some people, their situations were a lot like yours was in the army. Theirs not to reason why...."

"Yeah, you sign on for the tour, and do what you're told. The war was the only thing that ever came between me and my old man and it still twists my guts to think about it. I suppose that explains why I signed up for the force. You could say I'm trying to make up for him, you know, right my father's wrongs."

Kate nodded. "I think I know, but, it doesn't have to be that complicated. There really was—always will be—those generational differences. It's just that now, we're not like those people in a room with an elephant that everybody is either trying to ignore or can't agree about. Today, we've still got a great big elephant, but most people can't even see it. New York is a wonderful place, I love it and I know I'm among the lucky ones. But I wouldn't want to live here without people like you. Where would this city be? Sure, some cops are not great on compassion and even honesty, but whenever I hear people trashing them, I want to say something about how they're all we've got between us and the muggers and rapists and all that other stuff that scares me, especially for my children."

Kate, whose head had somehow found a place on Irving's shoulder, sat upright. "It's like that final scene in The Caine Mutiny, remember it? The lawyer—and the mutineers are counting on him to absolutely destroy Captain Queeg. Once in court, he does a switcheroo. He's Jewish, you see. So he tells about what Hitler was doing in Germany, making people into soap. Then he gets sort of carried away as he realizes the truth. Before the war, regular Navy men like Queeg, were the only defense we had against that kind of horror. So we shouldn't be too quick to condemn the Queegs of this world. They're like you cops, standing between us and that—the tragedy, the atrocity, the street shit—all that stuff. How do you keep it from breaking your heart?"

Quinn answered softly, stroking Kate's hair, "By just doing what I can. And when you've been around for awhile, you take another exam like I did to make Lieutenant, so you get to do more paperwork and less street work. I'm still getting used to that idea. I only just got the promotion. Well, last year anyway. There are still a lot of things I'm learning about the job. But the tragic, heartbreaking part? What was that word you used before, that your Grandmother said, about her heart?"

"Oh you mean heartscald. She used it a lot. My Gran had the soul of an Irish poet, but you'd know about that, wouldn't you?"

"Not really, the poetic one in my house was my mother. She taught English and poetry was a very important part of her life. But my old man. He was a roughneck, really. Except with my Mom. Even today, when they're in their seventies, he treats her with a kind of courtliness. I just love seeing them together."

"So your getting divorced must have been difficult for them, strange, even."

"Well, it was strange for me too. I married Donna right after graduation. I got a brand-new, army dress uniform and her folks gave one of those outrageous Italian weddings, I mean big and lavish. Donna's folks own a chain of bakeries and they don't mind spending money. It was out of my hands, really. I think I got married without having any idea of who Donna really was, except she was beautiful.

Irving Quinn had not talked this much for a long time. It felt good. "Right after the wedding, I went away to war and when I got back, there was this gorgeous, young dress designer waiting for me. Of course, we had a kid right away. Eric; he's going to law school. and then we had John; I think he's twenty. He goes to Cornell."

Kate was too polite to ask why a father would have to think about his son's age. Then she remembered that Tom never knew her exact age either. Avi too, sometimes had to ask, "How old does that make you?" when Joel or Dee Dee had a birthday. Maybe it was a male-thing, something genetic.

Quinn was abashed. He hadn't talked about himself at such length to anybody except the counselor to whom he and Donna had gone, hoping to save their marriage. The last session was followed by one of the worst fights they had ever had. He moved out of the house in Great Neck that night. It was more than a year before the divorce was finalized.

"Kate, is that you?" It was Maureen. Irving and Kate were startled. How long had she been standing there in the small corridor off the living room? "I thought I heard voices. Are you okay?"

"Yes, Mom. I'm fine. You remember Irving Quinn. He took me to a big Greek party. We didn't wake you did we?"

"No, no. I just wanted to check." She repeated, "I thought I heard voices. I'll just go back to bed. See you in the morning. Good night, Lieutenant Quinn."

He was on his feet. "Yeah, good night, uh, Mrs. Cassidy." He had stammered like a schoolboy.

That's it, Kate thought. My mother's going back to Larchmont tomorrow. Goddamn it! She felt like a teenager in her own home. She could have strangled her. How could she be so angry with her well-meaning mother? Very simple, she answered her own question. Mothers never stop being mothers and daughters never stop being daughters. She had learned that by watching Maureen and Deidre, each one certain she was right, clashing again and again.

Straightening his tie, Quinn said, "It's really terribly late and I know you're dead tired. You're still on the bench, so to speak. You've got to get some rest and I have to go too. Tomorrow's a working day for me."

Kate stood, reached for his hand and held it as he stepped back into his shoes. Now, her head reached just below his chin. This time, when he kissed her, they clung together much longer. In fact, the red light at 79th Street would have changed several times before they finally separated and Kate reluctantly led Irving Quinn to the door.

After slowly closing it, Kate stood, looking at the blank, steel door as if she were watching, with ex-ray vision, Quinn's progress toward the elevator. She rested her forehead against the metal for a long moment. Finally, she shook herself, wondering if she ought to be grateful for her mother's presence in the apartment. Yes, she decided, if Mom had not been here, who knows what might have happened. Then, hugging herself, she went into her own bedroom and sat perfectly still, looking at her face in the mirror. Slowly, thoughtfully, she began to remove her makeup.

Chapter Nine

AT ABOUT EIGHT in the morning Irving Quinn buzzed at the suite in the Waldorf. Tom Cassidy opened the door quickly, as if he had been standing by. He was dressed casually in well-tailored, pleated slacks and a turtle-neck sweater. Expensive, Quinn guessed. Cashmere, probably;. The sweater, draping in soft folds, seemed to be at least a size too large for his too-thin frame. Quinn thought, God, the guy looks like a typical old alky, except he's better dressed.

Tom Cassidy poured some very good room-service coffee from the wheeled-in table "Something to eat? There are some mini-Danish under that napkin."

"No, thanks. I stopped for breakfast near the precinct house. Cops need grease for breakfast. Keeps the mind sharp."

Cassidy took in the well-muscled, trim body of the younger man and thought, he doesn't eat much grease. Or else he works out—hard.

"So, all I want you to do is tell me about that first night you got into town."

"Well, it's pretty simple. My flight was delayed in Chicago, but I always guarantee my rooms here, so I wasn't worried about having a place to stay. Of course, I could stay at Kate's place, but frankly, I've grown to like my own company and hotels are where I'm the most comfortable.

"Anyway, I took the limo and checked in here about midnight, maybe later. I was beat. I always have a rough time with jet lag. Doesn't matter which direction, east or west. Nowadays the cross-country trips are getting harder and harder."

Quinn took in Tom's jaundiced skin and saw that the whites of his eyes were the color of scrambled eggs. He thought, this guy's liver is probably working at twenty percent efficiency, if that much. There was no sign that Cassidy had been drinking. His hand was steady as he poured coffee, his speech was precise. In a word, the man was sober. But drunk or sober, the man was very ill.

"I hit the bed and conked out. Just like that." He snapped his fingers. "My meeting wasn't scheduled until the afternoon, so I figured I'd run into Kate's studio to watch her show. You see, Kate and I keep in very close touch, always have. And after Avi died, I made sure we talked on the phone often and I even turned down work on the Coast so I could do projects in New York. I know she's got her mother. And Joel and DeeDee were home for months, but when things are tough for Kate, it's me she turns to.

"I don't mean to say anything bad about Maureen. She's been a good mother. But fathers and daughters—well, that's something else again." You got any girls?"

"No, just a couple of sons. But I think I know what you're saying. I've often wondered what it would be like to have a girl."

"Especially a girl like our Kate."

Quinn fumbled in his pocket for his notebook. "So, you left the hotel, at what time the next morning?"

"I don't know. You could check at the desk. I always leave my door card. Not a good idea to have your door card swiped in New York, is it?"

"That's good advice. I wish more out-of-towners were as careful as that."

"Well, I'm not really an out-of-towner. Remember, I used to live here."

"Didn't you once work here, at this hotel?"

"Yeah, but that was a long, long time ago. I was a bellhop. That's how I paid for my acting lessons. We all did jobs like that; waiters, busboys, bellhops, shoeshine. When I look back on it....The things people will do to get into show business."

"When it pays off, it pays off big, though, doesn't it?"

"Sure, for the one hundreth of one percent of those who make the big time. Maureen and I are the only ones I can think of from Freddy Sherwood's early classes who not only stayed in the business, but actually were successful."

"Freddy Sherwood? Have I heard that name?"

"Probably. He's gotta be ninety if he's a day, but as late as ten years ago, he had a hit show on Broadway. Lee Strasberg and Freddy Sherwood; those are the two names everybody knows. But this town is crawling with great actors, directors and teachers. And don't let anybody tell you the theater is dead. It's not. Of course, I'm not a theater man myself, but I owe everything to Freddy.

"Even today, when I tell an actor to do this or that or create some kind of business, I owe a debt to Freddy." He opened the napkin and took a small piece of pastry. "You sure you won't have one of these? They're baked right here at the Waldorf, nothing better."

"Well, Danish is one of my weaknesses." Quinn selected the light-colored one he knew would be sweet, vanilla-lemon scented cheese. Another reason, he thought for never leaving New York. They don't know how to make decent Danish pastry anywhere else. Before putting the small confection into his mouth, he said, "I'll bet you can't get these things, made like this, even in Denmark."

The two men finished their coffee and Lieutenant Quinn stood, ready to leave. "Well, I guess that covers your activities the night before the accident."

"Didn't you say, or was it Rudy—that the mirror had been rigged with squibs? So that means we're not talking about any accident. Isn't that why you're here? To make sure I'm not the guy who rigged it?"

"You know anything about squibs?"

"Lieutenant, don't be disingenuous with me. You know I've been in the movie business for thirty years or more. I've shot more explosions and blown up more buildings than may have happened in real life in World War Two and Korea combined. Of course I know about squibs and how they work. But if you're suggesting that I'd rig a mirror to fall and hurt my daughter, you've got to be out of your mind."

"Mr. Cassidy, it wasn't your daughter who was killed. It was someone whom you might very well have a motive for killing. It's no secret, after all, that your former wife, Maureen Cassidy, had an affair with Jim Vandersagen the Summer you were in basic training at Fort Dix."

A small vein in Tom's temple was visible and throbbing. The guy's gotta have a nasty headache, thought Quinn, but that's too bad. I'm conducting a murder investigation and it's giving me a headache too.

"I don't know about other people Lieutenant, but I know that when Maureen and I were divorced, we each went our separate ways. Whatever happened in the past, I left there. I had no reason whatsoever for wanting Jim Vandersagen dead, believe me. What's more, I'm not sure Jim was the only one. After all, Kate was right there too, and you haven't convinced me that she wasn't also the target of whoever rigged that mirror to fall."

Tom Cassidy started toward the door of the suite. "I know you've got important police business to do today, Lieutenant, so I'll let you get on with it. I've got a full schedule myself."

Kate slept late the next day and Maureen made a simple breakfast of toast, jam and low-fat cream cheese. There was a pot of coffee, made according to Kate's written instructions, which she had taped to the shelf on which the coffee-maker stood. Maureen put everything on a simple, white bed-tray. In a slender vase, she put one of the red roses that were sent yesterday—the third bouquet since the accident—by Rudy Macklin. With a spray of baby's breath and one fern leaf, the red rose no longer seemed vulgar. Especially, Maureen thought, in the Baccarat crystal bud vase she had given Kate for one of her birthdays, or was it an anniversary?

Kate answered the discreet knock. "Come on in, Mom. I'm awake." As her mother put the tray on the bedside table and poured a cup of coffee for each of them, Kate said, "Wow, this is first-class service. What'd I do to deserve this?"

"You know perfectly well. It's a peace offering. Here I am a guest in your home, and you ah entertainin' uh gentleman callah," Maureen giggled. She had used her fake Southern accent—pure Blanche

DuBois. "And there I was in my robe and slippers, sneaking up on you. I really wasn't expecting to see that cop there. Honest."

"Of course, not." She patted the bed. "Sit down. How could you know?. You weren't here when he came to pick me up for the big Greek party. You got my note, though, didn't you?"

"Sure. You said you were going out and that you'd be home late. Period. I didn't know you were going out on a date with a cop."

"Well, it wasn't a real date. He just had these tickets for one of those affairs at the Armory. You know, lots of bourzouki music and men dancing around with dollar bills on their foreheads..."

"My God," Maureen said, "Just like Molfetta's"

"What's Molfetta's"

"It used to be the best, and the cheapest Greek restaurant in town. When we were young, starving actors, we'd go there and scarf up all that fabulous food, reeking of garlic, but plenty—we were always hungry. And we'd drink that horrible retsina. Then, afterwards, we'd go upstairs where there was a band and a show and all that crazy music; with wailing clarinets and the men dancing with each other. Did they do that one where they get down on one leg and paste dollar bills to their sweaty foreheads?"

"That's just like last night." Kate said. "What happened to the restaurant? Did it close down like every other great place you used to go to when you were young?"

"Oh, I guess so. These days, a new restaurant opens every day and three more go out of business. Now we go to Thai and Korean places because they're like the cheap Greek and Italian and Chinese places I remember."

"Anything's better than cooking, right?"

"Oh, I can cook a meal if I have to, but honestly, Kate, how much cooking does a woman do when she lives alone? These days, if I'm at home I take out one of those frozen things, pop it into the microwave and get on with whatever else I've got to do, like learn lines for the next days' shooting, for example."

"But, you're not shooting anything now are you? Does it feel awful to be out of a job?"

"That's what I was hoping to tell you last night. Wait. She leapt off the bed and went into the room next door, her room whenever she stayed in town. She was back in a couple of minutes with something in her hand. Then Maureen stood in front of the mirror facing Kate's bed and put on a snow-white, beautifully-styled wig. She was transformed from a still-youthful woman into a handsome matriarch. "Voila! What do you think?"

"What do I think? What the hell's that for? You planning to play Marie Antionette?"

"Not quite. I've been dickering over this for weeks now, but I didn't want to spoil my luck by talking about it. But yesterday, I clinched the deal. Anyway Bobby Glass did. What an agent that guy is; he really earns his percentage."

"What's the deal, Mom? A new soap?"

"Yeah, but better. It's a series, in the most prime of prime time. Right here in River City, at our favorite network, JGV. My God, Adele's going to be my boss too. I hope she keeps her mitts off this show. Bobby says their new VP of programming is the best thing to ever happen to the network, but he likes to be left alone.

"Anyway," Maureen posed with the wig on her head. "Do I look like the last of a line of gold-mining and banking millionaires in San Francisco? The show's going to be called Telegraph Hill or maybe, San Francisco; same sort of format as Dallas, except I won't be sweet like Miss Ellie. I'm going to play one mean, bitchy lady. I can hardly wait. We shoot the pilot next week."

"Wait a minute. Doesn't that mean you'll have to go to San Francisco to shoot the series? You absolutely hate California!"

"No problem, darling. All the exteriors will be done out there, but the interiors, at least for starters, will be done in the studio here. That's because more than half the actors are from New York and they don't want to move out to the Coast until they find out whether or not the show's a hit."

"Well, you didn't spend much time among the unemployed, did you?" Kate was smiling at her mother. I'm glad you're going to stick around. But, why the white wig? What's the matter with your own hair?"

"Oh I guess I didn't tell you. I've decided to stop coloring it. It's mostly white by now anyway, and I realized I had one of two options. I could switch to white hair—the wig's for the transition. Or I could get another face-lift. Well, the wig hurts less, costs less and I can let myself ease into being an old lady instead of looking like every other sixtyish actress trying to look thirty-five. We all know it's a losing battle, and I'm not going to fight it anymore."

Kate was silent. She didn't know whether to express surprise and pleasure or to act sympathetic. Even with her own mother, perhaps most with Maureen, Kate knew the matter of confronting one's aging could be like a time bomb going off in a woman's psyche. Among her own friends, she had observed the arrival of milestone birthdays as events of major, often traumatically painful transition. And here was her mother, a woman who had based her entire life on the strength of her beauty and allure, casually planning to grow old.

Kate herself had faced her fortieth birthday and the shock of sudden widowhood within the same year. Only in the last few months, as the Home show took hold, had she begun to relax and come to terms with her new status. If Kate could handle aging this easily, it would augur well for the future twenty or thirty years away.

The telephone rang and Kate picked it up. "Hi Daddy," she said. "I hope you're still planning to take me to lunch today."

Maureen backed silently out of the room to allow Kate to talk privately with her father. By the time the call was finished, Maureen's bags were packed and she was ready to return home to the house in Larchmont.

During this, her last week of freedom, she had dozens of chores to do before settling into the routine of being a television actress. And, she thought of what she had glimpsed the night before when she inadvertently surprised Irving Quinn and Kate. She reasoned, if Kate is ready for a romance that might lead her to a second chance at happiness, I'd better not get in the way.

Maureen paid for storing her car in an uptown garage for nearly three weeks. The charge would have paid the rent for a month on a small apartment. She made her way across town and headed North in light traffic. At least she could think.

Thinking for Maureen really meant worrying. What was that Kate had said about Adele Vandersagen? Would she really fire her, not renew her option, despite the fact that Kate's show was a big hit? Jealous, angry women behave in strange ways and even murder is not inconceivable. I ought to know, she thought, I've played enough of them in my lifetime. Maureen had not shared her fears with Kate. But surely, the woman was worth watching. She made a mental note to mention Adele Vandersagen the next time she talked to Irving Quinn. He'll think I'm meddling. But where Kate's safety was concerned, Maureen resolved to stop worrying about what other people thought. I'm her mother, and if I don't do it, who will?

If Deirdre were alive, she thought, you can be sure, she wouldn't give a damn about who thought she was meddling. Deirdre would just give that cop the full benefit of her opinions complete with a perfectly mapped-out plan of action. Oh, Ma, she thought, keep a good watch on our Katy.

Maureen Cassidy was so deeply absorbed in thoughts of all that had happened in the past two weeks, she was unprepared to pay when she got to the toll gates at New Rochelle. She was surprised and annoyed that she had not refilled the coin holder in the small compartment in the console between the front seats. Driving to New York was no longer a regular habit. Normally, she preferred the train. Now, she was forced to fumble in her purse and had to endure the hostile stare of the young woman who took her money and made change.

"Well, she thought, I'd be angry too, if I had to stand on my feet for an eight-hour shift, breathing carbon monoxide fumes all day, taking money and making change. It was probably a lot worse than having been a waitress at Schrafft's. She gave the woman an extra cordial smile and "Thank you." It seemed to help.

How many times, she thought of those days, had she lost a tip because, still furious over something, she had forgotten to smile?

Maureen knew a whole lot about anger. Hadn't she spent fourteen years being furious nearly all the time when she was married to Tom? Once he had accused her of being a grudge-holder. "You're damned right I'm a grudge-holder," she had flared at him. "You spend every waking minute of our lives trying to make me feel rotten about myself. You never let a day go by without some kind of insult. Oh, I don't remember all of them, but there are some I'll never forget!"

If nothing else, divorcing Tom Cassidy had given Maureen a chance to look more closely at what Kate, in her younger generation's stark language, had called "your shit-load of anger." Well, she had, finally, stopped hating him, but whether or not the anger was still part of her, she would only find out by spending time with Tom, something she declined even when he was trying his best to be civil.

"I've never been able to understand the so-called civilized divorce, where people remain 'the best of friends.'" She was complaining to Kate who, now and then, would invite Maureen to join her and Tom for dinner. She supposed children never quite accept the fact that their parents prefer to remain apart. To hell with Tom Cassidy, she thought. There's more to worry about, like murder, for example.

Not only Jim's, but there was still the uncertainty about Kate. After all, Maureen reasoned, if Tom and I thought they were having an affair, why not somebody else, his wife Adele, perhaps. Or, quite possibly, some crazed, jealous girlfriend, of which there would, no doubt, be plenty. Just so Kate is safe, just keep her safe. Though she professed to no longer believe in God, she was praying.

As she approached her house, Maureen asked herself a straightforward question about Jim Vandersagen. Was she glad he was dead? Yes, she had to admit that his death, at least, put an end to her panic at having seen Kate and him together that night at Sardi's.

During the drive from New York, Maureen had allowed herself to think, in fact, to concentrate, on Jim Vandersagen's death. There were so many angles. She hoped that Lieutenant Quinn would soon have it all figured out. Did he have any idea that there might be a connection between a suspected love affair and the murder?

Even now, she caught her breath at the idea of Kate and Jim Vandersagen as lovers. That monster! For years and years, he had used his money and position of power in a compulsive pursuit of young women. Few newspaper editorialists, especially in his own properties, called him to account for his behavior. It appeared that, for Vandersagen, there had never been a moment of enlightenment for women, that they had remained forever locked into blocks of cultural amber that would not permit them to evolve. She heard herself breathing hard and realized that even now, after more than forty years, she was still filled with rage and humiliation, another reservoir of anger of which she could not rid herself.

"And to hell with you too, Vandersagen," she said aloud, as she pressed the button to raise the garage door. What she saw instantly wiped her mind free of all thoughts about either Tom Cassidy or Jim Vandersagen.

The lock on the inner door from the garage to the house had been broken. Warily, she went into the kitchen, then through the dining room. A quick check in the living room told her that thieves had made a thorough job of ransacking the place and removing every object of value.

Blank spaces on the walls indicated that she had lost the small Manet and a larger Chagall, the only valuable paintings. The stereo and entertainment cabinet had been stripped of its components. Missing too was the Degas bronze of a dancer, a small gem she had recently bought at an auction.

She flew up the stairs to the bedrooms where she normally kept little of value except a few pieces of jewelry. She had never developed a taste for ostentatious jewels, but the really valuable pieces—a three-carat diamond ring, for example, that Tom had bought for her on their tenth anniversary, plus several others, lay safely in the vault at the local bank. The contents of her jewelry case were strewn across the bedspread. The thief knew exactly what to take, ignoring costume pieces. Except for a string of amber beads, probably mistaken for plastic, there was nothing of value left behind.

The thief, or thieves, the detectives from the Larchmont police department, speculated, must have known she was away. She had not secured the house properly. Newspapers had accumulated and the house had remained shuttered and dark during the entire period she was at Kate's. It made sense. And she had to admit, she had not given a thought to security beyond locking the doors. She had forgotten to shut off mail and newspapers as she normally would if she expected to be away for any length of time. She had thought of nothing but Kate.

Methodically, though her heart was pounding, she went from room to room, giving the local police officers as complete a list as she could of missing objects. When she was done, she said, "I hope that's everything." Then she burst into tears. "Dammit, God double dammit! Why does everything have to happen at once?"

The detective, Mario something, handed her a wad of Kleenex from the box on the kitchen counter. He was making coffee. "You got any brandy in the house?"

"Yeah, I think so," Maureen sniffed. "Unless the bastards cleaned out the liquor cabinet too. In the living room, the glassed-door cabinet. Do you see it?" She called to the other cop who had gone to look.

Detective Mario Scala poured a healthy tot of brandy into a kitchen glass and said, "Drink it." Maureen obeyed, though she grimaced as the liquor burned its way down.

When the coffee was done, he poured three mugs, one for each of them and said, "Tell me again. Exactly how many days were you down in the city and who knew you'd be gone?"

Maureen explained that she had not taken the usual precautions against burglary because she was distracted by her daughter's accident.

"Oh yeah, right. I read about that in the paper. She's the one does that great Come Home thing. My wife loves that show. She's been wanting to get tickets, but there's a waiting list for years. You think, maybe...?

"Oh, of course. Please, just write your wife's name and address on that pad over there and I'll see to it that my daughter gets the tickets sent out right away. Will four be enough? That's usually the limit."

"Four's plenty. My wife and my daughter and even my mother-in-law can go. That'll be terrific, Mrs. Cassidy. Thanks. Now, we gotta go. But don't worry, we'll get to work on this case right away. You gonna file a report with your insurance company?"

"Yeah, I guess I'd better." She was grateful that her insurance agent was close by, handling everything; her car, homeowners' coverage. Some things, paintings, for example, were individually insured.

Maureen sat, her feet apart in an ungraceful sprawl. "I'll probably never see them again. It's not money, I care about. I love those pictures. I wanted Kate to have them when I die." Then she put her hands to her face and sobbed softly.

"Ma'am, Mrs. Cassidy? We gotta go. But would you do something first? Call a locksmith, get all the locks on the house changed and get your garage door-opener code changed. Do it right now. He touched her shoulder, but gently. Do that first. Then you can have hysterics. Is there anybody you want me to call to come and stay with you? Your daughter?"

Sweet Jesus! Kate's just getting herself back together. How could she call her? "No, thanks for all your help. I've got a friend in New Rochelle. She can be here in twenty minutes."

CHAPTER TEN

SISTER MARIA PATRICE, nee Carla Rodino, was a teaching nun at a Catholic girls' school in New Rochelle and when she had a rare day to herself, she would drive her battered old Chevy to Maureen's house, where the two friends would talk for hours as if each visit were the last. Often six months went by before Carla could find enough free time for another visit. "Don't forget, I'm married to Jesus and it's worse than having a real, live husband."

That sort of cynicism was creeping into Carla voice more and more often. She described herself as, "Cheap labor. I work for subsistence so stuck-up Catholic girls from Westchester can get a first-class education at cut-rate prices."

Maureen was shocked the first time Carla mentioned leaving the order and becoming a paid, civilian schoolteacher, "If I'm not too old," she had worried.

"Well, over sixty is pretty far gone for starting a whole new career, isn't it?" Maureen had asked.

"I know, but God forgive me, I'm so sick of being the handmaiden of the Lord. It's a thankless job, I'm bored to tears and if I don't do something, I think I'm going to choke to death."

"That bad?"

"Yes, it's that bad. Oh, how I wish I had married and had a houseful of kids."

"And been a mother during the baby-boomers' revolution?"

"Well, maybe I was better off after all. The only worries I had at that point were the girls at school. And they were a real handful, let me tell you."

When Maureen rang the school, the Mother Superior's secretary said, "I'm sorry, Mrs. Cassidy, but Sister Maria Patrice has gone on a retreat. We don't expect her back until the end of the month. Is it urgent? We can reach her, if we have to."

"No, never mind. Just tell her to call me when she gets back, will you?"

It was hours before she finished telephoning and watching the locksmith change all the locks. He told her to disable to garage door-opener until new equipment could be installed. Her insurance man was very comforting. "We'll get everything organized from this end. Don't you worry about a thing."

Easy for him to say, Maureen thought, as she went from room to room, trying to make order of the chaos everything had become. To nobody in particular she said, "Jim Vandersagen, you son-of-a-bitch, all of this is your fault!"

She fell into an exhausted sleep that was interrupted an hour later by Andy Feuerman's frantic pounding on the front door.

"You don't think I'm going to let you sleep here alone after something like this, do you?" He had driven for hours from his vacation lodge in the Adirondaks, where his answering service had relayed Maureen's message. Andy had the good sense to give her the sleeping pill he had brought along. Then he kissed her before going down the hall to Deirdre's old room to spend the rest of the night. Now, maybe the stubborn woman would reconsider and marry him.

For a long time, Maureen simply had not considered remarriage an option. And, though she did not mention it, she still felt it would be awkward to explain to Andy that, despite the reinterpretation of

Church dogma prohibiting remarriage, and her new-found freedom to profess no belief in a personal god, her inner self had not yet resolved the question.

Of course, the restraints of the Church had never been of concern to Tom.

After the divorce, Tom had remarried twice, once immediately after the final decree, a so-called rebound marriage to an actress. It lasted three years and then was dissolved by mutual agreement. Then, after a ten-year hiatus, Tom tried marriage a third time. His wife was a writer in Hollywood whose hectic life meant they saw little of one another for months on end. The third marriage had remained intact, if tentatively, until Tom and the writer separated at the end of the eighties, when they called it quits with a formal divorce.

Since then, Tom, as far as Maureen knew, not only lived alone, he had forsworn the company of women. She didn't know, nor had she ever asked, what his reasons were for the choice. But when she saw him two weeks ago, for the first time since she had watched him on television, accepting the Oscar, she knew that Tom probably preferred to be alone with what was clearly his failing health.

Kate knew it too. Not long ago she had asked Maureen what she should do about her father's, "trouble with the bottle."

Maureen had explained as honestly as she could. "You can't do it for him. He's got to acknowledge it first. Oh yeah, there are those intervention programs, but I don't know how well you're going to manage that by yourself." She left unsaid the fact that Kate would not be able to count on her for help. When she and Tom were through, she had sworn never to be involved with him again. Until the day the mirror fell and Kate was hurt, she had maintained a cool detachment from Tom Cassidy.

Though everyone in Hollywood and New York acknowledged that Cassidy had lost interest in new projects, his existing films continued to return massive amounts of money. Thanks to a first-class management team, Tom was financially secure. He once told Kate, "The trouble with my life is that I've done everything I've ever wanted to do, and I'm tired."

But he did not retire. Instead, he began to work on the Durrell project. It was an exciting year for Tom. He was the talk of the industry and Maureen remembered the pang of envy she had felt on hearing of his success. Here she was, still doing journeyman's work as an actress and Tom, meanwhile, had become an artist, acknowledged by his peers.

She had complained to Kate, "I'm sick of hearing about the great work Tom Cassidy's doing."

"Why, Mom? Don't you think it's true?"

"Oh yes, I believe every word. I guess that's the problem. I think," it was hard for her to admit, "maybe I'm a little jealous."

Kate had reassured her. "There's nothing to be jealous of. You're as fine an actress as anyone. He's a director. You've never had any ambitions along those lines, have you?"

Maureen had to say she had never dreamed of directing, but somehow, she envied Tom. Maybe it was the fact that, after the divorce he had spread his wings and did new and different work, while she had remained behind, her life changing little.

There was Kate to raise. Deirdre, of course, was indispensable in those years. Kate became an angry, rebellious teenager who, more than once had screamed, "I'm going to live with Dad!" She thought, but did not say aloud, and you two old bitches can just stay here and squabble forever.

One Summer, Kate did go to California to try living with Tom and his second wife. The woman was an unwilling partner in the arrangement. She wanted no part of step-motherhood and Kate had sensed it instantly. No effort on Tom's part could improve the situation. So, Kate spent an utterly miserable two months sulking by the swimming pool or riding alone out in the San Fernando Valley, until everybody agreed, they'd all be happier if she went home to Larchmont.

It was a year or more before Tom was successful in repairing the damaged relationship with his daughter. As for Kate, no matter how nasty the quarrels with her mother and grandmother, she never again said she wanted to live with Tom. The next four years were, as Maureen described them, "the special hell reserved for mothers of teenage daughters."

God knows, Maureen thought about that period, it might have been worse if Kate hadn't been able to work off some of her rage and confusion by alternating between Deirdre and Maureen. It was as if, when she had finally vanquished one of her two enemies, she could then turn and wreak havoc on the other, always secure in the knowledge that either her mother or grandmother would be there as a refuge.

Then too, Tom would come to New York and he and Kate would spend days together, after which she would return home, refreshed and ready once again to do battle with Deirdre or Maureen, depending who was the most accessible for a fight.

If DeeDee were giving her mother that kind of grief, Maureen had no way of knowing for Kate had never complained about her daughter. "Probably afraid I'd laugh in her face and tell her she deserved it," she had ruefully observed in a conversation with Carla.

Sister Maria Patrice had some particularly keen insights into the behavior of teenage girls. After thirty-five years of teaching and being in loco parentis, she told Maureen, "I have spent many a night on my knees begging forgiveness for my wicked fantasies of murdering a whole dormitory full of them."

Maureen was grateful for Carla's sympathetic ear, but she learned that the strurm und drang of the teen years must be endured, like passing through a hurricane. She learned, only after the fact, that she and Kate had survived. Things got less terrifying, but no less unpredictable after Kate went away to college.

Then, finally, the waters were still, the fury was spent and Kate was married and living in Boston with Avi and two babies. She racked up hundreds of dollars of telephone charges talking to Deirdre and Maureen.

She had not said so, but they knew Kate was lonely. She had left all her friends in the New York area and she was feeling trapped in the tiny house in a working-class section of the city—all they could afford on Avi's salary as a reporter on the Globe.

After a particularly difficult phone call during which Kate had begun to cry, Maureen had a sudden inspiration. "Katy," she said tentatively, "how would you feel if Gran came up there for a few days? You know, just long enough to give you a break." Maureen held her breath.

"Would she? Oh, Mom, I miss her so much. And DeeDee's teething right now and we're both so miserable. Gran would know how to handle this wouldn't she?"

"Of course, she would, darling." Maureen sounded more confident that she felt. How would Deirdre respond to the idea?

"Well, it's about time, she asked for me. Up there all by herself in that terrible place." Deirdre had never been to Boston, but somehow she believed that Kate was living among savages.

Maureen drove Deirdre and a trunk full of luggage and "necessaries," things that her mother was certain Kate could not obtain in that "unholy place." Neither Maureen nor Kate could understand the source of this mistrust of Boston nor Deirdre's perception of it as alien and inhospitable, but it was that which drove her toward what she believed was her granddaughter's rescue.

There was nothing in this world that Deirdre did with more enthusiasm than leap to the rescue of Kate if she thought it was called for.

As it evolved, Deirdre's part in the lives of Avi and Kate and their two children would last for nearly seven years.

At first, after her mother was settled in Boston and Maureen found herself living alone for the first time in her life, she was like a bather, suspiciously testing the sea, one toe at-a-time.

In the early seventies, to be a still-beautiful woman, free of child and parent, was a heady experience indeed. The first time she spent the night at a man's apartment in New York, after they'd gone to dinner and the theater, Maureen kept wondering if she shouldn't call Deirdre to let her know where she was. Then she remembered. There was nobody, not a single, living soul, to whom she need explain where she was and what she was doing. This, she thought, is the first time in my life I've ever been entirely free. The only sobering thought was that sex without the sacrament of marriage was still a mortal sin. That first year, Maureen would not go to confession, so took no communion, until just before Christmas. At least, she thought, I'll be free until then.

Of course, after years of abstinence, the first man with whom she had sex was the first one she fell in love with. If she had been searching for an unsuitable match, she could not have chosen better than an affair with Jerry Maxwell, Max, as he was known. Now, nearly twenty years later, Maureen looked back on what she had dubbed the Maxwell affair and laughed at the woman she was then.

Naive, romantic, utterly without the wisdom to judge a man's true nature, she had allowed Jerry Maxwell to break her heart. And she had allowed it to happen slowly, as if she wished to prolong the agony.

What she didn't know then was what every woman learns eventually—that there are ways to decide quickly whether or not a man is worth the trouble.

Today, Maureen felt she had the wisdom to judge, and quite possibly, Andy Feuerman was a man worth the trouble. She was all the more certain now, when she was feeling so completely shattered by all the traumatic events of the last weeks, here was Andy, behaving exactly as she would have him behave. He was thoughtful, unobtrusive, helpful, efficient—he could even cook. She could hear her mother's voice from the grave, telling her not to let this one get away. And as for Andy's being Jewish, well, Maureen silently reminded Deirdre of her beloved grandson-in-law.

At first, it had taken a monumental effort to make her see that Avi, a Jew, was not the devil incarnate. But before long, Deirdre had come to love Avi in that fierce way Irishwomen have of loving sons. Kate had more than once complained to Maureen, "She thinks he's a saint, for God's sake, constantly reminding me that Avi is the only man in the world the equal of her Danny O'Hearn."

Considerable help in the matter of being single was Maureen's friend, an actress like herself, though Carlotta Cheney had long since quit the theater to run a talent agency in partnership with her husband. When he died, she continued to manage quite successfully on her own.

Lottie was an old hand at sexual warfare by the time Maureen entered the arena. At first she tried to educate her friend, but later, she observed, "You can't teach a woman anything about men. She's gotta find out for herself. Look at me,"

She explained. "I've dated everybody from millionaires, to starving poets. Millionaires, as a group, I would say are the most cold-hearted. Henry Kissinger was right when he said money and power are aphrodisiacs. The trouble with rich and powerful men is, they're so accustomed to having women fall all over them, they never develop the skills it takes to be kind or loving. Typically, rich men never get beyond the window dressing: beauty, brains, social position—all that stuff. To them, having a relationship is like trading on the New York Stock Exchange. They want to know what kind of return they're going to get on their investment. They're not looking for love and someone to care about them—they have servants for that. A rich man's idea of an ideal woman is one whose beauty, maybe even brains and social standing are apparent enough to tell the world that he is an operator. And the awe and envy of other men is plenty of return on his investment."

"But who does that leave?" Maureen had wailed. I've got enough money of my own. I don't need somebody else's. What about the others, the ones without money and power?"

"Now you're talking trouble. Let's say you've fallen for a starving actor; you know how stupid that is." Lottie wrinkled her nose in distaste. "You got your share of those when you were in acting school yourself. And, I ask you, is there anybody more self-absorbed than an actor?"

At that point Lottie and Maureen simply collapsed laughing at all the actors they had known during the past forty years. There were the Mama's boys, not necessarily gay, but definitely in the control of stage mothers. There were the strivers, people who would grind anyone into the dust on their way to an audition. No, actors were definitely out.

After the Maxwell affair, Maureen was wary, but more than once she become involved with a man only to learn he was married. She had seen Lottie drift from one married man to another, always hoping she'd find one who cared enough for her to act on the meaningless phrases, "We're just waiting until the children are grown." or, "If I try for a divorce now, she'll destroy my career." and the topper, "We don't have sex. I can't see how she could be pregnant."

Finally, Lottie made a vow that she would never so much as eat dinner with a married man; no ifs, ands or other rationalizations. Maureen learned the lesson well. She learned too, about the other side of the seduction coin. She discovered that men are not all rapacious users of women and that when a woman spends the night with him, he feels painfully rejected if she chooses not to see him again.

In fact, Maureen was even now, repairing the damage to a forty-year friendship with an artist whom she and Tom had known when they were young.

His name was, by now, a famous one, with paintings hanging in MOMA and a contract with a major gallery. Ten years earlier, when the artist's wife had died suddenly, he called on Maureen. He was an ardent suitor, having, he confessed, been in love with her for years.

Maureen had made the mistake of going to bed with him. The artist assumed that sexual consent meant that Maureen returned his feelings. She did not. And, worse, she found his passion overwhelming. Rejecting him meant she would lose the one thing about him she wished most to keep, his friendship.

"What should I do?" She had explained the situation to Lottie.

"Do? There's nothing you can do. Just let it cool off. Maybe later, you can invite him to a party and make a point of introducing him to the most beautiful woman you know. If he doesn't want to stay friends, well, he just won't come."

So Maureen introduced the artist to another actress, younger and far more beautiful than she. The problem was, the actress fell in love with the artist and now Maureen had to listen to her lament as she wailed that he had broken her heart.

"I swear, Lottie," Maureen had said, "that's the last time I'm going to play matchmaker. I can't manage my own romances. How the hell am I going to help with somebody else's?" That was the point at which she decided that she would stay single, stop sleeping around and concentrate on her work.

Maureen had partaken of the riches at the banquet of the sexual revolution and now was suffering from indigestion. The freedom to come and go was still hers and she would continue to enjoy it. As for casual sex, very different today, considering the AIDS factor, it was still hers to choose, but now, she decided, it would be on her terms. Looking for Mr. Goodbar was not only undignified, it was fruitless. It had taught her something about men, however. What she learned was that men, like all human beings, are frightfully complex creatures, with frailties perhaps greater than those of some women, and that one risks doing great harm by not being cautious and considerate.

It was at about this point in Maureen's life when she was forced back into the role of Deirdre's daughter one again. But this time, the rules had changed. Deirdre had to come back from Boston because she could no longer be trusted with the safety of Kate's two young children.

"Mom, she nearly burned the house down last week!" Kate was crying. She's doing weird things. She gets lost on the way to the store. A month ago we found her near Faneuil Hall screaming at a bunch of people on the street. The police brought her home." Kate's sobs were muffled, but Maureen heard them.

Quickly, Maureen went to Boston and brought her mother to New York. A second series of exhaustive neurological tests eventually proved that Deirdre was suffering from the disease that went by a terrifying name: Alzheimer's Disease.

"You mean this dementia you say my mother has, isn't curable?" The neurologist at New York Hospital had given Maureen the same test results and prognosis as those at the Leahy Clinic in Boston.

"Just take her home and see that she's kept safe."

That was it. No medicine, no elaborate treatment. No hope, even. Nothing, just keep her safe and wait until she dies. Maureen took six months off from the show, learning to care for her mother and watching her grow worse each day. Now, finally, she understood what Deirdre had always meant when she had run on about the chain. "Don't break the chain. 'tis all we have that binds us."

The heartscald that Deirdre knew so well was now Maureen's and Kate's. They looked into dozens of situations and finally chose one that seemed less heartless and brusque than the others. But both Kate and Maureen were silent and grim with trepidation and a sense of guilt as they took Deirdre to the nursing home.

They were met with firm kindness and a take-charge attitude. The Sisters of Charity, still, stubbornly clinging to their magnificent habits, looked like animated Christmas angels, exuding an air of peaceful certainty. In a quiet backwater in Eastern Connecticut, the sisters provided the calm and dignity that reassured the bewildered Deirdre and soothed Kate and Maureen. But, after they left, they cried all the way down to Larchmont, reassuring one another that they had done the very best they could under the circumstances.

It would be two years before Deirdre's body followed her mind into death. As they sat in the old neighborhood church from which Maureen knew her once-lucid mother would have wished to be buried, Kate, Avi and their children were surrounded by mourners who had been Deirdre's first friends in New York. Some for fifty years.

In the front pew of the Church, only Tom was missing. He had been unable to return from Europe in time for the funeral. Maureen was relieved at not having to see him.

The mass was, mercifully, not too long and the priest, young enough to be Deirdre's grandson, seemed distracted and in a rush to get it overwith. How sad, Maureen thought. He never even met my mother. It didn't seem right. The old priest from this church had, himself, died a few months earlier. She prayed, more out of habit than piety, for the souls of Deirdre as well as the old priest.

Later, at the cemetery, during the graveside services, Maureen saw the man in the wheelchair. He was very old, wizened, wrapped in a blanket against the March wind. He wept openly. It was Liam Gerrity.

Maureen held tightly to Kate's hand as the last wilted rose fell softly on Deirdre's casket. And she never took her eyes from the face of Gerrity, glaring at him across the open grave. She saw no sign from him that he had the slightest idea of who she was. May you burn in hell everlasting she thought, just before the final "Amen."

After the funeral, Maureen, in sorry resignation, acknowledged, that her mother would never again be in the house except as a memory in snapshots or in phrases, when she heard herself repeating the very voice-tones and phrases Deirdre had once spoken

Months later, on a quiet Sunday morning, after having gone to church to pray for Deirdre's soul, Maureen went into her mother's long-abandoned room to begin, at last, the job of sorting through the things she had left behind. These paltry possessions held Deirdre's ghost in every tissue-wrapped and lovingly-stored object. Maureen realized with a jolt, this was the first time in her life she had ever performed the ritual of combing through the material remnants of another person's life.

She sighed. How few things there were. Deirdre had begun her life in America with very little and departed with not much more. She never had cared much for clothes or what she called "nickety-nacks."

As for money, she had used it for charity and gifts. She always bought extravagant gifts for Kate's children though they were often inappropriate. For Maureen she believed in practical things—a set of dish towels and matching apron was her idea of a nice Christmas present. And she was still buying dolls for Kate when she was a sophomore at Country Day.

Deirdre had a good head for money, having earned her own way for so many years. She had maintained a checking account since the middle fifties. There, in the top drawer of the dresser were the neatly-filed envelopes containing each year's collection of canceled checks and bank statements. Maureen set them aside to look at when she finished with the clothing and possessions.

Sadly, she folded the once-a-year, special-occasion dresses that Deirdre had accumulated, never discarding one. There was a mauve, knee-length evening gown, circa 1929, barely worn, very fragile, Deirdre's first fancy American dress. Maureen thought it belonged in a museum. She did not remember ever having seen her mother wearing it. Careful not to shake loose the bead fringe, she set it aside. Other clothing went into the box marked for the Saint Vincent de Paul thrift shop.

Then she tackled the tall chest in which she found Deirdre's few items of lace-trimmed underwear. They were slips, mostly, given through the years, by Kate. Many of them were still folded in tissue-lined boxes, never worn. And, scattered through the drawers were empty bottles that had once held perfume. Even now, she caught the faint fragrance of Shalimar, Deirdre's favorite. Those had come from Tom who once said a man can't make a mistake giving a woman perfume or flowers, but that flowers didn't last long enough.

She worked her way through mounds of old letters from obscure relatives in Ireland, postcards, mass cards dating from funerals half a century passed. The detritus of her mother's life lay gathered into neat piles, some things to be given away, the rest to be disposed of as trash.

Maureen flipped idly through the canceled checks, year by year. Some were written to Bloomingdale's where Deirdre continued to shop long after it had become an upscale, overpriced fashion center. It was one of the few Third Avenue landmarks that had not disappeared. There were checks that recorded payments for dental, medical and optometry services that Deirdre had insisted she do for herself. And each year there was a check to the beauty shop for the permanent wave she got every November. Maureen could almost hear the remark she made every year, "...so the kinks'll be out of me hair before Christmas."

And then Maureen realized that each year there were twelve checks, one a month, for increasingly larger amounts, beginning in the late sixties, through the start of the year when Deirdre's mental state began to deteriorate. Each check was to the same payee, The *Smaragdus Association.*

In all, there were monthly Association payments for nearly fifteen years, totaling thousands of dollars. The endorsements were fuzzy, difficult-to-read and rubber-stamped. What, she wondered, was the *Smaragdus Association?*

Maureen had her answer the following week, when Avi investigated. *Smaragdus,* as it was known, had an address in Long Island City, just across the 59th Street Bridge, in a rundown building housing a bar more typical of the old Third Avenue than the semi-industrial neighborhood where it was located, brooding among foundries and electrical wholesalers, on Roosevelt Avenue.

Avi described the place graphically, in his reporters' style. Maureen said, "It sounds exactly like the old saloon on Third Avenue where we lived upstairs, Gerrity's."

Avi said, "That's the name of the owner of the place. It's on their license, see." He held up a copy of the computer printout. One of Avi's researchers told him that Gerrity's on Roosevelt Avenue had been one of the better-known Irish bars that regularly collected funds which were passed into the hands of the IRA for the purchase of arms and explosives.

"You mean that's what this *Smaragdus* Association or whatever they call it is—just a cover for gun-running to the IRA?" Kate was fascinated. "I wonder who *Smaragdus* is?"

"Not who," said Avi. "What. It's the Latinized version of a Greek word for emerald."

"Of course, like the *Emerald Society,* another weeping and wailing bunch from the old country. They're probably fronting for the IRA too." Maureen was furious. "Goddammit, even after she's dead, I have to be worrying about those bloodsucking leeches—with their saints and martyrs, going about taking money from old ladies and then blowing up a lot of innocent people. They never give up, do they? Gerrity's, for God's sake! I don't know why it should come as a surprise."

Avi explained, "There must be hundreds of places like this one all over the United States and Canada. Somebody sets up a society or a benevolent association or something of the sort, but everybody knows their real purpose."

Kate wanted to know, "Why doesn't the government stop them?"

"First, you have to make a case," Avi told her. "It's very complicated. And these funnels for money and arms come and go like gypsy camps. The minute there's a hint of trouble, they just pack up their tents and fade away. Then some other group springs up in another place with another fanciful title."

"But my mother sent them money for fifteen years! She wrote her last check just before her mind started to go and you and Kate took over her personal affairs."

Avi nodded. "That's consistent with what we know about the deal. Gerrity's bar in Long Island City was closed down a few years ago. It's a greasy spoon now. The owner, Liam Gerrity, is retired and living with one of his daughters in Jackson Heights."

"So that's where she went all those years when she took the day off to go to the city—wherever the IRA had a fund-raising location. My mother never did have any sense where Ireland was concerned. Nothing, no sacrifice was too great, it didn't matter how many people were killed, as long it was for the Goddammed IRA."

Kate leapt to her grandmother's defense. "There you go again, being judgmental. You and Daddy. You never could let people handle their own lives in their own way."

Judgmental? Maureen guessed that described her and Tom. Especially Tom. He was a master at telling other people how they ought to feel. She remembered suddenly, the day she and Tom had sat with Kate while her friend, Judy, lay fighting for her life after a bungled suicide attempt. Judy's mother was furious with her daughter, saying, "How could she do such a thing! I swear, if she ever tries this again, I hope she makes it. She has no right to put us through this kind of agony!"

Tom had whispered something about how inappropriate it was for the woman to be angry at a time like this. And Maureen had barely been able to refrain from telling him he was wrong. Anger was exactly what she would have felt if it had been Kate lying there. No, enraged. Indeed, how could a young person be willing to inflict such pain upon her parents?

"I guess you're right. It was her life, after all. But really, Kate, your Gran sometimes did get carried away. Guns and bombs. My stubborn old mother never stopped. All that time, she was still fighting for Danny O'Hearn's dreams. Poor Ma."

"Maybe not so poor," said Kate. After all, except for us, that was the only life she ever had. Keeping the romantic dream alive—that's all she was doing."

"Yeah," said Maureen. "But with Liam Gerrity—the scum of the earth!" Swiftly, her mouth set in a grim line, she took the papers Avi had given her and, together with the bundle of canceled checks, threw them into the trash. Neither Avi nor Kate seemed to hear her mutter, "That's where you belong, you filthy old pig."

CHAPTER ELEVEN

MAUREEN WAITED UNTIL the following day to call Kate to tell her about the burglary. Now she was less likely to break down and cry. Quickly, she explained and reassured her daughter that she was unharmed in all but spirit. "It's really not bad except—I think I know how it feels to be raped." Kate heard the anguish in her mother's voice and Andy saw Maureen's face contorted by the anxiety she was trying to cover by speaking too rapidly.

She gave Andy a grateful look and accepted the cup of coffee he offered. Her voice smiling, she said, Andy's here. He came down last night so I'm just fine."

"Mom, I hate to take advantage of you like this, but I've been trying to get you to sell the place for years now. Wouldn't this be the right time to take my advice?"

"Of course," Maureen said. She certainly had no further reason for living so far from the studios in New York. And these days, with the train schedule cut back, those nights when she wanted to stay late in the city, she usually slept at Kate's. Yes, she thought, it really is time to put the place on the market and find an apartment. "Yes, of course, you're right. But don't expect me to make a decision right now—about anything."

No matter how Maureen tried to justify it, her reason for staying in Larchmont was long gone. The last and final link with the past had been nothing more than a small item in the local newspaper, a story about the new owner of the yacht once named *Sea Lancer*. Jim Vandersagen's beloved boat was sold to a Californian and would no longer be moored at the Larchmont Club.

How many years had she driven by the club while doing errands? She never admitted, even to herself, that seeing *Sea Lancer*'s tall mast, towering over all the other boats, gave her a bit of a kick. Passing the club or going by another road was not a conscious choice. It was just something she did now and then, remembering that first party for Freddy Sherwood's troupe, just before they went to the Cape. For Maureen, it had been the ultimate in glamour—like something in a movie. Even now she could recall the long, clean line of the bow and the compact, but fully-equipped galley, not much larger than a closet, in which, Jim had assured her, a chef could prepare a banquet.

Now, finally, her connection with Larchmont could be severed. Why, indeed, hold on to a house that was much too big, too rundown, and now, having been violated, much too unpleasant? Yes, she would put the place on the market and start looking for an apartment to buy, somewhere on the opposite side of the park, away from Kate, but only a taxi ride away.

Kate said, "I'll get my friend Ellie Abrams to work on it as soon as possible. She's a terrific real estate lady, and if she marries that Lloyd whatsisname with all the megabucks, she'll be the next Leona Helmsley."

"But nicer, I hope. Ellie Abrams is a darling girl. Okay, you can tell her to call me and I'll try to get together with her before my new show begins. You're going to start taping your show again next week, you said?"

"Yeah," Kate sounded tentative. "That is, I think so, unless Adele decides to fire me even before the season is over. "

"Why would she do that? Your ratings are holding up. The Network should be damned glad to have you. Everybody knows the magazine format is running out of steam. But your show is still, as they say, golden."

"Maybe, but they also say, nothing lasts forever. And if Adele is mad enough, she'll fire me in any case, even if it means cutting profits. You don't know, but I talked to some of the people who heard her the day Jim died. She was ranting on about me; called me some nasty names. She was having a fight with Jim. I suppose she was crazed with jealousy, though there wasn't anything to be jealous about. He told me she's suspicious of every woman in his life, even when nothing's going on."

Maureen resisted the impulse to remind Kate that, in Jim Vandersagen's life, where women were concerned, there was never a time when *nothing* was going on. She also refrained from asking a pointed question about Kate's relationship with Jim. Andy's presence in the room deterred her. Now was not the moment to try to discover the real meaning of what she had seen the night she glimpsed them across the room at Sardi's, though she had come to what seemed the obvious conclusion. Surely, she thought, they were behaving like two people in the throes of a new love affair. Someday, she would find out. But, she thought, let it be for now. The man was dead. Perhaps sometime in the future Kate would tell her the truth.

Andy Feuerman was busily whipping eggs—his recipe called for halving the number of egg yolks—"though, my mother would faint if she saw me throwing away perfectly good egg yolks."

He had cooked—"cremated," Maureen said—bacon so that it was low in fat. Then he set out three kinds of preserves for the toast, no butter. "A good breakfast, and one that won't break your heart," he said, putting a plateful of food on the table Maureen with an exaggerated flourish.

"That's what comes of having worked as a waiter all those Summers in the Catskills. What a great jumping-off place for a kid from the Bronx who turned out to be the last of the honest arbitrageurs on Wall Street."

After the downfall of Milkin, Boesky and other junk bond sellers and deal-makers, Andy Feuerman's company had stood nearly alone, millions of dollars in the red, but with its reputation unsullied. Now, almost a decade later, Andy was quietly putting together investments, mergers and acquisitions—playing by the rules and, to the chagrin of his former competitors, making lots of money.

Maureen ate slowly, savoring every bite—how she loved to have someone cook for her. Spoiled, she supposed, after all the years of Deirdre's indulgence.

Marrying Andy would mean having a cook, not working except for the fun of it and most important, not having to worry about getting too old to work in television. She had enough money to live decently but she had never been obscenely rich. Andy was obscenely rich, though he lived quite simply. Yeah, she told herself, the way Andy lived could serve as a model for the very rich. His name never appeared in the paper except in the business pages. He enjoyed life and gave to charity nearly as much as he was reputed to earn. Yes, marrying him would not be a poor choice by any standards—even her friend Lottie's

Once, she had asked him a direct question about his wealth. "Andy, you're one of the ten richest men in New York, you have everything anyone could want and you have an impeccable reputation as a philanthropist. How do you feel about all that?"

Andy didn't hesitate. "I like it."

Yes, she ought to tell Lottie about this guy. Andy would prove to be the exception. Maureen thought, it is quite possible to find a nice man—and if he happens to be rich....She smiled, remembering Mae West's line: "It's better to be rich and healthy than poor and sick."

But, would she want to stop working? Probably. Television acting certainly wasn't glamorous; it was hard work. And she went off, mentally into her new apartment—probably in the East Sixties—choosing where and how she would display her pictures. Then she was hauled back into reality. Her pictures were gone. She'd never see them again. Before she could wrestle with the depressing problem of the burglary, the phone rang.

It was Sister Maria Patrice. "Hi, it's me, Carla. What's up? I got an urgent message from the school."

"Oh, Carla, I'm sorry, I didn't mean to interrupt your retreat." She told her briefly about the burglary. "But Andy's here now and everything is under control. Where are you?"

"I'm right next door in New Rochelle, taking care of the business I went on the retreat for."

"What kind of business? I thought a retreat was for prayer and meditation."

"It is. And that's what I was doing. I was meditating and praying and making up my mind about my next move."

"What do you mean, 'move'? You going somewhere?"

"Yes, you could say that. I'm going back to the real world. I've decided to leave the Order at the end of the Fall semester or sooner, if they can find a replacement for me. I'm going to be a civilian again."

Andy, seeing Maureen's stunned look, said, "Is something wrong? Is your friend okay?"

She shook her head, still unable to speak. Then she said, "But, Carla, you've been a nun for more than forty years!"

"Yeah. Isn't that long enough?"

"But you can't just give it all up. Just like that." Maureen snapped her fingers.

"Don't sound so shocked, dear heart. I've been thinking about doing this for more than ten years. It's just something I have to do before I die."

"But, *how* will you live? *Where* will you live?" Maureen's head was like a beehive of buzzing questions.

"*Where* may be a question, but one I can manage. As for how, you know my father turned the shoe repair business over to Dominick, And my brother didn't lose any time in re-inventing it as a little goldmine. The *SHOE STOP* shops that you see all over town throw off plenty of money and Dom keeps selling franchises like MacDonalds— well, not quite like MacDonalds, but enough. Anyway, he says my share of the business amounts to half a million dollars right this minute. And that's without counting the regular income from the franchises. So, money's no problem. The only problem I can see is what am I going to do with the rest of my life."

Maureen said, "Yeah, what are you going to do?"

Carla laughed. "You sound the way you did when we were in the sixth grade. There are so many things I want to do, I can't begin to name them. But for starters, how about travel? Do you realize the only time I've ever been out of the United States was on a nuns' trip to the Vatican? All those years of teaching teenage girls about the world, and I never got to see any of it. Of course, I'll need a traveling companiion at first. Wanna come with me?"

"Oh, I can't. At least, I can't right now. I've got a new show. I'm playing the matriarch. Oh, my God, Carla, I have so much to tell you. You've got to come over as soon as you can. This is beginning to look like one of those years. I sure hope you can come over tonight. I've got something to show you." She thought, I've got empty spaces to show you. But she'd tell Carla about that later.

Andy watched as Maureen listened. Then she said, "Yes, tonight. You said you don't have to go back to work until Monday." She repeated Carla's question, "Will Andy be here tonight?" She looked at him.

He shook his head and said, "No, I've got to get back to town."

"Good, see you at six." Maureen put the phone down. "Carla's leaving the Order. She's not going to be a nun anymore. I can't believe it. Forty years! After all that time she decides she wasn't cut out for the religious life."

Andy laughed at Maureen's puzzled look. "Same thing with some marriages. I've known people to stay together forty years or more and then get a divorce. I always wonder what took them so long."

"Where were we?" Finishing his second cup of coffee, Andy continued to describe Jim Vandersagen's funeral. He wondered, "How come you weren't there? Didn't Adele ask you?"

"Oh, yes, I got an engraved invitation, but I was feeling so miserable that day and, it was raining, if you remember. I just decided to stay in bed. Nobody missed me, did they?"

"Well, nobody specifically asked why you weren't there, but it was such a zoo, I really didn't talk to a lot of people. Sure gave me the shivers, though. It was so strange. The memory of Steve Ross's funeral is still fresh, so everybody was comparing the two guys. People were wondering exactly what Vandersagen had been doing about putting his communications conglomerate together. The rumors were thicker than the flowers. Of course, there were lots of *Time Warner* people and the movie crowd too. They were all over the place with those insincere condolences, but I don't think Adele was fooled. She knows the world's full of sharks. I must say, she looked stunning in black."

Maureen said, "Then, you don't think she's a grieving widow?"

"I don't know. She seemed pretty sad to me. But, gorgeous!"

"What is she going to do?"

"That's what everybody is speculating about. I said they're sharks. You get the feeling they're all swimming around waiting for the feeding frenzy to begin. You know what I mean? Everybody is speculating about what's to become of the whole network, the newspapers—all that stuff. And nobody knows what she's going to do. Maybe Adele has plans, but so far she hasn't told anybody. Everyone knows there's a board meeting this week and the word is that she's going to spring something then. I'd say the telecommunications and media markets all have the shakes right now. And not only because of Jim Vandersagen's death. Remember, back in the sixties, when Dustin Hoffman's father looks at this kid floating around in the family swimming pool? Then he says one word; 'plastics.' What was the name of that movie? I think it was *The Graduate*."

"Yeah. Well that's how things are today. Only it's a million times bigger than that. It's everything, telephone, TV, movies, the whole *schmere*. And the word is *telecommunications*."

"Cute word. I suppose you're involved in a big way with those whatchamacallits, or is just a single whatchamacallit?"

"Not really, though it's possible that if there's a different company, a new one formed by gathering in some peripherals, for example, we might be called in to put together a new public offering. That's really what I do best, though I've got plenty of competition."

"What do you mean by a new public offering?"

"Well JGV is an enormous operation right now, but it's probably about to undergo a huge change. Not too different from what happened with *Viacom* and *Paramount* or *Time Warner*, for that matter. You see, there's this whole new set of technologies...have you heard about the *Information Superhighway*?"

"Yes, but it's only a name to me, something I see in news headlines. It's all going to be bunched altogether, isn't it? News, telephones, television, movies, everything, and you'll be able to get it right in your house on the TV screen, through the wires?"

"That's as good a description as I've heard," said Andy. "Though, it's much more complex than that at the administrative and financial ends. There will be a great deal of money changing hands. Some people will emerge richer than Croesus; others might lose their shirts. One thing is sure. There's going to be a lot of speculating about the next move Adele Vandersagen makes, if she gets control of the company."

"Doesn't she have that now? With Jim gone, she inherits his share, and that means she gets control of the company, doesn't she?"

"I'm not sure. Vandersagen has two sons, and there are some Kenyons with a good chunk of stock. But, my guess is that Adele is working quietly to grab as much as she can. She's got a good business mind, that woman. I've dealt with her in the past and she's always been level-headed and very savvy. Abner Kenyon's little girl is nobody's fool."

"That is, unless she killed her husband." Maureen raised an eyebrow.

Andy laughed. "You don't think she's the one who done 'im in, do you?"

"How should I know? All I'm sure of is that the police questioned her very closely."

"They questioned you too, didn't they?"

"Of course. I suppose everybody who was in the studio that day came under the scrutiny of Lieutenant Quinn. Did I tell you his first name is Irving?"

"Well, you won't have to worry about that if you marry me. You can still be Maureen Cassidy, because, frankly Maureen Feuerman seems just as silly as Irving Quinn. You *are* considering my proposal, aren't you?"

"Yes," Maureen laughed, glad to be off the subject of the Vandersagens. "I'm thinking about it and I promise you, you'll have an answer just as soon as I can clear my head enough to think intelligently. So much has happened. I think I know how Alice felt slipping down the rabbit hole."

Irving Quinn had just finished putting his desk in order after having spread more than a dozen folders and notes over the surface. Of the thirty or more people who had been interviewed, he was about to narrow his suspect list down to less than five or six.

As usual, since having given up cigarettes a year earlier, he felt the urge to smoke whenever the task he was doing reached a critical point. But, he noticed, the urges were becoming less frequent and much less intense. The things he had read about conditioned response seemed to be true. Hmm, Pavlov's dog, he thought. How many years does it take before you really kick the tobacco habit? If somebody offered him a smoke right now....idiot! Once, during the early stages of withdrawal, an NYPD psychologist said she thought he had an addictive personality. How do you figure something like that? he wondered. In any case, he was thankful that tobacco had been his only vice, having steered clear of heavy boozing after watching a favorite uncle die and knowing his own father was a lifelong member of AA. Probably got a real genetic predilection, he thought. To say nothing of the kind of job that would drive anybody to drink.

The phone's shrill electronic ring interrupted his reverie. "Quinn."

It was Alex, who had been watching the Waldorf since early in the morning. "He just went up to her apartment. The brother, Gil. You want me to stay here and see how long he stays up there?"

"Yeah, that's a good idea. I don't think it's especially significant, though. After all, he is her brother and she never said anything about not being on good terms with him."

"Okay, boss, I'll stay with it. You still want 24-hour surveillance of the hotel?"

"Yeah, sure. I want to know who sees Adele and I'm also interested in Tom Cassidy. You say you haven't seen him in the lobby for two days?"

"That's right. But, I know he's up there, because one of the guys has been keeping track of room service, and they're going up there, regular."

After the call, Irving selected the files for Tom Cassidy, Maureen Cassidy, Rudy Macklin, Adele Vandersagen and her brother. The file on Kate Cassidy lay face down on his desk. He didn't need to turn it. He knew her telephone number by heart. He was irritated. He thought, you damned fool, she's still a suspect!

Kate was feeling well enough to enjoy the quiet of her apartment. From the living room she could see the remains of Autumn's annual show in Central Park. How lucky I am, she thought. I'd never give up this view if I had to scrub floors to be able to pay the upkeep on the apartment.

In fact, she would have to do much more than that to continue paying the cost of maintenance on the eight-room, corner apartment on the twenty-first floor of one of the best buildings on Central Park West.

When she and Avi had bought the place, they were strapped for cash and terrified of the financial trap they were certain awaited them. As always, when Kate had concerns, she called Tom. And Tom was at the point in his career where money was starting to accumulate faster than he could spend it.

Avi had a bit of trouble accepting the generous gift Tom had made—the entire down-payment plus a trust fund covering ten years of mortgage payments. "I feel like a kid," he had complained. "I'm nearly thirty-eight years old and I can't provide a home for my family without help from my father-in-law, you know, coming *up* with the *down.*"

Kate quickly pointed out, "Of course you can provide a home for us. Look at that lovely house we had in North Andover. Nobody paid for that but you. But, oh, Avi, this is the place I've wanted all my life! Don't make me turn it down just because it troubles you to take my father's money. You'll be making plenty when you get up to speed at the *Times*. But, if we don't take this now, while we have a chance, it'll never come around again. Please, please," she had begged.

Within two years, Avi had published a book, had a byline at the *Times*, and best of all, got a weekend news show at WJGV. A few years later, writing a huge check to Tom, in repayment of what he insisted on calling a loan, was one of Avi's last important acts before his death.

Though it would never compensate Kate for the shock and horror of losing her husband in so brutal and senseless an attack, it helped to know that she and the children need not be in want.

Maureen and Kate had once talked about the the lives of people who grow up without constantly worrying about money—as Kate had—and how different it had been for herself and Dierdre. Maureen had struggled to put into prespective Kate's life and her children's—never experiencing real poverty, and Dierdre's with her infant Maureen.

Being poor when you're a kid. How could Maureen tell Kate what it was really like? Only Deirdre understood poverty's inexorable power to shame, to corrode and to distort one's vision. To be poor meant much more than simply having barely enough money for basic necesseties—it defined one's place in society. Even today, when Maureen wore fine clothes or jewels, she felt as if it were a betrayal of Deirdre for whom the shame would remain locked within, shaping her every waking thought until merciful senility delivered her from such concerns.

Kate had seen some of the obvious after-effects of Deirdre's life of poverty, especially when she or Maureen would take Gran shopping at the A&P supermarket. They would cringe as she shouted across the aisles, "Don't buy them carrots. They're two cents cheaper at Grand Union!" Heads would turn among the well-bred matrons with their shopping carts. Everyone heard Deirdre instructing the butcher, "Don't be afraid to use the knife. I ain't payin' fer fat. I don't want that pot roast to shrink like one a them heads they sell in Pago Pago!"

In time, Kate and Maureen learned the art of being poker-faced while Deirdre called attention to herself by shouting, pinching, comparing and altogether being a highly visible and audible embarrassment. Later, when Deirdre had made friends with some Italian and Irish grandmothers who also attended daily mass at the local church, Maureen would pick up two or three of them, drop them at the store together, like a gaggle of gray geese, to haggle, pinch and complain as a group. When the shopping was done, she would drive by, help load their groceries and then take them home.

Before Kate learned to drive it was Maureen's weekly task and as time passed, she learned to dread the Saturday shopping trips. The supermarket forays became known as Mom's "wet head-cloth-days" since the first time Tom came in late one afternoon. With an ironic display of sympathy, after finding Maureen, prostrate on the sofa with a cold cloth on her head, he said, "I see you took your mother shopping again."

Now, Kate was luxuriating on Central Park West, her link with the supermarket was the telephone—she probably was one of the few in hundreds of thousands of women in New York who had regular contact with that special breed of young males known as grocery boys. A great distance, not measured in miles, lay between this apartment and her mother's old place on Third Avenue. For Kate, it was no more than a handful of family stories. The rest had disappeared and today, all she knew of Third Avenue was upscale shopping at Bloomingdale's and Barney's.

Maureen was gratified that her only child should enjoy the benefits of wealth, and that her grandchildren would not suffer the agonies of having to learn, painstakingly, some of the ways of privilege.

If Kate had no memory of poverty, Maureen had enough for the two of them, and she had no doubt that, like her mother, she would never lose that touch of mistrust and anxiety about money until her memory too would fade into oblivion.

Tom had grown up impoverished too, but he was not, never had been, obsessed by it. since his father's family though originally Irish, dated from the 18th century in Connecticut, where they enjoyed status as *Yankees*. His mother was the descendant of French Canadians, nominally Catholic, but rather more casual than the Irish immigrants of the last century. To have been Irish in the years following the famine, was to know, on intimate terms, the fears of poverty, if not outright starvation. To Kate they were quaint family fables. But to Maureen and Deirdre they were daily fare. Even now Maureen could mimic Deirdre perfectly, as she put a plate on the table, saying, "Eat now for ye don't know if ye'll eat tomorrow." or "Pray the Lord you don't go to bed hungry another day."

God knows, thought Kate, looking at the leaves being blown about the Central Park sheep meadow, there are people down there with no place to sleep tonight, but I can't fix it. Sometimes, her conscience was a terrible trouble to Kate. Then she'd write a check for an unusually amount to whatever charity solicitation had come in the mail that day.

But today, it was too early for the mail. She would catch up on *Vanity Fair* and *The New Yorker*. The phone rang. She caught herself wishing the voice would be that of Irving Quinn.

It was Adele Vandersagen. Hearing Adele say, "Kate? I didn't wake you, did I?" dropped Kate's stomach downward at roughly the same rate as an earthward-bound meteorite.

"No," the smile in her voice concealed her trepidation. "I was just enjoying my last few days of recuperation."

"Good." Adele sounded pleased and then, very business-like, she said, "Kate, I wonder if you'd like to come over here and have some breakfast with me. I have a little proposition I'd like to make before I go to the board meeting this afternoon. I know you're going back to work next week and, well, I think this will be good for both of us. You sure you're feeling okay?"

"Sure, fine." Kate was puzzled. Adele was being much too pleasant for someone about to do a hatchet job. "I can be there in about half an hour. Would that be alright?"

"Sure," said Adele. "Is there anything special you'd like for breakfast?"

"Mm, no. Anything. Anything except eggs, of course."

"Okay," Adele said. "Too bad isn't it? Nobody gets to enjoy eggs anymore. I've given them up too. I hope somebody soon discovers that a soft, runny four-minute egg with buttered toast is exactly what it takes if you want to keep your figure and live to be ninety. See you."

Kate was unable to think clearly. Adele? What could she possibly want except to fire her? Maybe Adele was from the old school, where firing people was done with a gentle hand and a kind voice. Well, she'd be ready for anything. And, she decided she'd look her best into the bargain.

As she skillfully put on her makeup she reviewed the conversation she'd had two days earlier with Tom.

"Oh, Daddy, I'm waiting for the shoe to drop. I've never been fired from anything before. I just know I'm going to do something stupid like cry."

"Nonsense," Tom had reassured her. "You'll do no such thing. If the stupid woman can't see how valuable you are to the success of the show she now owns, she's a bigger fool than I thought. Katy, darling. Look at it this way. The show is called *Come Home with Kate*. What are they going to do, hire somebody else and call it *Come Home with Susie Jo* and feature recipes for grits and hog jowls?"

Tom had done his best Arkansas drawl and had Kate laughing so hard, she said, "I gotta go, Daddy or I'll pee my pants."

Funny, she thought, he hadn't answered his phone last night. And now there wasn't time to call him. She promised herself she'd go directly to Tom's suite after breakfast with Adele and, no matter what news she got, she'd try again to convince him to check into the Fletcher Clinic. Better do it, she thought, before he goes back to California. At Fletcher, she thought, I can keep an eye on him and make sure he gets the right kind of aftercare. The Fletcher Clinic claimed a success rate with alcoholics equal to, if not better than Betty Ford.

The Waldorf Towers elevator was unobtrusive. If you didn't know, you might think it was a service elevator, set apart from the bank of regular hotel elevators.

Nervously, Kate waited for the door to open, watching the light that indicated the elevator was on its way down. The concierge had been alerted and was pleasant, but not subservient, as he led her away from his desk. "Mrs. Vandersagen is sending the elevator for you right away. It won't be a long wait."

"Thank you," Kate said. Before he turned to go, the man stared at her for a moment. She could almost read the question he was too well-trained to ask. He wondered where he had seen her before.

Since the start of her weekly show, she had gathered a small, but fiercely loyal following. Her fans tended to be women, though, because hers was an evening magazine format, research had shown there were many men as well. What appealed to them was the inclusion of shows about building and hardware generously sprinkled among the cooking, decorating and gardening segments.

How much the show meant to her was only now clear as she felt nearly faint with the fear of losing it. What would she do? Magazine articles? Certainly, she had enough material to write hundreds, but Kate knew, better than most people, how reclusive one must be to write. Even at the research stage where Avi would be out, digging for material, he once told her how he had felt like a hermit, "Just me and the copy."

Kate knew that, without the show, she might get on the next plane to Ireland where Dee Dee was studying. She knew if she should do that, she would be too clinging, too demanding of daughterly loyalty.

Soon after Avi's death Audry Hoffman had said, "Let her go. That's how she's handling the death of her father. She's like a little bird with a healthy pair of wings and she's scared, but she's also very anxious to try them out. She can't do that if you follow her. And she can't feel safe unless she believes you are certain she is safe."

Easy for her to say, Kate thought. She doesn't have a twenty year-old daughter living in Dublin without a soul to look after her. As for Joel, he'd be furious if she showed up in Tel Aviv. "He's got the same problem as she does." Doctor Hoffman told her. "But it's harder for him because boys simply do not allow their mothers to provide comfort while they search for their manhood."

"Search for their manhood" was a phrase Kate was hearing often these days. Maybe, she wondered, we ought to have a second *Bar Mitzvah* when a guy gets to be twenty-one. A *Bar Mitzvah* with drums and booze and throwing up and all the stupid things she remembered watching Avi and his buddies doing when they were in college. Weren't these, after all, manhood rituals? Perhaps if they were to become more stylized, ritualized, even sacred, it could be done and completed, so the boy and his parents could get on with their lives. The elevator's arrival shut off further speculation about her children. Now, Kate began to worry about Adele.

Aside from whether or not she was about to lose her job, was she about to confront the person who killed Jim Vandersagen? More chilling was the thought that Irving Quinn had posited. Had she been a target too?. And, if Adele killed Jim, and had tried to kill her too, what was she doing riding up in this tiny box to the apartment of a woman who, if she cared to, could dispatch her without anyone ever knowing that she was here?. Well, him, she thought, of the concierge.

Oh, my God, Kate thought, Irving doesn't know I'm here. She had more or less promised to tell him where she went and for how long. There hadn't been time, nor, she had to admit, had it seemed important to call Quinn to let him know her every move. The only person she had tried to call, her father, was not answering his phone. She was rapidly rising toward Adele's floor and suddenly, she decided to go back down again. She would ask to meet in the lobby, someplace more public and safe than an apartment where anything could happen. Frantically, Kate looked around for a button to push to reverse the elevator. There was a panel of buttons; She located the one marked *up*, another *down*. Trying to control her panic, she pressed *down*. But the car continued its ascent. She didn't dare try the other, the red one, labeled *emergency*. God knows, she thought, I don't want to have the whole damned hotel in an uproar. Why not? her other self asked. Because, she answered herself, sometimes it's better to be dead than embarrassed.

Kate drew a breath, a deep one, for she realized it was too late, in any case. The elevator was slowing. Quit being a baby, she told herself.

Such self-lecturing had always helped in the face of danger. Here goes, she thought, as the elevator slid to a liquid-smooth stop. Squaring her shoulders, Kate wore an artificial smile and tried not to bite her lower lip, as the metal door opened with a faint slurring sound.

"Good morning," said a cheerful Adele Vandersagen. Well, Kate thought before she replied, at least she doesn't look like a killer.

Once inside the apartment, Kate was pleased to see the woman Adele called Mina. People don't usually murder their guests before witnesses. And she was grateful too for the freshly-brewed coffee. The morning was cold and windy and she had waited an eternity for a cab. Beneath the soft leather of her boots, she realized she had lost all sensation in her toes. Cold? Fear? Whatever. It was too late to do much except keep an eye on the door for a hurried exit, if need be. One thing, though, Kate thought. Being fired was beginning to seem less frightening.

"Here, let me have your coat. Oh," Adele stopped and stroked the lining. "Sealskin, and on the inside. Great idea. You can keep warm without alerting all the crazies with paint cans. She held up the coat and admired the silken outer shell, cut like a raincoat; at first glance, very casual, but to someone who understood clothes, a luxurious solution to the problem of keeping warm through a New York Autumn and Winter.

"Avi made me buy it two years ago. I love it. And, it's really very practical."

"Of course, Avi Ginzburg. I remember the week he was killed. It must of have been awful for you. To lose him like that. So suddenly." She stopped.

"Um, yes." Kate felt that nothing she could say would be adequate. After all, Adele's husband had been murdered too. Was she really mourning? If she had killed Jim, she couldn't be suffering too terribly, could she?

To cover her confusion, Kate made polite conversation. "It's so hard, isn't it?" She knew she sounded like a lame brain, but there were mice running around on a tiny Ferris wheel somewhere inside her head.

Adele led her guest from the entry into the living room where the glowing colors of the trees in Central Park turned each French door into a panel of brilliant color.

Kate said, "I've got a view from the other side of the park. Aren't the colors spectacular this year?"

"They sure are. I suppose one good rainstorm will shake all the leaves loose and then New York'll put on its Winter coat. Can't say I'm looking forward to it."

"No, Winter here really isn't too great, I agree. But then, we've got so many things going on, and they're all indoors. That's how I cope. I go to the theater and the opera and the ballet." Kate realized she had been speaking too fast and slowed down a bit to conceal her anxiety.

Adele led Kate back toward a sofa and gestured for her to sit. "That's it, lots of light and color. Opening nights, all that stuff. Jim just loves, I mean loved it."

"I am so sorry. Jim was very special to me too. He's the reason I'm doing the show. Or he was, I mean…"

"Well, we're both widows, and at least you understand. Of course, in my case, it's not quite the same is it?"

"How do you mean?" Kate was still sitting at the very edge of the sofa, with her full woolen skirt falling to the floor as she leaned forward.

"Well, surely you know that Lieutenant Quinn thinks I'm a suspect."

"Does he?" Kate was sure her voice was cracking like that of a teenage boy whose register keeps changing.

"Of course. Everybody at the studio heard the little spat we had that morning in the Green Room, so naturally, I'm supposed to have killed my husband. Isn't that ridiculous?"

Not to me, thought Kate. "Do you have any idea of who it was who might have done it?"

"Oh, God, if I had, don't you think I would have told the cop?" She took a sip of her coffee and indicated that Kate should help herself to cream and sugar. "Breakfast will be here in a few minutes. Croissants and jam okay with you?"

"Fine." Kate tasted the coffee. Delicious, pure Colombian she was sure.

"So, you haven't asked me yet. Aren't you curious about why I brought you up here this morning?"

"Well, naturally, I..."

"Look, before we go any further, let me set your mind at rest. I know you must be worrying about the things I said to Jim that day in Green Room. Whatever else you've heard about me, and I'll bet it's plenty, only one thing is true. I've got a bad temper and a big mouth. And that kind of thing can get a woman in a lot of trouble. I know. But you need to understand where I was coming from."

Kate was silent.

"I don't know now, and I didn't know then, what, if anything was going on between you and Jim. But I'll admit I suspected...well, I suspected the worst. Not because of you, or who you are. But because of Jim. I've put up with his infidelities for a lot of years. Mostly, it was because I loved him, but partly too, because my business interests are so tightly bound with his, that there was no way I was going to let him slip away. I know that sounds greedy and self-serving, but the fact is, my marriage to Jim was more of an *alliance*, in the sense that the French use the term.

"You see, my dowry, to use a really old-fashioned word, was why Jim married me in the first place. Oh, sure I was nuts about him, but it was my Daddy who finally made the choice. Understand, I wouldn't have married someone I didn't love just to please my Daddy. But, on the other hand, my Daddy was not about to let me marry some dude without anything to bring to the table. You following me?"

"I think so. But I was married on a beach, in a red dress and we didn't have any money in the bank."

Adele laughed. "Oh a real hippie wedding, was it?"

"Yeah. We used to believe you could live without money."

"I can't say I ever believed anything quite so romantic. You must have been very much in love."

Suddenly, to Kate's utter dismay, she began to cry. She knew it was not just grief over Avi's death. It must have been something more immediate, a relaxation of the tension which had been building since Adele's early call and that she no longer felt afraid.

"Here," Adele said, handing her a box of tissues. "I sure hope I don't affect everybody like that. Mostly, I irritate people."

Kate laughed just as suddenly as she had cried. "Funny, I always thought that was my problem."

"Well, I think it's because we're both women with minds and that, in itself irritates people. Anyway, to get back to Jim and you, what I was really wondering was....This isn't as easy as it looks. How in hell do I ask a woman whether or not she was sleeping with my husband? Well, that is the question. Were you?"

"Was I what?" Kate had been blowing her nose.

"What I mean is, I never could figure out what was going on with you and him. It wasn't like the other women. Some of them were real bimbos—no problem there—others were harder to figure. Then there was you. Right after you started the show and Avi was killed, there were times when Jim never stopped talking about you. It was "Kate" this and "Kate" that, until I was sure he was going to ask me for a divorce. So that's why I'm asking, what exactly was going on between you and Jim?"

"It's hard to explain, but I'll try. You see, when Jim bought the Boston station and it became a JGV affiliate, that just happened to coincide with Avi going to the *Times*. At that point, since we were moving to New York, Jim asked Avi to do the Sunday show. He had caught my interview segments on the Boston station and said he had an idea about a similar show for the network, was I interested? *Was I?*"

"All I had been worrying about was moving back to New York and having nothing to do all day but watch my mother on the soaps. Ugh! So the ...*Home*...show was like a life-preserver for me. And I loved Jim's determination to keep it wholesome, and not celebrity-focused, instead of trying to compete with Geraldo, Rosie and Oprah. He thought the market was saturated with gut-wrenching issues on talk shows and people doing flack work for their latest books and movies. He wanted to give them information. Why am I telling you all this?. You probably know that, don't you?"

"Oh sure," Adele said. "In fact, it was my idea originally. But, go on.

"Well, you know how well the show did. I swear, I've never been happier in my life. The kids were grown. Dee Dee had just started her freshman year at U.Conn., Joel was doing splendidly, and I was so busy, what with the show and the new apartment. Life was almost too perfect."

"That's when, as my Daddy would have said, 'the snake comes up outta the grass and bites you in the ass.'"

"Yeah. That's about right. I'd taped about eight shows, so when Avi died, I was able to take time out to do all the horrible things you have to do." She stopped.

"I know," Adele said. I think funerals are important though. They give you something you absolutely have to focus on. You've got to get it together and organize things. The only alternative is to let someone else do it, and, if you're like me, you just couldn't let another person arrange your husband's funeral."

"True. And it gave me and the kids all that stuff to work out, with very little time to just sit and cry. Oh, you cry alright, but, well...you do understand."

"What about you and Jim, later, I mean?"

"Well, he was just about the kindest, dearest boss anybody could have. We went into reruns two weeks early, so I'd have more time. And he'd call practically every day. Then he'd take me to lunch or dinner when he was in town. I'd started to depend on him the way I used to on Avi, or, when I was a little kid, my father."

"Is that the way you felt about him, like a daughter? No other feelings?"

"At first, yes. But later, well, I have to be honest with you. I must have been starting to feel different. Understand, I'm not a home wrecker and I never had designs on Jim. You've got to believe that. But, yes, naturally, well... I think I was beginning to fall in love with him. I don't know for sure what I was feeling, but he had begun to be very important to me. I never told anybody, mostly because I wasn't sure myself."

"You know, of course, that he and your mother once had a steamy love affair; up on Cape Cod, at that first Summer theater. You knew that, didn't you?"

Kate's face grew the ash-white color of the bone china coffee cup. Adele read the shock and consternation that not even a well-trained actress could hide. And Kate was a TV journalist who had never been an actress. She thought, Kate must know something else, probably more specific than mere rumors about her mother and Jim. Adele had believed that the affair was common knowledge. Now she wasn't sure. And she was remorseful at having blundered into uncharted territory, putting Kate into near-panic. Was it possible that she didn't know the story about her mother and Jim?

Hearing Adele's matter-of-fact reference, Kate experienced, once again, the visceral sensation that comes upon learning something utterly inconceivable, that will forever after change your life. She was silent for a full fifteen seconds before she spoke again. And Adele, who realized she had unwittingly tapped into Kate's most private, inner thoughts, waited without saying a word.

"Yes, or rather no, not until my mother went crazy the night she saw us in Sardi's."

"What do you mean?"

Kate described the night when she had wrestled with the idea of starting something more serious than platonic friendship with Jim. That night in Sardi's, having drunk two superbly-mixed Manhattans, she decided to plunge ahead. After nearly two years of widowhood, Kate was achingly ready for what is politely termed, *romance*. In fact, she was falling in love, or so it seemed as the sexual magnet of Jim Vandersagen manifested itself, despite his age—sixty-five wasn't old for a man like Jim. Boldly, she was stroking his knee, something she had not dared before. And she whispered into his ear, "Haven't you ever thought about taking me along on one of your sailing trips? We could go to the Bahamas and..."

Before Jim could respond, Maureen saw her daughter's face. It was quite simply, the face of a young woman who was bent on seduction. That was the moment when Maureen got up and soon left the restauran, in a state of extreme agitation. And Kate, having watched as her mother turned pale and left the table, knew that something was terribly wrong. She started to go after her, but Jim said, "Don't."

To Adele, she explained, "I was about to find out why he stopped me. But first, let me set your mind at rest. Except for that momentary lapse of my own good judgment, there was never anything between Jim and me except very warm friendship.

When he saw my mother walk out like that, Jim decided to tell me the truth about why he had been so interested in me. What he told me was something that stopped me dead in my tracks. Of course, I was embarrassed at having behaved like such a bitch-in-heat, but there was more to it than that."

Adele waited, fascinated and even a bit afraid of what she would hear next.

Kate began to tell the story slowly, at first unable to defend against a freshet of tears. "It was only three weeks before he died, and I never really got a chance to tell him how much I cared about him." She mopped her face with the Kleenex Adele gave her, then she went on.

"First, I want to repeat what I said before. I never slept with your husband." She suddenly stopped and asked, "But how did you know that my mother and Jim once had an affair? Until that night I had never heard anybody say a word about it."

Adele's response was delayed while she poured more coffee.

"Naturally, you wouldn't. People don't tell daughters about their mothers' sex lives. And it was a long time ago anyway. But in my case it was just another fact. You see, before my Daddy would let me marry Jim, he had him investigated. I mean, he knew everything about him including his shoe size and how many fillings he had in his teeth. Then, to complete the picture, he had a psychologist draw up a profile of Jim Vandersagen, so Daddy knew things about him, maybe Jim didn't even know about himself."

"So, of course, you knew about my mother?"

"Oh, God, not just your mother, but a hundred other girls as well, both in and out of his marriage to the cucumber princess?"

"You mean his first wife?"

"Yeah. If a woman were married to a man for twenty-five years, she probably wouldn't know as much as I did before I married Jim. I knew about the girls, the rumors that he ran off with profits from the Cape Cod theater. They weren't true, by the way. The Playhouse just lost money and that partner of his, Macklin? Yeah, well, he had mortgaged that property to the hilt and when the theater project went bust, the guy just lost everything. But almost all the other rumors you heard about Jim were true—the womanizing, the not-so-honest business dealings, everything."

"And, knowing all that, you married him anyway?"

"Well, as I said, I was crazy in love with the guy."

Chapter Twelve

Sister Maria Patrice, dressed in old, worn jeans and a grey sweatshirt was helping Maureen restore order to the house left in disarray by the burglars. The living room bore mute evidence to the systematic looting. The two friends worked in no particular pattern as they attempted to restore the room to a semblance of its normal order, though they hurried as if to erase completely all evidence of the violation.

"They sure didn't miss much, did they?" Carla was picking up books, their pages opened as if the volumes had been shaken in a search for hidden papers or cash. "Remember when we were kids and we used to find things in the pages of books from the library? I once found a five-dollar bill."

"Yeah," Maureen said, "and your mother made you take it back to the library."

"That's probably why I wound up becoming a nun. My family was very keen on keeping to the moral high ground." She sneezed. "Whew! I think those guys did you a favor. How long has it been since these things were dusted?"

"My God, I don't know. Probably not since before my mother left for Boston. No, not that long, but I wouldn't be surprised if the last time I touched them was four or five years ago. Kate's right. This place has outlived its usefulness in my life. It's time to pare down to the essentials and move to a smaller place. I hardly spend any time here anyway, except to sleep."

"But you loved this house, didn't you? You and Tom had to scrimp and struggle to get it. And what about Kate? Doesn't she want the place?"

No, Kate's a city person. She had enough of the suburbs when her own kids were little. She always hated the fact that she had to drive so far from North Andover whenever she wanted to go into Boston. She's right, Carla. I'm going to sell it and put it all behind me."

"All the memories too? Even for me, this house has special meaning. I never told you, but when I was a young nun and got that first job teaching in New Rochelle, I was so miserable, I don't think I would have been able to hold out, except for the fact that you were living so close by. Being able to come here when I could get some time off probably saved my sanity."

"I had no idea. I thought you loved being a nun. I used to envy you because I thought you had figured out the secret of living simply. I would tell myself the key to happiness was simplicity. My life was such a rash of work and being a mother, to say nothing of being a daughter. And, until Tom left, I was trying to be a model wife as well." She stopped, rueful. "As I recall, I wasn't terribly good at any of them either."

"Well, it wasn't all bad was it? I remember having some incredible laughs here, especially when your mother was still around." Carla stood and brushed her dusty hands on her jeans. "Remember when she was getting ready to become a citizen, and we spent that weekend rehearsing her?"

"Which one is Washington, the one with the beard and the Hat?" Deirdre could never distinguish between Lincoln and Washington.

"No," nine year-old Kate had said, "that's Lincoln. Washington is the one with the white hair. Remember, Gran, white for Washington and, for Lincoln..." She struggled for a mnemonic and finally offered something she hoped would work. "Try *Blackguard*, that what they called him in the South. I learned it in school."

"Blackguard. What a terrible thing to say about a president!" Deirdre had become a patriot in light of her pending citizenship, though she remained as confused as ever.

"Sure, Black, like Abe Lincoln's Hat."

"Deirdre tried again to distinguish between the two presidents. "White hair Washington; Black hat Lincoln. Why on earth do ye have to know that to be a citizen? I've lived all this time without bein' one. Maybe I ought to just ferget the whole idea. Why is it so important anyway? With all them judges askin' questions."

"Because," Maureen urged. "We want you to be able to vote for John Kennedy. Imagine, Ma, an Irishman for President of the United States!"

It was an idea that spurred Deirdre to new effort. She wanted passionately to be able to vote in the next election.

"And, remember, how she kept telling me I should study too, so I could vote?" Carla laughed. "I couldn't convince her that I was born in America."

"Yeah, my mother thought with a name like yours, you couldn't possibly be a citizen without going through the process. God, Carla, sometimes, I miss her terribly."

"The way you two used to fight, I find that hard to believe."

"I know. But it's true, I think about her every day. Especially the way she was about this house. She was so proud, she kept it so clean and beautiful, especially the garden. Do you remember her roses?"

The two women made lunch, and finished it quickly. But they lingered over their coffee.

Then Maureen asked, "Carla, are you absolutely certain about this? Leaving the Order, I mean?"

"It shocks you, doesn't it? The idea of a nun giving it up and going back to the world. But, believe me, if you were to look at the statistics, you'd be amazed at how many nuns are doing exactly that. The world is changing, the schools are changing. Everything's changing except the orthodoxy of the Church. But, in fact, even that will have to change ultimately. I won't go on about it, boring you, but I told you to think of me the way you would any other woman who decided late in life to leave a marriage."

"But, what worries me is, will you still be a Catholic?"

"Maureen, sweetie, I don't know whether I'm a Catholic right now, while I'm still, officially a nun. I don't even know what a Catholic is supposed to be." Carla blew her nose with a wad of Kleenex.

"It's hard, isn't it? But, you still know right from wrong. You still know what's sinful and what isn't. You're not confused about those things are you?"

Carla searched for ways to explain her doubts and the conclusions she had reached while wrestling with the decision she had made. "I don't think I can explain it, at least not in so many words. I've read a lot of books written by women religious who have passed through these same doorways, and I'm still not sure that what I'm doing is the right thing. All I know is I gotta do it." She stood and gathered dishes and cups. "And don't forget, my family is going to want an explanation too, and I don't think I have any idea of what to say to them."

"Well," Maureen hurried to reassure her friend. "Whatever you do, you'll still have me on your side." They hugged and Maureen was silent; so was Carla. It was a long moment before either dared speak.

Maureen broke the silence. "Maybe you should try my mother's little trick. You know the one, with Saint Peter?"

Carla laughed. "I remember vaguely. Isn't that where you put the statue of Saint Peter in a room, facing the wall, until you get the thing you've been praying for."

"That's right. But, remember, you must not turn his face *into* the room, or it will never happen.

"How many days does the poor guy have to stay that way? Was it nine days, or something like that?"

"No, nine days; you're thinking of a *Novena*. That's to the Holy Mother." Maureen was laughing now.

Carla played the game. "Are you trying to tell me Saint Peter's more powerful than the Holy Mother?"

Maureen was time-shifted into school where she and Carla had begun their explorations into the arcane world of saints and supplication. Maureen explained. "He's not more powerful, just different. But Saint Peter, with his face to the wall; that's not something you should do every day. It's got to be for something really special."

"Like what?"

"Like when my mother was trying to save money for a trip to Ireland and I needed six fillings in my teeth."

"Well, you were lucky she had the money for the fillings, never mind the trip. We'd better get back to work. Saint Peter, facing the wall or not, isn't going to get this place put in shape for the real estate lady to start showing it to prospective buyers."

Irving Quinn rang Kate's house and got her answering machine with its brief, almost rude message. "I'm busy now, but I'll get back to you as soon as I can." *Beep*

"It's Quinn, Irving. I've been trying to reach you since early this morning. Call me at the precinct." He wanted to say something soft, sexy maybe, the kind of things people say when they aren't sitting at a cluttered desk in a New York City Police Department cubbyhole of an office.

Quinn looked around and through the glass that separated him from the crowded room of desks with busy cops telephoning, using computers, interviewing and, of course, drinking coffee. He knew his people were whispering about how the boss was going to lose a few nuts and bolts with all that jasmine tea. He was restless, not getting anywhere and he knew the Captain would soon start pressuring him to shelve the Vandersagen murder case and start working on others in the pipeline.

Heads turned as Irving Quinn opened his door and went to the coffee station and poured himself a cup. He could almost hear them thinking, that's more like it.

Someone shouted that there was a Maureen Cassidy who wanted to speak to him. He turned back toward his office, managing to spill only a few drops of coffee on the nondescript floor where it would hardly be noticed.

Quickly, Maureen described the scene with a list of items stolen. She said, "I know this will sound silly, but I can't help wondering if there's any connection between this and that other thing—you know, the, uhm, the accident."

"Mrs. Cassidy, there was no accident. It was a homicide." Then afraid, he had been rude, he said, "I'm sorry to hear that your house was broken into. I know it must be a terrible shock to you. You say, there were newspapers and mail accumulating. That's like a red flag to burglars. I'm really sorry you had to find out this way." Then he continued. "Do your local police have any ideas?"

"Not a clue, as far as I can see. But, Lieutenant, I'm really worried about Kate. How do I know they weren't here looking for her, or for something that belongs to her. Do you think I'm being paranoid?"

"God, no. Your house has been burglarized. You say it was turned inside out. Sure, it could have been nothing more than a coincidence, but I wouldn't rule out a connection. Trouble is, I can't quite put it together yet. Not at this point, anyway." They ended the call with promises to keep in touch if anything should develop.

Lieutenant Irving Quinn had what he thought of as a secret vice. He liked to read, or at least, peruse, the *New York Daily News*. His sense of guilt was a legacy of his English teacher-mother who believed the tabloid, as journalism, was not only lowbrow, but probably, corrupting to the mind. He remembered that his father sometimes sneaked a copy into the house, concealing it under his uniform coat. Then, father and son would go down to the basement to read the sports pages before they tore them to bits and buried them beneath the garbage at the very bottom of the can.

Years later, during the early years of his wife's fashion design career, it was important to scan the so-called bibles, *Women's Wear*, *The News* and other print media for mention of who had worn what; created by which designer. One's name in a major column, for example, could mean that a young dress designer's career was launched and steaming forward to success. A Suzy mention meant she had arrived. The first time Donna Quinn's name appeared in the Suzy column, Irving took her to the fanciest restaurant on Long Island to celebrate her triumph.

It was no flash in the dress dummy's pan. As Donna rose to the heights on Seventh and Fifth Avenues, her husband, an NYPD sergeant then, had two choices. He could remain obscure and become known as Mr. Donna Quinn, or he could study and take the exam for Lieutenant, with an eye to further career development—Captain maybe, or even Commissioner. Or, he could quit and go to law school.

Periodically, Donna would suggest law school. Finally, he exploded. "I'm a cop. I like being a cop. I don't want to go to law school so you can tell everybody your husband's an attorney. Cop was good enough for my father and it's good enough for me!" He left, slamming the door—the first time in their marriage—not the last.

Despite the divorce, his habit of looking for Donna's name in the gossip columns had not disappeared. Must be like smoking, he thought. This morning, as always, he looked briefly at all the city papers that were routinely delivered to the precinct. The Captain considered newspapers one information tool that had not yet been replaced by computers.

Today, after looking at the sports section, he glanced at the front page—another shooting in the Bronx. Then he flipped to the entertainment and gossip writers. There, buried in the middle of one column, he read the item: "Tom Cassidy, the director, lunched at the Four Seasons with Wendell Carson. Must have been listening to the writer pitching a story. We didn't see who bought lunch."

Quinn carefully folded the paper and added it to the pile near the coffee pot where Jonah Smith was filling his cup. "Want some? Jonah asked.

"No, thanks. Say, didn't you and Alex tell me that Tom Cassidy hadn't left the Waldorf all day yesterday?"

"Yeah, as far as I know. We've kept the lobby elevators covered as well as all the doors. He never left the hotel."

"I wouldn't be too sure of that. You got the direct-dial number for the manager? Whatsis name? Webber?"

"Yeah, Fred Webber. Here it is." Smith had punched it up on the computer, in a name, address and telephone log for the Vandersagen case. "Sure beats lookin' through a rolodex, doesn't it?"

"And it dials the number too, if you ask it?"

"Sure," said Sergeant Smith; he loved that machine. "Watch. All it takes is a coupla key strokes. See?"

"I'll pick it up at my desk. Line three, right?"

After confirming an appointment with Fred Webber, Quinn walked the seven blocks from the precinct to the Waldorf, fighting against a typical late Fall wind that made New York feel as cold as he imagined Moscow would be. Why, he thought, must the great cities of the world have such terrible weather? Donna had taken him to Paris the year Saks Fifth Avenue opened a Donna Quinn boutique and it had rained and snowed the entire week.

Well, at least, he thought, this isn't Paris. Irving Quinn, was one of those New Yorkers who knew he could never be happy in any other city, another reason, he remembered, that prompted Donna's demand for a divorce. She wanted to buy a second home in the South of France and Irving had furiously refused saying, "Godammit, I don't make enough money for us to have a second house—not even a shack in Maine."

With Donna's cool reminder that she had enough money, he abruptly walked out of the house in Great Neck. Donna filed for divorce six months later. Since then, he had been happily living in a creaking old building on the West Side, complete with rats the size of house cats. The promotion to Lieutenant, at least, meant he could move to better quarters. That is, if he ever got the time to go apartment hunting. He made a mental note to check out a decent building not far from the precinct house.

He wondered whether or not Kate had a secret wish to live in France. He hoped not. Then, as he reached Park Avenue and the Waldorf loomed ahead, Irving Quinn redirected his thoughts to the matter at hand, investigating the mysterious movements of one Tom Cassidy. He hurried forward, his head thrust into the collar of his Burberry, wishing he hadn't been too macho to put in the wool liner. He stopped for a moment for a word with the undercover cop in the lobby and then went directly to the manager's office.

Fred Webber, the urbane, multi-lingual manager of the Waldorf greeted the lieutenant with hot coffee in a silver pot. It was infinitely better than the sludgy brew he was accustomed to at the precinct.

"So, you say that Mr. Cassidy sometimes comes and goes by way of the employees door?"

"Oh yes, many of our guests do that in order to avoid the public and the press."

"But we have a man on the employees' door, and he wasn't seen. Is there another way in or out?"

"There are several. One, through the basement, opens out into the next block, though that one is usually not known to our ordinary guests."

"What do you mean? Isn't Cassidy an ordinary guest?"

"Of course, but he's one of the few who once worked here as a bellboy. He still keeps some of his things down there in the locker room."

"Does he rent that locker from you? Do you have access to it?"

"No, he doesn't rent it. It's hotel property. We just let him use it as a courtesy."

"Then you won't mind if I go down there and examine it, will you?"

At the Waldorf Towers apartment, Kate Cassidy and Adele Vandersagen had finished breakfast and a long, intimate talk about Jim, each woman with a different perspective about him. When they were finished, the coffee table was strewn with crumpled Kleenex.

Then they were through. It was as if they had held a private service for him. The spirit of Jim Vandersagen was finally laid to rest by the last two women to whom he had been most closely bound.

Following Adele into the bedroom seemed perfectly natural. "Come on in and we'll talk while I get dressed." They were like two close friends who had known one another for years. Strange, Kate thought. She didn't usually make friends so quickly. Adele slipped off the light caftan she had been wearing to reveal a beautifully embroidered slip. "I'm almost ready, but I gotta put my face on first."

Putting the finishing touches to her *toilette*, Adele continued to explain. "I've been living like a hermit ever since Jim's funeral. The phone hasn't exactly been ringing off the hook either. Not that I've ever had that many friends in New York. But still....I wonder if they're avoiding me."

"Nonsense," Kate said. They're doing what people always do when a woman's husband dies. They get this crazy idea that she doesn't want to be disturbed. After Avi was buried and the kids went back to school, I even had that problem with my own mother. I thought I'd go nuts trying to convince her and my friends that what I wanted the most was to be with people and out, doing things and going places. Otherwise, you just sit and brood. You're not going to do that, are you?"

"I'm going to try not to," Adele said getting up from the dressing table and crossing to the closet. Kate, wishing to change the subject to something more cheerful, asked, "What's it like in Texas? Do they have fancy private schools for millionaire's daughters?"

"They do, sure. But my Daddy wasn't any millionaire, at least not while I was a kid. He didn't get rich until I was in college. So I went to the public school in the suburb where we lived, outside of Dallas. And I did what every good-looking girl does in high school in Texas, if she's lucky enough..."

Kate was laughing now and interrupted, "You became a cheerleader, right?"

"How did you know?"

"My God, Adele, don't you watch television? They had that show about the mother who tried to murder the other kid or the kid's mother, so *her* daughter could get on the team. I hear the competition is fierce."

"Yeah, it is. But can you imagine anything more stupid, dressing up like baby whores and jumpin' around while a bunch of hormone-loaded teenage boys go out and get themselves nearly killed, with broken bones, playing a game that's too hard even for professionals."

"You're from Texas and you're knocking football? You could get your citizenship revoked for that, you know."

"Not really. I'm telling you this in the confines of my apartment and it's your death warrant if you tell anyone." She went to the desk and rummaged through some papers.

"We've talked about everything except what I asked you up here for." She held up a piece of paper that she had taken from a manila folder. "Ah, here it is." She handed it to Kate. "Read it. I've got to go to the to the bathroom before I leave."

Sitting on the bed, Kate read the document which carefully spelled out a renewed option for her to do the show for another three years. She could see no equivocation, no hedging, nothing that looked like a trap.

Adele stayed in the bathroom an inordinately long time, enough, Kate thought, for her the read the document word for word. She reappeared soundlessly, leaving the door behind her unlatched. Kate was startled, as Adele spoke. "Now, there it is all spelled out." She gestured toward the renewed option with her own signature in all the proper places. "All you have to do is sign it at the red X and you can do the show for another three years, if the ratings hold up. Your lawyer can check it out and have me reword it, but I need this one today."

Kate was finishing the last paragraph. The language was straightforward without many terms in legalese, and now, after her third reading, she was satisfied. "You said, on the phone, you wanted something in return. What was it?"

"Not very much, believe me. First of all, how many shares of JGV do you have?"

"I don't know exactly. There were the ones in Avi's profit-sharing deal and we bought some too. And, of course, I've got some through profit-sharing as well."

"Would you say you've got more than three thousand?"

Kate thought a minute. "Probably more like five. Why?"

"Because, that's the favor I want. I need your proxy so that, if I've played my cards right, I'm going to have enough votes to consolidate my position as Chairman. Excuse me, I mean chairperson."

"But I thought you already had enough votes or shares or whatever, with Jim's, uh, the stuff he left you."

"I thought so too, but that was before I heard from Jim's son, James, Junior. It seems, the little prince wants to leave his home in Europe permanently and replace his father as chairman of the board."

"Just like that?" Kate snapped her fingers.

"Yeah. I'm sure his mother put him up to it. In the first place, he hardly knows zip about the telecommunications business and even less about how it works in America. He's been living in France since he was ten years old."

"Are you sure there's going to be a battle? Maybe all he wants is a job."

"You know, Jim was right. You are too sweet and too innocent. Look, when somebody who has never even shown his face in the office before his father's death, suddenly shows up the day after the funeral, telling me he expects to take an active part in the business, that raises my hackles. I'm like a mountain lion. I'm always alert and I can smell danger. Believe me, I know something's up. I'm pretty sure, though, between your shares and everything in the Kenyon camp, I can beat the little coyote cub at his own game."

"Well, sure. If that's what you want the proxy for, I have no problem with that. Where do I sign?"

"I've got proxy forms at the office. You can ride down in the taxi with me, and sign them before the meeting starts." Still in her slip, she went to the closet and quickly selected something to wear. She held up a subdued, but beautifully cut, wool crepe, teal blue suit with silver buttons. "Do you like this outfit? It's got a matching wool cape trimmed in gray fox."

Kate was genuinely impressed. "It's gorgeous." She said.

"I suppose people keep expecting me to show up in buckskins and fringes, but, frankly, I like pretty clothes. I just wish I were as tall as you are so I could wear those great big hats. I think a big hat makes people sit up and take notice, don't you?"

"I don't know," Kate was honest. The only hat I own is a Russian fur thing I only wear in the dead of Winter, when you can't stay outside unless you've got your head covered."

"Well, I think you're making a mistake. You've got the figure for it. You're thin and tall and you'd look terrific in something sweeping and dramatic."

Adele, hatless, settled the cape over her shoulders, letting the fox trim fall in a perfect vertical to her knees. There was no fur at the hem and the suit skirt was just visible two inches below the bottom of the cape. Dark stockings, and shoes in the same color as the suit, effectively masked the fact that Adele was neither very tall, nor very thin. But, her neck was long and her hair was cut short to emphasize its length. The reddish blonde color was so skillfully done that one hardly realized it covered her natural color, medium brown with gray streaks. Altogether, Adele Vandersagen looked the very model of a woman of means, endowed with the brains and skill to take an active part in a complex business rather than just be a silent stockholder.

Kate, with her blonde hair in far from perfect order, felt at a slight disadvantage compared with Adele. She sensed Kate's discomfort. "Here, use this, though, unless you want some hair spray, the wind's going to blow your hair about anyway." She offered a hairbrush.

"Thanks," said Kate. She thought, and you were afraid she was going to hurt you? Adele Vandersagen may indeed have been short-tempered—that was something she could understand, having lived with Maureen and Deirdre. But Kate felt completely at ease, like a schoolgirl getting ready, with a friend, for some kind of adventure.

"Well, we're actually early." Adele said. "I guess I must be more anxious about this board meeting than I realized. I have to admit, getting that call from young Jim, Junior really got my blood up. He hardly said word one to me at his old man's funeral, but there's nothing shy about him when it comes to wanting to step into his shoes."

Kate refrained from comment. She hadn't seen Jim's sons at the funeral, nor would she have recognized them. There were so many people attending the services at the huge church on Park Avenue that, despite seating for several hundred people, the place was packed with standees. Kate was lucky enough to be seated in a pew at the rear.

Given the press of mourners, it was no surprise that Kate did not remember anyone in particular. Unless one had been specifically looking for Jim's son, he would have been indistinguishable from the dozens of men, dressed in dark suits, who sat in the front pews. The son must have been very near the open casket containing the perfectly embalmed body of Jim Vandersagen. The best funeral director in New York had skillfully concealed the fact of Jim's broken neck. And the makeup was so well applied, those who looked at it had all agreed, "He looks as if he's asleep." As Irving Quinn observed the visitors one by one, stepping up to view the corpse, he made a mental note that even the rich and famous must rely on clichés to help them bear up under the strain of confronting death which neither riches nor fame had spared one of their own.

Kate had deliberately chosen to sit near the door, in the last row, because she was still feeling the effects of her injuries and wanted to be able to beat a hasty retreat. When the service was over, Irving Quinn had sat down beside her. Her head was reeling and she was near to passing out in the overheated church. Quinn swiftly led her to the vestibule where he turned her over to Jonah Smith, saying, "Put her in a cab." He turned to go back inside, but not before squeezing her good arm, saying softly, "I'll call you later."

Adele snapped her fingers before Kate's face. "Hey, wake up. I know there are better places than here, but...."

Kate was doing a lot of that—drifting off in the middle of something to think about encounters with Irving Quinn. She didn't need a psychiatrist to explain the reason.

"You're more than welcome to join me at the board meeting, if you want to see how all this is going to play out." Adele checked the contents of a black leather briefcase that was the essence of understatement. Kate guessed it would have a price tag in the thousand-dollar range. Mmm, she thought, like my coat. You only realize it's expensive when you examine it closely. Adele's gloves and handbag, also black, gave off the same air of unostentatious luxury.

Kate remembered when she was in high school, how Maureen had taken her shopping to teach her the subtleties of quality that made high-priced clothing and accessories worth the expense. That was long before her mother could more than nibble around the edges of buying them. But Kate was not an apt pupil in any case. By the time Maureen was earning a star's salary, and could afford fine clothes for her daughter, Kate was in college. It was the seventies and she was in the vanguard, looking like a beggar when rags and the look of poverty were all the rage.

Kate remembered how it infuriated Maureen when she would show up in Larchmont on weekends, wearing dirty, torn jeans, no bra and unironed shirts. Filthy sandaled feet were the final break in Maureen's resolve not to carp at her. Even Deirdre had found it difficult to defend her. Well, Kate thought now, I am learning to enjoy spending money, though she realized she would never need or want to match Adele Vandersagen in the pursuit of luxury.

"I don't think I'll stay at the meeting with you, but I will sign the papers first. Then I want to come back here and pick up my father for lunch. Is it okay if I call him before we leave?"

Adele said, "Sure, use the phone in there." She pointed to the door to another bedroom, a twin of the one where Adele had been dressing.

The room was well-decorated in the style Kate thought of as *safe*. There was nothing particularly beautiful about it, but she could see, it would be soothing for sleep or late-night television-viewing. It was not unlike the bedroom she and Avi had shared. The phone, a standard Waldorf house model was beside the bed. She sat down and realized the phone line was not linked to the switchboard. She had to dial the hotel's number first, then ask for her father's room. Aloud, she said "Come on, Daddy. Pick it up. You said you were going to wait for my call this morning. Please, Daddy, you promised." Frustrated, she slammed down the instrument harder than she intended.

In the doorway to the living room where Adele waited, Kate crossed to where she had left her purse. "I'm afraid he doesn't answer." Silently, she prayed that Tom had not gone out to lose himself in one of the city's thousands of bars.

Kate accepted her coat from the closet, handed to her by Mina who had appeared silently. "Adele, you said you're early. Would you mind terribly, if I just ran up to my Dad's room. I kinda want to check on him, before we leave the hotel."

"Sure, no problem," Adele said. Kate's anxiety was perfectly understandable, given Tom Cassidy's reputation as a lush. Painfully, she remembered her own worries as a teenager when her mother, Betty Kenyon, had taken to her room for hours and days, just herself and the booze. God, she thought, we were so lucky my Mamma died like a heroine, falling from a horse, instead of in some institution where Daddy said she belonged. Abner Kenyon was climbing socially and he was not about to let his wife's love affair with the bottle stand in his way.

"I'll just stop at the desk." Kate seemed unembarrassed. "They'll let me in. I've had to do it before when, you know...." She didn't explain. Having shared so many intimacies, she was feeling very positive about Adele Vandersagen—she had a new friend.

The women went out into the vestibule. The elevator cab was in the same position as it had been when Kate arrived nearly three hours earlier. Its sliding door was closed. "I can't believe we've had such a nice visit," Adele said, pushing the button to open the door.

"Yeah, look at the time. It's almost noon."

"Go on," Adele said, making a sweeping hand gesture to indicate that Kate should enter the elevator before her. She waited in the rear of the cab, expecting Adele to follow. But Mina opened the apartment door. "Mrs. Vandersagen. There's a call for you. It's your lawyer."

"Oh," said Adele. "I've got to talk to him. You go ahead and check on your father. I'll wait for you in the lobby. If there's any real delay, you can page me. Okay?"

"Okay," said Kate, stepping into the elevator. She pushed the button marked *Down*.

The door slid shut as silently as it had opened. The motor started to hum and the cab jarred slightly, beginning its descent. Then Kate heard a sound. It was muffled, but she thought it was an explosion of some sort. The elevator car suddenly lurched and began to drop as if in a free-fall. Kate thought, My God, she *is* trying to kill me!

Within seconds, she was thrown against the wall, then, as she tried to keep her footing, the elevator came to a shuddering stop. Her head banged against the waist-high, brass rail and she fell in a heap. She was in great pain—her ribcage hurt, her head was aching—but she was conscious and miraculously, she thought, alive. The elevator had fallen no more than half a dozen feet before it was arrested by the safety device that had been standard on American-made elevators since before the middle of the twentieth century.

Gingerly, breathing shallowly to minimize the pain, Kate got to her feet. The lights had gone out, leaving only a small, red emergency lamp which cast an eerie glow in the tiny space. She looked through the diamond-shaped window and saw a most depressing sight, a dark brick wall. She was trapped.

Like most people in a similar situation, she panicked. Then she stopped and fought for calm and clear thinking. She groped among the buttons on the control panel. Was there a small flashlight in her purse? She couldn't remember. In the dim red light, squinting, she could just barely make out the button marked *Emergency*. Good. First she tried pressing it firmly. Nothing. She banged it with her fist. Again, nothing. Then, as her sense of entrapment rose to the level of pure hysteria, she began to scream.

There was no response to Kate's voice. She began to pound the walls of the small container in which she was suspended, hanging, for all she knew, by a thread. If she knew more, she would have been less frightened, but to Kate, who was somewhat claustrophobic in any case, this was becoming a matter of urgency bordering on the absolute edge of sanity.

"Dear God, Holy Mother of Jesus, I've got to get out of here." She remembered all the prayers she had not uttered since Deirdre's funeral, the *Our Fathers* and the *Hail Marys* as well as the *Apostles' Creed* and a few Hebrew prayers Avi had taught her. Then she stopped and, thinking of what she was doing, laughed despite her terror. I guess, she thought, it's true what they say about no atheists in foxholes. Then she banged the walls again and started to scream once more.

This time, she directed her voice to each of the four corners of the car, hoping there might be a way it would carry to someone, somewhere within the labyrinth of the gigantic hotel building.

Within half an hour, though it seemed more like twice that long, she was rewarded by the sound of footsteps over her head. There was someone on the roof of the car. Please God, she thought don't let it be Adele, coming to finish the job.

Above her a square panel opened and she heard something for which she had almost stopped hoping. It was the sound of a man's voice with a distinct New York City accent.

When Kate looked up, she saw a large head, made larger still by the NYFD fireman's helmet it bore. The head said, "Don't worry, lady, we'll have you otta there in a coupla minutes. You awright? Ya wanna say something? Please, lady. Answer me. Y'awright?

Kate was so relieved, she could only nod. Finally, the fireman beamed his powerful flashlight at her and saw her tear-stained face.

"Yes, yes. I'm alright," she managed to say. "Please, somebody call Lieutenant Quinn. Please." Then she began to cry again.

"We're from the fire department. Now, don't panic." Then the fireman was shouting to someone over his head. Next, she saw him coming down into the cab, feet first. Gracefully, like a cat, despite the heavy canvas coat he wore, the man dropped and stood beside her. With an ax in one hand and the flashlight in the other, he allowed Kate to lean against his shoulder and, awkwardly, but firmly, he held her in his arms as Kate succumbed to the wracking sobs against which she had been fighting during the agonizing wait for rescue. The fireman quickly put her into a harness and she was hoisted upwards, through the opening in the elevator car. Then she was passed through several pairs of hands until she was released in the vestibule of Adele Vandersagen's apartment. The small space was crowded with people and the door to Adele's apartment was ajar. Inside, she could see, standing in a knot, Adele, Alex Karalopulous and mercifully, Irving Quinn.

On unsteady feet, she walked into the room and pointed her finger at Adele. "You! You tried to kill me. It didn't work at the studio, so you thought you'd finish the job here." Then she turn to Quinn, "Irving, arrest this woman for the murder of her husband and for trying to murder me too." She was trying hard not to cry and she saw that her outstretched hand was shaking.

Quinn spoke first. "Kate, you don't understand. Look, you've had a terrible experience. Are you hurt?"

She was furious. "No, dammit. I'm not hurt. And, no thanks to *her* I'm not dead either. Well, aren't you going to arrest her?"

Quinn knew better than to smile. "Kate, you're mistaken. Adele didn't try to kill you. We're here because Adele called us. She called to have you rescued."

"Sure, that's because the ruby slippers didn't work. What should we do, pour water over her and make her disappear? For God's sake, Irving, can't you see what she did? She got me up here, so she could kill me in a disabled elevator. I go to the movies. I know that's the way it's supposed to work."

Adele stepped toward Kate who held out her hand, palm outward. "Don't come any closer, or I swear, I'll tear your eyes out." Now that she was safe again, Kate was angry and she noted with a small degree of satisfaction how her fury frightened Adele who paled and stepped back, saying, "Kate, no. I didn't...."

"Listen, to me, Kate." Quinn had taken her by the shoulders and gently pushed her down into a chair. He turned and took a glass of something that Mina had been holding on a small tray. "Drink that." he ordered.

Kate drank it. It was cognac, something she had never developed a taste for. Funny, she thought, they're still bringing cognac to people in a crisis. Just like the movies. "Just like the movies," she said aloud.

"That's the point," Quinn said. "It's not just like the movies. If this were a movie, you'd be dead."

"What are you talking about? She tried to kill me, didn't she?"

"No, she didn't." Quinn was patient. "When Adele came out to take the elevator, it wasn't working. She said she was going to meet you in the lobby after you checked on your father. Right?"

"Yeah, but she never did, she thought I'd be lying dead at the bottom on the elevator shaft, except it didn't work. Too bad, wasn't it Adele?" Kate glared at her.

"Will you shut up for minute, while I explain." Quinn said it softly.

"Look, that elevator was tampered with alright. There's no question, it was designed to kill somebody this morning, but you're mistaken if you think it was you."

"Why not me? She wasn't expecting anybody else, was she?"

Quinn drew his hand through his graying, but still abundant dark hair. The gesture reminded her of the way Avi would rake his hair with his fingers when he was upset. "Look, I'm trying to explain. Listen, dammit!"

Kate was silent. She took another sip of the cognac—not bad, considering she never drank straight spirits.

"The only person who knew you were coming here today was Adele, right? Not me, not your father, not your mother, not Rudy Macklin, nobody, right?"

Kate nodded.

"Then don't you see? You weren't the intended victim at all. It was Adele. Somebody was trying to kill her, not you. The phone call was one of those unexpected elements. If it hadn't rung when it did, she'd have ridden down in the elevator with you. Then both of you might have been trapped down there together." God knows, he thought, what Kate would have done to Adele in that case—just the two of them, alone together for thirty minutes. He shuddered inwardly.

"But why did she do it? Why did she get me to ride alone and nearly get killed? I don't understand."

Quinn said, "I know you don't, but I think I'm beginning to. Look, are you sure you're alright? I've got to get on with this thing, and I've got to move fast. I'm going to leave you here with Alex. You sure you're okay?"

"Why do you have to leave me here? I don't want to stay in *her* apartment. How do I know she won't try it again."

"Kate," Adele said quietly. Believe me. I did not try to kill you. I don't know anything, I mean anything at all about elevators. How could I have set it up to explode and fall? You've got to understand. Look, do you remember this. You came up here. The elevator was working perfectly, remember?" Kate nodded.

"Okay, then, do you remember my leaving this apartment at any time? If I had tampered with the elevator, when would I have done it? I never left the apartment."

"No, maybe not, except you could have."

"When? When could I have left the apartment, set dynamite or whatever to blow up the elevator cables, and return to pour a second cup of coffee? Tell me that!"

"Well, I went into the bedroom to make a phone call. You could have done it then."

"Oh sure. You were on the phone how long? Two, three minutes? In that time I was supposed to go out, get up to where the cables are, up onto the roof, probably, I don't know. And then I was supposed to find the elevator cables and set dynamite. All in three minutes?"

"You could have pre-set them and just pushed a remote, like with the mirrors in the studio." Kate looked at Alex. who had been watching, fascinated. "Couldn't she, Alex? Wouldn't that be possible?"

Alex was looking distinctly uncomfortable. "Sounds like it makes sense, but the Lieutenant, he said you got nothin' to worry about. She's not the one."

"Easy for you to say," Kate told him. You're not the one who was sitting in a falling-down elevator screaming. And what do you mean, 'she's not the one'? Does he know who is?"

"That's what he said. Told me to keep you here until he calls me."

"Mina," Adele said, "Do you think you can find something for a few sandwiches? If not, I can get something sent up. The service elevators are still working okay, aren't they."

"No, problem, Mrs. Vandersagen." Mina disappeared into the kitchen.

"You mean, there are other elevators?" Kate said. Then she answered her own question. Of course, it's just like my building. We have a service hall for all the apartments on each floor. So, there are elevators that the public never sees." She was still snubbing Adele, not entirely certain of her innocence. "Alex, does that mean that somebody could have come up in the service elevator and got up on the roof or wherever the cables are—all that while Adele and I were in the apartment this morning?"

"Something like that. The boss didn't spell it out. He just wants you to wait here, okay?"

"Adele?" Kate was tentative. "You weren't trying to *kill* me?"

"No, of course not, why should I? But...."

Kate finished the thought. "Someone was trying to kill you then, right?"

Now it was Adele who turned pale. "Why me? Oh I know there's a whole lotta folks that don't like my style. It's a burden you carry when you come East from Texas. But I'm damned if I can think of anybody who dislikes me enough to want to pure kill me" She went across to her favorite spot on the sofa and sat down heavily.

Kate joined her and silently held out the remains of her glass. With a look of puzzled gratitude, Adele took it.

Chapter Thirteen

L<small>IEUTENANT</small> Q<small>UINN</small>, his face set, concentrated upon the task before him. After leaving a somewhat-mollified Kate in the care of Alex, he went back to Fred Webber's office. He put his head in the doorway. "Okay, that's under control, I suppose. Your people said they would have the Vandersagen elevator working as soon as they can assess the damage and get the cables repaired. I'd like to go down to look at that locker now."

Fred Webber had stayed unruffled after the call came with the report of an accident. Even as fire emergency crews rushed up to the Vandersagen elevator to rescue Kate, he had remained cool. Now, with his usual decorum, he listened to Quinn telephoning Jonah Smith, "Yeah. Meet me at the Waldorf. I'll be with Mr. Webber, the manager. His secretary will know where we are. We should be ready to move as soon as we find what we're looking for in that locker room."

Webber, diffident, but deeply concerned about what was going on, asked, "Is it possible for you to tell me exactly what happened to the lady?"

Quinn realized that when he got the call during his meeting with Fred Webber, he had raced out of his office and gone up to Adele's apartment without much of an explanation.

"They told you there was an elevator accident?" Quinn said.

"Yes, I knew that. And the Fire Department explained that the lady was rescued and in good condition. But, I don't understand. The maintenance chief said the cables were damaged. How could that be? We are very meticulous about our safety standards in this hotel."

Fred Webber's question went beyond mere curiosity. His proprietary concerns were understandable. There was the hotel's reputation to consider.

Quinn hastened to reassure him. "I don't think there's any more to it than what you already know. The Fire Department confirmed that somebody rigged explosive charges on the elevator cables. Presumably, the objective was to murder Mrs. Vandersagen, but it didn't work."

"*Mein Gott!*" Mr. Webber's lapse into one of his three native languages was the only indication that he was distressed. "At least it did not happen in one of the public elevators. Are the Fire Department people all finished? We told the guests it was a wastebasket fire."

"Yeah, but I guess you'll have a great deal of paperwork to worry about—with the city and all; the building department and stuff like that." Quinn knew how it was to be in thrall to the webs of red tape in New York's various departments.

Webber said something that sounded like, "*Wheesh, city*—papers; it's nothing. Just so the newspapers and the television don't get hold of it. Can you imagine if word got out that one of our elevators almost fell?" He shook his head to ward off the unthinkable. "What was going on up there?"

"Well, it's scary alright. But everything's under control for the moment. The Fire Marshal said the explosive charges were probably set by someone who had a key to the rooftop hatchway leading to the cables for the Vandersagen's Tower elevator. They were rigged to go off only when a person *inside* the cab pushed the *Down* button. And, they were heavy enough charges to blow all the cables. In other words, someone wanted that elevator to fall, all the way. Twenty stories! It seems, someone in this hotel is hell bent on murder. But, there's something I don't understand. The firemen said the elevator didn't fall, not very far anyway. How come?"

Webber had recovered from his fright and was the urbane hotel manager again. "Well it's very simple really. We can thank God for modern elevators with their built-in safety devices."

"I want to know all about how they work. But could you tell me on the way down to the basement? I need to take a look in that locker."

As they walked to the elevator and waited, Fred Webber explained.

"The safety devices work quite ingeniously. It's as if there were pairs of wings in the elevator shaft. There are sensors that report whether or not the cab is descending faster than normal. If so, the wings open automatically and catch the cab, so to speak, before it can go down too far. It's what you might call a safety net. Today, all elevators must have them. You know, in the old days, there were many accidents. Cables would break, the elevator would plummet, and pouf! people would die, like in the old movies."

"Yeah," said Quinn. "I remember those old movies." Webber and Quinn stepped into a service elevator, padded on all sides with movers' quilts. At the touch of a button, the cab descended smoothly and quietly to the basement.

Jonah Smith, along with a uniformed patrolman, met them as they stepped off the elevator into an area crowded with chairs, tables and rolling carts—the usual paraphernalia of hotel operation that the public rarely sees except when they are covered with damask linens that disguise their utilitarian ugliness.

Webber then led the cops to a far corner where a block of six lockers, apparently no longer in regular use, had been shoved against a wall. Webber opened the doors to all of them with a single key. There was a moldy old bellhop uniform in one of them. The five others were filled with an array of materials that included squibs, wires, tools, timing devices—everything, in fact, that proved Irving Quinn had found all the evidence he needed to convict Tom Cassidy of the Jim Vandersagen murder and today's attempt on the life of Adele.

Cassidy had either been stockpiling the materials for a long period or, more likely, he had brought them in his luggage on his last trip from California.

"Too bad." Quinn said to Jonah Smith. "If we had more extensive scanning for explosives in checked-in luggage on domestic flights, this guy might have been stopped at the gate at LAX."

Smith wanted to be certain. "You're pretty sure that's what he did, brought the stuff with him? He didn't buy it here, in New York?"

"Not likely. He's got access to several special effects labs on the Coast and they probably have enough stuff to blow up half the city. We talked to some of them. They've worked with him for years. These explosive devices are available any time he wants them. Anyway, the crime lab has identified this stuff. Beside the two or three shops in Los Angeles, these particular squibs are only available at one place in New York. And we checked them out. The New York people know Tom Cassidy, but they said he hasn't ever bought any explosives from them."

Quinn let the wrappers from several squibs drift through his fingers. "See, he must have taken these apart to get an extra large charge for the elevator cables, because a single one of them simply isn't strong enough to blow something that heavy. I wonder how much stuff he used."

"Crime lab will be able to tell, won't they?" Jonah wanted to know.

"Oh, sure. But what bothers me is, why? Why kill Jim Vandersagen? And then, only a few weeks later, why does he try to kill Adele? It doesn't make sense."

He slammed the locker doors and made sure the yellow evidence tape was in place as the policemen and a very nervous Fred Webber prepared to leave the basement.

Quinn nodded that he was finished. "Mr. Webber, is there an office I can use? I need to make a couple of private calls and make some notes—I don't want to get too far away from the hotel."

"Of course. I understand perfectly. You can use my office. It's the most private. You just dial nine for local calls."

"Don't worry, I've got a cell phone and so do my sergeants." Even hotel managers had to worry about the small stuff these days.

Maureen was in Larchmont, putting the final touches on the house, readying it for showing to the buying public. Not bad, she told herself. The place should sell quickly. The phone interrupted. That's probably the real estate broker, she thought. She was totally unprepared to hear from Irving Quinn.

Maureen was on the alert instantly. "What's wrong?"

"Nothing's wrong. It's just that we've finally got a breakthrough in the Vandersagen case and—well, I think you ought to come down here."

"Down where? Kate! Is Kate alright? Has that lunatic done something else? Is my daughter alright?"

"Yeah, don't worry. Kate's fine. But, look, I think you ought to come down here, the Waldorf. Kate's okay. She's up in Adele Vandersagen's apartment and, well, it's just—I think you ought to be here."

Maureen didn't waste time, trying to get Irving Quinn to supply further details. She sensed he had something important to tell her, but he made it clear he would say no more on the phone except, "How soon can you be here?"

"Okay," Maureen said. "at this hour of the day, it shouldn't be more than thirty minutes to the midtown exit on the FDR Drive, and then, if I catch the lights, I can be at the Waldorf in another ten minutes. Will that be okay?"

"Fine." Quinn said. Webber's secretary had set him up in a small room within the manager's office suite, a perfect command post. Jonah Smith and a uniformed patrolman stood by.

Quinn said to the sergeant, "I'm expecting Maureen Cassidy. She's on her way here. Would you go out front and make sure she puts her car in the garage? Bring her up here. Then, stay handy. When I'm finished with her, I'll let you know when we can move."

"You got it," said Jonah Smith, moving surprisingly swiftly for a man of such bulk. The uniformed cop watched and waited while Quinn made a series of calls to downtown. Then he said, "I've got a job for you. I want you to take the car and go down to city hall, siren screaming, if you have to. You'll be picking up a warrant. Get it back here in absolutely record time, okay?"

"Okay, sir." The patrolman then wanted to know. "Should I bring it here to this office?"

"No, bring it to the..." He looked at his notes to make sure he had it right, "eighteenth floor. We'll be waiting at the elevator for you. Alright, go."

Then there was little more to do but wait. Quinn called the precinct for further coverage to make sure his quarry would not escape. Within fifteen minutes, the Waldorf Astoria had a cop at every exit, including those not covered earlier. Quinn told Webber's secretary that her boss and he would be on the eighteenth floor and would she please send Mrs. Cassidy up there when she arrived?

"Yes, Lieutenant." Fred Webber's secretary had been in the hotel business for fifteen years. Unflappable was how she saw herself and she was right.

As Webber and Quinn waited on the eighteenth floor, they talked about the years when Tom Cassidy had worked as a bellboy.

"You understand, this is all hearsay. I was still a young apprentice in Geneva. I didn't even get here until the early seventies."

"So a bellboy would know every nook and cranny in the hotel? Places the ordinary guest would know nothing about."

"Naturally. A hotel like this one is like a small world of its own. Why, just the networks of corridors alone..."

Maureen arrived breathlessly, as if she had run all the way from Larchmont. When she got off the elevator she demanded, "What's going on. Where's my daughter?"

Quickly, Irving Quinn told her the story and reassured Maureen that Kate was unharmed.

"I'm going to see her right now. How do I get there?"

Fred Webber, ever mindful of the impact these affairs might have on the hotel's image as an oasis of civility, said, "I will escort you Madame. Please come with me."

Maureen followed but not without asking Quinn, "You're going to arrest him, aren't you?"

"Why do you say that?"

Though the elevator had arrived, Maureen ignored it and Webber had to wait for her, his body language betraying neither impatience nor anxiety.

"We both know he did it. He's the one who killed Jim, isn't he?"

"I don't know that for sure. What makes you think that?"

"Oh Lieutenant, stop being cute. I thought it was Tom from the very moment I knew he was in the studio that day. I'm sure he's the one who did it and what's more I know why."

"Maybe you ought to sit down here," he pointed to a sofa facing the bank of elevators as one, going down, arrived and stopped, its door opening smoothly.

Fred Webber, with the instincts of a born hotelier, understanding that he was not meant to overhear, stepped into the elevator, pushed the *hold* button and said, "I shall be in the lobby. Then I shall escort you to the Tower. And, Lieutenant, you have the key for the service elevator, do you not?"

Quinn looked down at the set of master keys which Webber had given him. "Yes, yeah, I've got it. Thanks."

The door closed and the hallway was empty except for Quinn and Maureen Cassidy. They might have been any two people, in a first class hotel, sitting quietly while awaiting an elevator. It was midday and nobody emerged from any of the rooms. In the silence only a slight hum indicated that they were in the center of a large hotel within the heart of a great city. Maureen found herself holding her breath, as if to put off having to reveal what she knew must be told.

Then she plunged ahead, taking Quinn back to the day she and Tom Cassidy had sat together outside the operating room in which Kate was being treated for the cuts and bruises from the falling mirror.

"I asked him flat out, 'Did you do it?' Of course, he denied it. And then he acted very indignant as if I had to be crazy to think he'd be capable of such a thing."

She painted the picture swiftly; the two people in the hospital corridor, trying to keep their voices low, but each becoming more excited.

"I'll tell you why I think you did it. You were afraid of the same thing I was afraid of, that she was having an affair with him."

"Well, it's true, even out on the Coast, people were talking about Kate and Jim Vandersagen. As her father, of course I was concerned. But, is that any reason to think I'd endanger her life?"

"I'll tell you what I think," said Maureen, hearing her voice rise in spite of her efforts to control it. "I think you set that mirror to fall but you get a nasty surprise right in the middle of everything when Kate showed up."

"You are off your head Maureen. You always were nuts and now that you're getting older, you're nuttier than usual."

The personal attack was always Tom's best defense when he quarreled with Maureen. This time, she tried to stay on track instead of exploding into hysteria.

"Oh, no you don't. You're not going to get away with it this time. Making me the crazy one doesn't get you off the hook. What I want to know is not that you did it. I'm absolutely convinced you did. But why? Why would you want to kill Jim Vandersagen?"

Tom shook his head. "You mean you don't know? Didn't you feel the same wild desire to kill him when you thought they were having it on? I'd think you would have, even more than I. After all, she's not really my daughter, is she?"

Maureen was silent. Tom knew he had delivered the telling blow.

In a very subdued voice, Maureen asked, "What makes you say that?"

Tom was not kind in his triumph. "Oh come off it, Maureen. I've known the truth about Kate since she was thirteen and I certainly guessed at it more than once long before that."

"What happened when she was thirteen?" Maureen held her head very rigidly, as if waiting for another blow.

"It was your mother, don't you remember? The day I was leaving you for good, when I was going to California for the first time and we were battling over my getting at least partial custody. She told me. Good old Deirdre. She probably thought she was doing you a favor, saving your daughter from her rotten old man.

"Well it nearly worked. For a couple of minutes there, I was ready to just chuck it all, you, Kate, the whole thing. But then, I realized something." He was near tears once again, as he had been that day.

"I realized I loved Kate. And that she *was* my daughter, even if she was the biological child of Jim Vandersagen. Christ! How could anybody overlook the fact that she looks just like him? It's true, I never made the connection until your mother spilled the beans, but from that point it was as obvious as rat shit in the sugar. But, I didn't see any reason to break Kate's heart any more than necessary. So I just kept my mouth shut and tried to be best possible father I could be."

"So, when you thought Kate was having an affair with her biological father, you decided to rig up a mirror that would kill him. You hadn't counted on Kate appearing out of nowhere to get nearly killed herself."

Tom shook his head. "I never did any such thing. That's your overheated imagination talking again. For all I know, you might have done it. After all, you had motive too, even stronger than mine."

In recounting the story to Irving Quinn. Maureen had tried to remain unemotional, paraphrasing the more hostile exchanges.

Guinn asked, "Was there anything else that led to you believe it was Tom?"

"Wasn't that enough? Now, what's this about Kate in another accident? I want to see her, and I want to see her now."

"Okay," said Quinn, standing. You just go on down in that elevator and Mr. Webber will take you to Adele Vandersagen's apartment, where your daughter is waiting for you. Be careful. She's going to need a lot of support, handling all this."

Maureen's first instinct was to snap something about not needing to be told how to look after her daughter, but she thought better of it. This Irving Quinn was alright. Kate could do lots worse. She said, "Lieutenant, Irving. Thanks for that. Kate will be okay with me. I'll talk to you later." She stepped into the elevator and was gone.

Immediately following Kate's rescue, when the initial excitement was over, Alex retreated toward the kitchen of the Vandersagen Apartment, leaving Kate and Adele together, silent, facing one another in the living room.

Kate stared and Adele, nervously fussed at a loose thread on the sofa cushion. Alex, from the kitchen doorway, was half expecting another outburst from Kate, but all he heard was the bubble and drip of the automatic coffee maker. The silence was far more unnerving since these were two women. He didn't like silent women. There was no way to guess what they were thinking. He preferred the yelling and sobbing which left no doubt that a woman was angry. Angry, he could handle. Not a sound, that was quite another thing. To fill the silence, Alex began a polite but meaningless conversation with Mina who offered him one of her excellent sandwiches.

There were voices; the women had begun to talk. Mina was soundlessly fussing in the cupboards. Then she excused herself, saying she had work to do. Alex had work too. In the confines of the apartment there was no natural place for a cop to wait. But the kitchen, at least, had a door so he was not forced to eavesdrop He closed it and sat at the table, idly looking at the supermarket tabloid Mina had thoughtfully provided for him. Well, he could always read about two-headed babies born to rock stars who were impregnated by space aliens who had kidnapped them and released them unharmed in the desert. Bored, yes. But the Boss told him to wait and that's a cop's job. Sitting in a comfortable kitchen sure beat the usual kind of waiting Alex was accustomed to. Then Mina came back and turned on the TV, so they both watched CNN which saved him the embarrassment of trying to make small talk.

Adele's voice was soft, finishing her explanation. "So, you see, my marriage to Jim Vandersagen wasn't exactly the idyll I wanted the police to think. After all, I might very well have been charged with trying to kill him."

"Yeah," Kate said. "When you add it all up, there couldn't be much doubt. But what was I supposed to do, tell Irving Quinn that I suspected my own father?"

"This has to be terribly hard for you."

"It's hard all right. But, Adele, it really is my fault Jim's dead. If only I'd said something!"

"Yeah, I know. It's probably got a whole lot to do with the generation thing, you know, in the sixties they called it a gap. I think today, it's more like a chasm, a grand canyon, even." Adele put down her coffee cup and stood. "I don't want food, which is a first for me. She went to the cabinet that opened to reveal the bar. "Let's have some more of that brandy. We're both still pretty well shaken up, and that's all the excuse I need. How about you?"

Kate said, "Oh sure, me too. Aren't people supposed to drink in situations like this?"

"If not now, when? This is really very good brandy. Same again?"

Kate held up her hand to indicate a small amount.

"At least, I shouldn't have to worry about the genetic thing," Kate said, taking a small sip. "Though, of course, there's the O'Hearn family. Who knows what kind of drunks they were."

"Well my mother wasn't Irish, not a bit, so that old myth doesn't mean too much." Adele shook off her shoes and tucked her feet under her rump on the sofa. "Speaking of family, don't feel too bad about not being able to close the gap between you and your mother. I don't think it's possible. For example, the two most progressive things my mother ever did were, let's see. First, she switched from Gordon's Gin to Stolichnaya after PepsiCo made the deal with the Soviet Union. Some deal, huh? They got Pepsi and we got some terrific vodka. Oh and yeah, the other big moment in my mother's life was the time she switched from forty years of Time magazine and signed up for Newsweek instead."

Unable to respond to Adele's attempt at humor, Kate shook her head. "You know Jim was so relieved when he told me that night. He had a picture of his mother. I couldn't believe it. When it was taken she was about the age I am now. I just looked and looked and it was like seeing myself in the mirror. Same eyes, same bone structure. I didn't want to believe him, though. I was furious. And at the same time I was horribly embarrassed. It was only a few weeks ago."

They were sitting in a side booth visible to the crowd. Kate's face was red with shame and the effort to keep from crying. She whispered fiercely, "How could you leave my mother pregnant like that, so she had to go and marry somebody else? Why didn't you do the decent thing?" It sounded old-fashioned, but Kate could not think of any other way to say it. "I was pregnant when Avi and I were married. He didn't abandon me." She was still smarting from having made a fool of herself. This man was her father! "Why did you leave her like that?"

"I didn't leave her. I told you. One morning she just cut me dead and she wouldn't even speak to me. God knows, I had no idea she was pregnant. I got an invitation to sail in a major race down in Bermuda, so naturally, I went. It was years before I even knew you existed—I mean as my daughter. But when I met you up in Boston that first time, I couldn't believe what I was seeing. It was as if my mother, had come back to life. You could be her twin."

"So you decided to find out all about me?"

"Yeah. I probably know a great deal more about you than Tom does, including your real birth weight. You certainly were not a premature baby, no matter what they told you."

"What do you mean?"

"Well, somebody changed your real weight from eight pounds, fourteen ounces to *three* pounds, fourteen. It only took a little of that white stuff on the original, which, by the way, I have actually seen."

"What do you mean?"

"Oh, I had the paper 'borrowed' so I could make sure. Don't worry, it was put back in the file room at the hospital. By now, it's probably been reduced to microfilm anyway. The copies for the city were probably filed with the three-pound number. And, you may not remember this, but I got some of your blood that time when the network had the Red Cross blood drive. The DNA lab test proves you're my daughter."

"I can't believe you went to all that trouble just to make sure I was your child. Why didn't you ever say anything?"

"Can't you see why? Look at you. You're beside yourself with rage and grief. Kate, I didn't want for this to happen. But I had to be near you. I never had a daughter and I knew Adele and I would never have kids. But tonight. Well, you see how it was. You had to know."

"But what am I supposed to tell my mother? Or my father?"

"You don't have to. Just go on as you always have. They're your real parents. Tom is—as much as Maureen. Just let's go on as we have. We'll be special friends with a secret that nobody else knows."

Adele was open-mouthed. "I had no idea Jim wanted a daughter. He didn't seem to mind when I found out I couldn't have a baby. For a while we talked about adopting, but then one day, he said he wasn't interested anymore. I wasn't too keen on having kids myself, so we just dropped it. Now I know why."

"So it looks like you're my stepmother, or something, doesn't it?"

Relieved to see Kate's spirits return, she laughed.

"Well, it is funny. But my God, Adele, he's dead. He was my father. I found him and then I lost him. It's like a soap, no it's more like grand opera. The only thing missing is a great soprano and some heartbreaking music. I wish I could figure out who killed him and who tried to kill you. Until today I didn't have the faintest idea, but now...Oh my God, Adele."

Alex, hearing the murmur of conversation from the living room, relaxed enough to eat sandwiches that Mina urged on him.

There was a sharp rap on the service door in the kitchen. The cop was on his feet instantly, swallowing quickly as Mina opened it. Maureen, swept into the room, hurriedly thanking Webber who was already on his way to the elevator.

She pointed to Alex and demanded, "Where's my daughter?"

Mina silently led Maureen into the living room where she watched panic appear abruptly on the faces of Adele and Kate.

Kate stood. Both mother and daughter stared for a moment and then Maureen spoke. "Kate. Oh, Kate, darling, I don't know how to tell you, but..."

"It's okay, Mom, I know. You don't have to explain."

"What do you mean, you know? What do you know?"

"I know about Jim, and that he was my biological father, and that..." She was unable to say more. The effort not to cry required her full attention. Maureen too was silent. Then she walked rapidly across the carpet to the windows where, for what seemed much longer than a minute or two, she looked at the Fall foliage in the distant park. Then she turned, facing the two women and walked toward Kate. The movement was so studied, it was as if there were a camera shooting the scene where she would stop only upon hearing the word *cut!*

How theatrical, even hammy, Adele thought. No wonder she never got further in her career than soap opera. Then she chided herself for so uncharitable an idea. After all, this was a difficult moment for everyone.

"But, Kate, how long have you known? Who told you?"

"Jim did. Look, sit down. I'll try to explain."

Maureen looked around as if she couldn't decide which of the seats she should take. Adele made up her mind for her. She gently led Maureen to a chair at a right angle to the one in which Kate had been sitting. Then with her hand, indicated that Kate should be reseated. From the bar, Adele got a glass and poured a generous three fingers of brandy into it. "Here," she said, handing the drink to Maureen.

Kate went on, "You remember, you asked me about my relationship with Jim?" Maureen nodded.

"Well, it was that night, the time you saw us in Sardi's. He told me everything. Mom, he swore he didn't know you were pregnant. He said you cut him dead and wouldn't speak to him. That's when he went away to Bermuda. And you married Daddy." She stopped for now she was in a flood of tears she could no longer contain.

"Anyway, he pulled out this picture of his mother. I couldn't believe what I was seeing. If I didn't know better, I'd have said it was a picture taken of me a few years ago. Same bones, same hair, same everything."

"What else did he say?" Maureen spoke in a monotone. Absently, she sipped from the glass in her hand. "Ugh! I don't really like straight spirits. Could I have some water, please?"

Adele was on her feet and halfway into the kitchen with the glass before Maureen spoke again. "But why? Why didn't you tell me or Tom or anybody. Why not me, especially?"

Kate was silent for a moment, thinking. Adele brought a silver pitcher of water and the glass on a small tray. Then she said, "Excuse me." and retreated to a corner of the room, too fascinated to leave, though she knew she ought to have disappeared discreetly.

Kate said, "I couldn't tell you. It was too embarrassing."

Maureen, her voice quavering, said, "But, I'm your own mother. Couldn't you have told me, at the very least?"

"Especially not you. Weren't there things you'd learned about your own mother, that you weren't ever able to talk about?"

Softly, Maureen said, "Oh, yes, oh, yes." She poured water into the glass of brandy and took a lengthy sip.

Adele knew, instantly, that Kate had touched a sensitive nerve in her mother. She saw nothing, no startling change in Maureen's face, but she knew, if there had been an electronic sensor, it would have fluctuated wildly, showing the rushing of blood, the sharp intake of breath and the leaping of adrenaline. She's a better actress than I give her credit for, thought Adele, finally turning to leave the room.

"Okay, it's true. I was pregnant with you when I married Tom." Maureen was silent.

"But why? Why didn't you tell Jim. That's what he said was driving him crazy. That you knew you were pregnant with his child, but you went and married another man."

Maureen said nothing. How could she explain the humiliating conversation she had overheard that night over the porch? Even now, she felt shamed and used as she recalled hearing Jim Vandersagen talking about her to a person she had never identified.

"It was all so long ago. I don't think I can explain. Things were so different in those days, so, almost Victorian. Anyway, I found out soon enough he was engaged to be married."

Without thinking Kate said, "Oh, yeah, the cucumber princess."

Maureen laughed. "Is that what you call her?"

"Yeah, don't you think it fits?"

"I guess you're right. I remember they had their picture in the Times Rotogravure. God, I was sick. Not only was I throwing up all the time, I was struggling to get enough work to keep us all from starving, and that bastard was in the Rotogravure. Oh, Katy, I am sorry, he was your real father, after all. I shouldn't have said that."

Kate said, "Don't worry about it, Mom. Jim had a terrible reputation with women. Adele told me. I know he was no angel."

Maureen nodded. "Anybody who knew Jim would hardly be shocked to hear him called a bastard. If you read the press, he was a lot worse, though they use much bigger words to describe what they mean."

Alex. put his head into the living room and announced to nobody in particular, "I've gotta leave now, but the lieutenant says could you wait just a coupla minutes? He's got something he wants to tell you."

CHAPTER FOURTEEN

Taking one elevator down and then another one up to the eighteenth floor, Alex knew Quinn was ready to make the bust. That Kate, he thought, she's not going to be too happy about seeing her old man in custody. But, he shrugged, every case of murder hurts a lot more people than just the victim.

"Mr. Cassidy?" Irving Quinn knocked on the door using the flat of his hand. The noise seemed shockingly loud in the quiet hotel hallway. "Tom Cassidy, open up. We have a warrant for your arrest."

Nothing. No sound; a *Do not disturb* sign. Quinn took the master key-card, inserted it into its slot and the door clicked open. He motioned to Jonah Smith to wait in the doorway to the corridor and for Alex to follow him.

The suite was a mess. There was an overturned bottle of whiskey and a pair of shoes on the floor in front of the sofa. The television set was on with the sound off. To the right, stood the half-opened door leading to the bedroom. Alex, looking at Quinn, silently asked if he should unholster his gun. Quinn shook his head.

Irving Quinn approached the door to the bedroom, and with his foot gently pushed it until it was fully open. On the tousled bed, curled under the coverlet was Tom Cassidy. Drunk, he thought, approaching more swiftly. He was within a foot of the bed when he stopped. Tom Cassidy was not drunk. He was dead.

Quickly, Quinn went into the bathroom. There, among the disarray of toilet articles he found the small plastic bottle. The label read "Seconal, One or Two tablets at bedtime. There were the usual overlapping warnings about drowsiness and operating machinery. The bottle was empty. The number 100 indicated how many pills had been in the prescription from a pharmacy in Beverly Hills, ordered by a Dr. Oberg.

"Well, he's asleep, alright," Quinn said. "Let's get on with what we have to do." Then he spotted the envelope on the bedside table. On hotel stationary, the note was addressed to Kate Cassidy. Oh, God, he thought, she can't even read this until it's been logged and examined. But turning it over, he saw that the flap had not been sealed.

"Okay, Alex, get her mother, not Kate, on the phone. I can't leave, but at least I can talk to her." He was thinking, and I won't have to be the one to tell Kate that her old man was a killer and a suicide to boot. He called Smith into the room and told him to turn the body for a better look. "Okay, you can call the M.E."

Quinn was very business-like to make his work seem less ugly, though, God knows, after twenty years, he still found horror in the bodies of the dead. Some cops had thicker hides, he thought. But for him, the reaction was always the same, revulsion, pity and the recurring shock at how quickly a *person* disappears and becomes *evidence*, *corpus*—an unappealing object to be disposed of as quickly as the law and decency will allow. Most people, Quinn knew, had no idea how quickly a dead person becomes nothing but a remnant. And Tom's corpse, yellowed by a failing liver, was going to be a real challenge to the undertaker's art.

Alex called him to the phone. "I've got the mother. Here."

He said, "Irving Quinn, Mrs. Cassidy?"

"Hello, Lieutenant. You wanted to talk to me?"

"Yes. There is no easy way to say this. He's dead. An overdose of sleeping pills combined with enough booze can be very effective." He hoped she would not think him cold-blooded, but experience had taught him, that directness was better than the circumlocutions young policemen stumble through in trying to spare people's sensibilities.

Having absorbed the initial shock of hearing that Tom had probably killed himself, she asked, "Was there a note?"

"Yeah. It's for Kate. I can't remove it from here and I can't leave for awhile, but, you want me to read it?"

"Please," Maureen said, dreading what she would hear.

With his rubber-gloved hand, he took the note paper by the edge and carefully opened it. He cleared his throat and plunged ahead:

Darling girl,

Don't find it impossible to forgive me for causing you so much pain. I realize now that only a coward deals with his problems as I have. But, when you talk to your mother, you'll understand how compelled I was to save you from disaster. I know you'll recover from all this and I've made sure that nothing will come between you and the job you love.

I'm sorry about the clinic. I just couldn't face that kind of thing at my age. This way is better. I've never stopped loving you.

Daddy

Maureen was silent. Quinn said "He must have known what he was doing. All that booze and God knows how many pills. He wanted to check out. I think he knew it would be easier on everybody if he did it this way."

"Yes, yes, I'm sure you're right."

"You'll tell Kate? I can't leave here, but please, please tell her I'll see her as soon as possible."

Silence. Then he said, "Maureen, are you okay? You'll tell her?"

"Yes, I'll tell her. I'll take her home."

When Maureen had gone into the bedroom to take the call she was fairly certain it would be to tell her of Tom's arrest and she was prepared to present the fact of it to Kate. But his death, worse, suicide, was another matter. After putting down the phone, she stood for a moment in the doorway. Then, like the actress she was, she set a serene expression on her face, and walked into the living room.

But Kate knew instantly that Maureen was more than distressed. Her hands were clenched and there was an almost imperceptible trembling to her head. She wondered if her mother could be showing early signs of Parkinson's disease. Then the tension broke suddenly and Maureen wailed, "Oh Katy, Katy. Your Daddy is going to burn forever. He'll live in everlasting hell. That stupid fool. A hundred pills. That Goddamned fool."

Her voice barely audible, Kate said, "He killed himself, didn't he? He always said he would if life got too complicated." Then she let her mother into her arms and they both wept softly.

Adele, having quickly assessed the situation, backed out of the room and called the garage, telling them to have Mrs. Cassidy's car out front in fifteen minutes. Kate and Maureen needed to go home. She would drive them herself, if necessary.

Why is it, she wondered, that some people's lives are so messy?. That was the only word that applied, messy. Tom Cassidy, from everything she had learned of him, was the kind of man that her father had always warned her against. Abner Kenyon once said, "Honey, don't get involved with any feller that cain't manage hisself. 'Cause, if you do, you can be sure, after he's made a mess of his own life, he's gonna make a bigger one of yours."

Adele helped Kate and Maureen into their coats, patting their shoulders as if to be warmly dressed would help dispel their sodden gloom. "Do you want me to come down with you?"

"No, no. Thanks, Adele. We're just going to drive across town—I want to be home and my mother—well, I'm going to keep her with me for a little while." Before she stepped into the service elevator, Kate added. "And don't worry about the proxy. You've got it. If you send a messenger, I'll sign it this afternoon."

"Don't worry about that now. I've already missed the meeting. There'll be another one later."

Once in the car, after having ceded the driver's seat to Kate, Maureen was silent. They were on an Eastbound street, heading for the park, when Kate exploded.

"Why, why, in the name of all that's holy, did you lie to me? Why didn't anybody tell me the truth! Now I've lost both my fathers. How can you spend a whole lifetime making believe something is what you want it to be instead of looking at it and facing it? Lies! A whole lifetime of lies! That's what you and Daddy gave me. Why? Why? Because of some mid-Victorian convention that said you had to be properly married. It didn't matter that you gave your kid a fake father and I had to wait forty years to find the real one. Then, then...."

Kate sobbed and fumbled in the car, looking for something to mop her eyes. She nearly hit a parked car. Maureen said quickly, "Pull over there," pointing to the only clear parking space on the street. It was the reserved diplomatic parking area for the French consulate.

"Here," she said, reaching into her purse for a hankie.

"You still using these?" Kate had given her a dozen Irish linen handkerchiefs five years earlier. "Nobody uses hankies anymore."

Then she shook her head. "Mommy, I'm so mad at you. I'm so mad at Daddy. I'm mad at Jim. Everybody. All of you. All liars. Why couldn't you just have told me the truth?"

"You don't understand...."

"You're damned right I don't understand. Don't you think I told Joel I was three months pregnant with him when I married Avi? Mom, this is the twentieth century. We don't have to play by those old stupid rules anymore. And Daddy. Oh, God, Mom, he must have been totally crazed. Why, why, in the name of heaven? What was he thinking? Why did he kill Jim? Jim was no threat to him. After all these years. Why now? Why did he have to kill Jim?"

Calmly now, Maureen said, "You don't really understand, do you?"

"What's to understand? He killed Jim and then his brain was so pickled in alcohol, he thought he could save my job by killing Adele."

"Well, I agree, that part was certainly the work of a crazy person"

"Oh, I suppose it's not crazy to rig up a two-hundred-pound mirror and have it kill somebody, maybe me as well?"

"That's not what I mean."

"Then, what do you mean?" Kate's nose was red, but she had stopped crying.

"I mean, he thought he was saving you from something really horrible."

"Horrible, like what? What's more horrible than the stupid, paranoid, idiotic things he was doing? You got something else you haven't told me?"

"No, but Tom really wasn't insane, you know. He was only trying to protect you."

"Protect me!" Kate was screaming again. "He commits a cold-blooded murder and I nearly cash-in too. That's protecting me? Protecting me from what?

"Incest." Maureen said the word quickly as if to rid her tongue of it in an instant.

"You mean.... Wait a minute. It was that night in Sardi's. What did you do, call him and say, 'Hurry, Tom, Kate's about to have sex with her own father'? Christ! Did you do that? Did you call him?"

"No, I swear it. I never said a word. He heard rumors out on the coast. The way you two were always together, the talk was getting really wild. Everybody thought you and Jim were lovers."

"My God. God! Mom, why didn't you just ask me? I would have told you what was going on. "Why in the Goddamned hell didn't you ask me?" And she began to sob again. "Stupid, stupid, stupid...."

A uniformed policeman leaned down and motioned for Kate to roll down the window. He said, "You can't park here. This is reserved for the consulate. Uh, you'll have to move." His young face was full of concern. "You okay? Wanna take a couple minutes to pull yourself together? But, then you really will have to move."

"It's okay, officer. I'll be okay in a minute. I'm just having a fight with my mother. And then we'll be out of here."

The cop backed off. Screw the French Counsel, he thought.

"So, Daddy just decided to blow up Adele's elevator too. What the hell's that got to do with incest?"

"I don't know anything about that. But Irving Quinn said something about your job. He was trying to save it for you."

"Oh, Jesus, now I know his mind really was blown apart. It was all my fault. I just kept bitching and moaning about how I was afraid Adele was going to fire me. So he decided to kill her too. Mom, the man was insane, you know that, don't you?"

"Yes, I know. But still, it's..."

"Still what? You think it's perfectly okay for a guy to go around killing people because he's afraid darling Kate's in danger of having sex with her biological father? I know it's a pretty scary idea, but *murder?* My God, Mom, you don't go around murdering people for something like that! And why Adele? Goddammit, why in hell did he think I couldn't save my own damned job?"

Suddenly, she was furious again, this time with no tears. "How dare he! Who the hell did he think he was, taking on my life as if it were his own personal responsibility? As for incest, even if it were true, which it wasn't, thanks to Jim's rescuing me from my own stupidity—is incest the worst things that can happen to a person? You think it would have been the end of the world for me?

"I'm not sure."

"What do you mean, you're not sure?" She looked at her mother and watched as Maureen lowered her eyes to look at the interlaced fingers of her gloved hands. They trembled slightly.

"Mom, you're hiding something. You can't do this anymore. Whatever it is, believe me, I'll understand. Tell me. Did you have anything to do with this mess?"

Silence. Then Kate was quiet too.

"Well, we're not moving from this spot. I don't care if they tow us away. You tell me right this minute. What were you doing that day in the studio? You were there, right on the set. You had your little black and white-stripped tote bag. Mom, tell me, now, or I swear, I'll call Irving Quinn and let him sweat it out of you. What were you doing that day? Oh, I'm going to lose my mind, I'm sure of it. Tom's craziness is contagious. You've got it too. But I'm not going to let this go any further."

Maureen was crying now. "He was such a fool. Poor Tom, such a fool. But he was afraid for you, just like I was. You were so vulnerable. I only wanted to save you."

Save me? You were going to save me too? What were you doing that day? You've always been overprotective. When I was a kid and I had that mild asthma, the *allergies*. The allergies. That's it!"

"Maureen sniffed. What do you mean. What about your allergies..."

"Stop it, Mom. I've just figured it out. Irving or somebody said it. Men rig up explosives, but women, well women are different. They use poison. You did it, didn't you? You put poison in the chocolate sauce!"

"Really, Kate, I don't know what you're talking about."

"Oh yes you do. You're the only one who knows that I'm allergic to chocolate and that I wouldn't touch the stuff. And just the week before

I was telling you how Jim likes to come on the set and taste stuff, even after Rudy gave strict orders to throw away anything standing on the counter for the shoot. Oh, yes you had it all figured out, but Tom beat you to it, didn't he? Irving said there were no toxins in Jim's body because he never swallowed the stuff. But, by God, you tried, didn't you? You tried to kill him too.

"No wonder I'm losing my mind. My whole damned family is nuts. Everybody. All lunatics. Gran sent her money to the IRA to buy guns, my real father discovers me one day when I'm all grown up, my Daddy, the big hero in my life, is a raging drunk. Poor Joel and Dee Dee—maybe they got better genes from Avi's side. I hope so."

Then Kate looked directly into Maureen's eyes. "You did it, didn't you? You put the poisoned chocolate sauce on the counter, didn't you?"

Maureen was silent.

"Mom, it's true isn't it? The only people who know about my allergy to chocolate are you and Joel and Dee Dee. Well, Tom too, but he wasn't in close touch that year when I was really getting sick. So all you had to do is put the jar on the counter, leave the top off and Jim would be sure to come along and take a nice, big mouthful, right?"

Maureen said nothing.

Now, Kate was backing out of the space in front of the consulate. "Okay, we'll go back to my house. We'll park the car in the garage and then you and I are going to talk."

Now, carefully making her way through the park, Kate kept up a running conversation. "So, what were you going to do the minute Jim keeled over dead after eating the chocolate sauce?"

Exasperated now, Maureen said, "Alright, I'll tell you. I had the original jar of sauce unopened in my tote bag. I was simply going to switch them in the excitement while everybody was trying to revive Jim."

"Brilliant! How were you going to make sure somebody else, a stagehand, say, wasn't also going to swipe a finger through the stuff?"

"That's why I was right there on the set, ready to make the switch."

"I was right. You are crazy. Do you realize, you could have killed somebody, a perfectly innocent person? What on earth made you think you could get away with something like that?"

"I don't know. I just knew I had to do something to keep Jim Vandersagen from doing to you what he did to..."

"What were you going to say? What, aside from getting you pregnant, did Jim Vandersagen do to you?"

"It's not something I can talk about."

"Yes it is. You're my mother and I have a right to know what drives a perfectly nice woman like you to do some asshole thing like trying to poison somebody with garden chemicals. Tell me!"

There was a traffic pileup on 79th Street. The car was warm and, with the windows rolled up, very quiet. The only sounds were muffled horns bleating their frustration and Maureen's quiet voice, telling Kate about the night she had overheard Jim discussing her. "When he called me an *'Irish piece'* I promised myself that one day, he'd pay for that. So, when I thought you and he...well, you know.... I just decided the time had come.

"I found an old can of insect stuff, really concentrated, like a thick, black syrup in the bottom of a bottle. It was so simple to doctor the jar of sauce. I don't think I really thought it through. I mean, I didn't know exactly what I was going to do except I took the original jar and put it into my tote bag. My poisoned one was the same brand as the one in the diet cookbook. So it was easy to make the switch." Maureen looked please with herself, as if she had been terribly clever.

"Alright," Kate said, inching the car forward toward the traffic light beyond the park exit. "Subject closed. Promise me, Mom, not even on your deathbed, you'll never say another word about this. What happened to the good jar of chocolate sauce?"

"New York is full of places to leave a nice jar of chocolate sauce."

"And what about the bottle with the insecticide? What were you planning to do with that?"

"We have a very fine recycling center in Larchmont, so I..."

"That's it!" Kate said, as they broke out of the jam and drove uptown. "Promise me you'll, never, never, ever in your entire life, ever, ever, try to help me. Even if you see me about to fall off a cliff."

"Don't talk nonsense. That's what mother's do when they see their daughters about to fall off a cliff, they act."

"Please, God," said Kate, I hope neither of my children ever start to fall when I'm around. I'd probably do something at least as stupid as you did."

"Probably." Maureen sighed.

There was light traffic Northbound on Central Park West, bringing Kate home quickly. She drove down the ramp into the building garage, taking a ticket from the attendant. "Hi, Miss Cassidy, ma'am. You gonna leave her here for a coupla weeks like last time?"

"Oh, my God," said Maureen. "The real estate woman. She was bringing somebody this afternoon. I've got to get back."

"She's got my number here in the city, doesn't she?"

"Yeah, and she can call the Service too, if she needs me. God, Katy, I'm so mixed up. I can't think straight."

"Me too. We've got a lot of work to do, don't we? I guess, in the end it's better this way. Daddy would have been miserable in that clinic. But still, I wish I could have gotten him there in time."

She chewed at the idea. "I could have helped him. I could have prevented it."

Maureen cut her short. "I know how you feel. But you couldn't have stopped him. There's no force on earth that could have stopped Tom Cassidy. We'll both have to spend a little time before we can understand that. But, believe me. We couldn't have stopped him."

"Yes, but Adele. What about her? You mean he was willing to go so far as to kill somebody just to save my job? Jim, yes, I think I can see how both of you could lose perspective. But you've got to admit, he had to be, well, I said it before, totally nuts. I guess booze really was the problem. His brain was just not working anymore. Like Gran's."

In the elevator to Kate's apartment, Maureen sighed. Yeah, I suppose it doesn't make much difference how your brain cells are destroyed—booze, disease. Oh, it's all so horrible."

Once inside the door of the apartment, mother and daughter took off their coats and gloves, stashed purses and then, silently, they hugged, each patting the other's back in mutual comfort. They smiled as they separated. Maureen went to the kitchen to make coffee and Kate to the telephone answering machine for her messages.

As she approached the phone, it began to ring. She decided to wait before picking up. The last thing she needed right now was some insurance salesman asking if she had disaster coverage.

She knew the voice. "Kate, it's Irving. If you're there, please pick up. If not, I'm back at work and you have the direct-dial number..."

Kate picked up the phone and said, "Did I ever tell you about the New Yorker who was so rich, he was accustomed to dialing the number of his bank, the Irving Trust Company, and saying 'Hello—Irving?'...?"

About the Author

Arline Potter was born in New York City not far from where the events of the story unfold. She has clear recollections of walking the avenues and looking in shop windows on Fifth. Her first spiritual home was probably the great New York Public Library where she dreamed of a career in the theater or (then) radio. Alas, she had no talent for acting, so she did the next best thing. She wrote lines for people who did.

"Writing fiction is so much fun. I feel like the child I once was, playing make believe. The background was always glamorous and the plots were most likely those of the last movies I had seen. But even then I knew how to make a character do my bidding."

Her current work is another mystery set in nearby coastal California, in a fictional community on the very real Monterey Bay.

9 781583 488492

Made in the USA
Lexington, KY
01 February 2012